ALSO BY PAIGE SHELTON

ALASKA WILD SERIES
Thin Ice
Cold Wind
Dark Night

SCOTTISH BOOKSHOP MYSTERY SERIES
The Cracked Spine
Of Books and Bagpipes
A Christmas Tartan (a mini-mystery)
Lost Books and Old Bones
The Loch Ness Papers
The Stolen Letter
Deadly Editions
The Burning Pages

COUNTRY COOKING SCHOOL MYSTERY SERIES
If Fried Chicken Could Fly
If Mashed Potatoes Could Dance
If Bread Could Rise to the Occasion
If Catfish Had Nine Lives
If Onions Could Spring Leeks

FARMERS MARKET MYSTERY SERIES
Farm Fresh Murder
Fruit of All Evil
Crops and Robbers
A Killer Maize
Red Hot Deadly Peppers (a mini-mystery)
Merry Market Murder
Bushel Full of Murder

DANGEROUS TYPE MYSTERY SERIES
To Helvetica and Back
Bookman Dead Style
Comic Sans Murder

WINTER'S END

A MYSTERY

PAIGE SHELTON

Minotaur Books

New York

First published in the United States by Minotaur Books,
an imprint of St. Martin's Publishing Group

WINTER'S END. Copyright © 2022 by Penelope Publishing LLC. All rights reserved. Printed in the United States of America. For information, address St. Martin's Publishing Group, 120 Broadway, New York, NY 10271.

www.minotaurbooks.com

Library of Congress Cataloging-in-Publication Data

Names: Shelton, Paige, author.
Title: Winter's end : a mystery / Paige Shelton.
Description: First edition. | New York : Minotaur Books, 2022. |
    Series: Alaska wild ; 4
Identifiers: LCCN 2022024430 | ISBN 9781250846594 (hardcover) |
    ISBN 9781250846600 (ebook)
Subjects: LCGFT: Detective and mystery fiction. | Novels.
Classification: LCC PS3619.H45345 W56 2022 | DDC 813/.6—dc23/
    eng/20220525
LC record available at https://lccn.loc.gov/2022024430

Our books may be purchased in bulk for promotional, educational, or business use. Please contact your local bookseller or the Macmillan Corporate and Premium Sales Department at 1-800-221-7945, extension 5442, or by email at MacmillanSpecialMarkets@macmillan.com.

First Edition: 2022

10 9 8 7 6 5 4 3 2 1

For Heidi and Marianne and Pat and Pat.
Your friendship means the world to me.

One

The End.

I looked at the words.

Then I grumbled and rolled the paper up the typewriter and grabbed the Wite-Out from my desk. It wasn't the end. Something was wrong with this story.

I just didn't know what it was.

I painted over the two words, then sighed. It was bad luck to leave them there for the universe to see if I was certain that the story wasn't finished or wasn't right, or something.

"What do you suppose the problem is?" I asked Gus. He was curled up on the dog bed next to my desk.

He raised eyebrows over his husky-blue eyes. Even if he hadn't been a purebred, I'd have thought he was the most beautiful dog ever. I adored him and sensed the feeling was mutual, particularly when ear scratches were involved.

"Well, maybe I'll read the whole thing to you, and you can help me figure it out."

He seemed lazily amenable. I laughed. "We have a walk soon. Kaye and Finn will be here in about thirty minutes. That okay?"

At the word *walk,* he perked up, though he didn't rise. He whined in agreement and then rested his head on his front paws again.

"Okay, I need to think about something else for a while. That's the only way to figure out what's wrong with a story, think about something completely different."

When I'd been tasked with finding homes for several dogs after their owner disappeared during the throes of the dark winter, local resident Kaye Miller had taken Finn. He was part Saint Bernard and part mystery breeds that were a concoction of smart and strong. The dogs had been members of a sled crew and had lived together for a long time. To give Gus and Finn a chance to see each other, Kaye and I had taken them out for a walk together once a month. When we'd first ventured outside, it had been mostly dark with challenging weather. Now, as we'd come into June, we were seeing much longer days and lots of thaw, which meant some mud but also temperatures that weren't always below freezing. It was still raining a lot but not today. The walk toward town down the road outside the shed might not be too terrible.

I looked forward to it, to seeing both Kaye and Finn. I couldn't say that Kaye and I were friends, but I'd enjoyed our time together, and I hoped we'd be able to walk the dogs more now that the weather might permit easier travel.

Truthfully, I was excited about *making* a friend, a woman close to my age, who based on our few times together, seemed to share a similar sense of humor.

I acknowledged that maybe excitement about such a thing was odd, perhaps immature for someone who was thirty. Did age matter when making friends? I really didn't know. I hadn't made very many of them over my lifetime. The strange turns of events in my life had kept me mostly a loner, though not an unhappy one.

"All right," I said to Gus, "I have thirty minutes for housekeeping."

I put attention to straightening my desk, making a few notes, and looking out the window. I hid the manuscript, including the page with the Wite-Out, sticking everything into one of the desk drawers.

Though more people than just the local police chief, Gril, now knew my real identity, Kaye wasn't one of them.

I opened the top middle drawer to replace the red pens I used, and my eyes landed on a piece of paper with a phone number, stalling my tasks. It was a number I'd dialed more times than I could count since it had been given to me around the same time the dogs had become my responsibility. For a couple months, a generic voice mail had picked up. I'd left messages. But around March, the voice mail greeting disappeared. Now it only rang and rang.

It was allegedly my father's number, but I doubted I'd ever know for sure if it was or had ever been.

I closed the drawer but then opened it again. I hadn't tried the number for a week or so. I'd told myself I was going to stop calling it. My father had left my mother and me when I was seven. He hadn't responded to any of the messages I'd left at the other end of this number. At some point, I needed to accept that he was never going to come back into my life and didn't want to—hadn't wanted to for a long time. I sighed and then closed the drawer yet again.

"Pathetic," I said to myself, then looked down at Gus. "I'm pathetic."

Gus lifted an uncertain eyebrow, as if not sure whether or not to agree.

My circumstances weren't typical. My life hadn't been, so maybe this experience was simply my *normal*, not pathetic. No, I decided quickly, this continued sense of longing for a father who didn't want to be in my life was most definitely pathetic. Maybe a little justified, sure, but I needed to get over it. I was trying—and it was only one of the reasons my life wasn't *normal*.

I'd come to Benedict, Alaska, directly from a hospital in Missouri. A week or so before that, I'd thrown myself out of a van after being kept inside it for three days by Travis Walker, a name I hadn't immediately remembered and a man who hadn't been caught yet. I'd felt compelled to run away and hide, thinking that no one could find me here. I'd been wrong about that, but I still felt mostly safe, and as far as I knew, Walker hadn't made his way here.

One of the secrets I lived was my pen name, Elizabeth Fairchild, and my actual career as a thriller writer. Here, most people knew me by my real name, Beth Rivers.

I grabbed some files from the corner of my desk and straightened them. They were filled with details on local events and things I used for my cover job, editor of the local paper, the *Petition*. This shed, the home office for the paper and a place I could hide to write my books, had served me well.

No matter how I worked to distract myself by straightening up, the phone number kept flashing through my mind. No, I wasn't going to call the number today.

I had wanted something else to think about, something to get my mind off the book, but now I would rather have been obsessing about it instead.

I'd channeled some anger into this new manuscript, using the story as a way to maybe work out some of my own. Maybe I wasn't doing it right. Maybe I wasn't being honest enough about it. It would come to me.

I had a therapist now to help me through my traumas and resentments. Leia had encouraged me to journal, but when I told her I thought I could finally use what I'd been through in one of my books, she said it might be a good idea. *Might*. She'd had some reservations and wanted to make sure that whatever I wrote didn't send me into a downward spiral. It hadn't, but I sensed a roadblock of some sort—both in my real life and in the book. It was as if I could see what was ahead, but it was awfully blurry.

No matter what, though, Leia was glad I was ready to write it down—or as she said, "write it out of me."

I stood and walked to the other desk in the shed. I gathered a remaining pile of flyers I'd been putting up around town the last few days and neatly restacked them. Though I'd published the date of tomorrow's big event in the *Petition*'s weekly editions for months now, the flyers had been extra reminders. Everyone was required to attend the event. If they didn't, they'd be searched for and inquired about until eyes were put on them.

Tomorrow was Benedict's annual Death Walk, wherein Gril, the local police chief, and Donner, the other member of the local law enforcement team as well as a park ranger, took a head count, hoping everyone survived the winter, and then searched the community for those who didn't report in.

The Death Walk was not only important but also exciting. I'd heard many Benedict residents speak about it in expectant tones.

Don't forget about the Walk.

Unless you're dead, be there.

I'd learned that this was another reason the Walk was so important. It gave the community something to look forward to and talk about, a social event.

Just as my eyes moved back toward the drawer with the phone number, I heard the rumble of a truck engine approaching.

"Oh good," I said, grateful for the distraction. "That must be them," I said to Gus as I made my way to the shed's door, happy to get out of my head, at least for a little while.

I opened it wide just as Kaye and Finn exited an old blue truck. I assumed the man behind the wheel was Warren, Kaye's husband. I hadn't met him yet. I stepped off the small landing from the shed, planning to introduce myself but was stopped by Finn and his happy greeting.

"Hey, boy," I said as I scratched behind his ears and he and Gus also said hello to each other.

"Hi, Beth," Kaye said as she joined us.

In that short few moments, Warren put the truck in reverse and backed onto the road. He smiled and waved in our direction before he turned and took off toward town.

"It's great to see you both," I said, smiling at Kaye.

"You too."

Kaye's light brown hair was always smooth and had been pulled back into a perfect ponytail every time I'd seen her. Her skin was pale, and her bright brown eyes seemed unbothered by whatever challenges tugged on the corners of so many people's eyes out here. I'd only lived in Alaska for about a year, and some parts of me felt stronger, more youthful even, but I'd experienced the stress of the winter, and I wondered how much it showed on me.

"Warren will pick us up later," she added.

"That works. Come on in for a second. Let the boys say hello to each other. I'll change into boots." I turned back toward the shed.

It became crowded quickly. Bobby Reardon had originally set up this old hunting shed with a tin roof to house the workings of a weekly paper, the *Petition*. Bobby had been dead a few years now, but it seemed everyone thought of him fondly. He'd always had a chair and a full bottle of whiskey at the ready for any visitors. I'd tried to continue his hospitality, but I didn't think as many people stopped by to chat with me as they had Bobby.

He'd decorated the place with old black-and-white movie posters and a few typewriters atop two desks. I'd added my own Royal, which I'd found a long time ago in a Missouri secondhand store. All of my novels' first drafts had been typed on it. Subsequent drafts had been done on my laptop, but I doubted I'd ever change up the tradition of typing on the Royal, no matter how difficult it might eventually be to stock up on Wite-Out in Benedict.

Two big dogs and two adult humans made the space tight, but the dogs didn't seem to mind.

"How have you been?" I asked as I sat in my chair and reached for the boots under my desk. I'd slipped into tennis shoes earlier that morning.

"Oh, I'm good."

I looked up at her funny tone.

She sent me a tight smile. "No, really, I am."

Other than the fact that she was close to my age, I knew only that she lived with her husband and in-laws out west about "a good five miles." She'd told me a little about her husband, Warren, and how well they seemed to get along but not much about her in-laws. One time she'd mentioned that two of Warren's brothers also lived there, and I'd said something about that making for a lot of people in the house. She'd changed the subject quickly. I hadn't asked anything more about it.

I'd meant to ask my landlord, Viola, about Kaye, but with so much else going on I never had. That small, strained tone in Kaye's voice made me wish I knew more about her situation.

"Yeah?" I asked.

Her tight smile relaxed into something more real. "Yes, definitely. Sorry, I do have something on my mind, but it's not bad. I'll tell you about it on the walk."

"Sounds good."

Once the boots, coats, hats, and leashes were in place, we left the shed and started down the road toward town. I was grateful it wasn't raining yet—and even more pleased that there wasn't a cloud in the sky. There would be soon enough.

"Warren reminded me to be on the lookout," Kaye said. "He's seen more bear cubs and mamas roaming around this year than in a while."

"Just yesterday I saw a mama black bear and two cubs walk right by the shed's window. It was quite the sight, and I was glad I was inside at the time. Gus sniffed curiously but didn't seem to be bothered by them. I could smell them through the window, and they were ripe."

Kaye laughed. "Finn isn't bothered by them, either. Elijah trained his dogs very well."

"He did." My heart sank a little at hearing his name. Everyone missed him and wondered where he'd gone. I was probably more curious than everyone else because I suspected that my mother had gone with him, and I wondered about her too, though she'd always been pretty good at taking care of herself.

Gus and Finn had both been part of Elijah's dogsled team. He'd taken care of his dogs, even to the point of keeping files on all of them with instructions where the dogs should go if something ever happened to him.

That's how I'd met Kaye. I'd called her one day to tell her she was listed as Finn's first possible connection and asked if she wanted to get together to talk about it.

She had. We'd met downtown at the one small restaurant, both ordering pancakes and coffee as we discussed if she was willing and ready to take care of the dog.

She'd been enthused. She'd owned dogs as a child but not since moving to Benedict from Montana and marrying Warren. I'd asked her if she wanted Warren to meet Finn first, but she'd said he would be fine. I'd had a moment or two of concern that maybe I hadn't been as thorough as I needed to be in checking out Finn's new home, but Kaye had been so excited about taking the dog that ultimately I'd accepted things as they were.

All the dogs had been placed in good homes, but nothing was perfect around here. There were no dog parks, and a veterinarian came through town only twice a month if the weather permitted. Wild animals were always a potential threat.

But I knew that the dogs were with people who would love them and do their best by them. I figured that was about all anyone could ask since I didn't think I could take care of all of them myself.

"How have you been?" Kaye asked as we set out. "I haven't seen you since our last walk. As small as this place is and with the weather improving, I thought I'd see more people over the last few weeks."

"I'm still in my first year. I wasn't sure what to expect. I have been out more but not a lot. Since I live downtown, I'm either there or here at the shed." I nodded back toward the building. "I felt moments of isolation during the winter, but it wasn't as bad as I thought it might be. Since I live in the same building as Viola, we had each other's company and our own rooms if we didn't want company. Downtown only shut down a few days, so most of the time we could walk a short distance and see someone else. How did you and your family do?"

Kaye smiled, but I wondered if it was forced, too. Maybe I was imagining things. "We did okay. It's a house full of people, and every winter I actually wish to get away"—she laughed once—"for a little isolation."

"Do you all get along? I mean, I'm not trying to be nosy, I just . . ."

"No worries. Sure, we get along. I mean, we all like and respect each other and for the most part we are cordial, but all that closeness can get old. You know?"

"I do. How do you get away when you want some alone time? Is the house big enough?"

"I take walks, I guess. The house is a funny place. It started as a cabin built by my father-in-law's father. It's been added on to for years. We all have our own spaces. I call them pods sometimes, but they're just added rooms and such. From the outside, to me it looks like something from a Willy Wonka movie but less colorful."

"How many people?"

"Six," she said with a notable eyebrow raise. "My husband, me, his parents, and two of his brothers."

"That's a lot of testosterone," I said, hoping to keep it light.

"I'd say. Even Camille, Warren's mother, seems that way." She laughed again, more genuinely this time.

It was such a gleeful noise that I laughed, too.

"Oh, it feels good to be out," she exclaimed. "Away from . . ."

"It does feel good." I paused. "Away from? Is that what you were talking about in the shed? What was bothering you?"

She nodded and then looked off into the distance to her right. It was a westerly glance, so I suspected she was thinking of her home. Or maybe not. Downtown was that direction, too. I recognized something in her profile. Though not as much as just a few minutes earlier when Warren had dropped her and Finn off, she looked bothered, something pinched her lips, squinted her eyes. There's immeasurable beauty to this land, but there can also be a void, something dug out by the dark and the cold. I'd felt it, though that space had been replenishing with the nicer weather. I wondered if she experienced the same thing, but I wanted to let her answer on her own time. I waited and watched as her expression relaxed some. She turned back to me and smiled weakly. "And I already feel much better."

I couldn't help but note that in addition to being outside, she was also away from her husband. Was that part of what had transformed her so quickly? She truly did appear to be a different person than the one who'd been dropped off only a few minutes earlier. Freer, maybe.

"I could do this all day, just walk," she said.

Maybe she just liked the outdoors.

"I hear you," I agreed.

We continued down the road in companionable silence for a short distance.

"Beth," Kaye said a few beats later. "Do you ever feel like you want to run away?"

I glanced at her. She didn't backpedal or try to shrug off her words.

"I've had that feeling before, yes. Why? Is that something you've been feeling?"

She sighed. "Oh, it's probably just the winter thaw, but, yes, I have been feeling that lately. Maybe I'll hop on the ferry and spend some time in Juneau. I don't know; I just need a getaway." She smiled almost apologetically. "I think I go through this every year. I can't be sure because I never remember this sense of melancholy—that's what Warren calls it, and he tells me it's an annual thing, whether I remember it or not. I really don't remember it. Isn't that strange?"

"That you don't remember it or that you go through it?"

"That I don't remember it."

I shrug. "I don't know, I think that's normal. I hear women forget the pain of childbirth, because if they didn't, they would never have another child."

The dogs had found something intriguing to sniff on the side of the road. We'd come to a stop. Kaye looked at me for a long moment, as if she was taking time to dissect my words. I thought tears might have sprung to her eyes, but she blinked them away before I could be sure.

Finally, she spoke, "That is an incredibly good point, Beth."

I nodded, and wanted to say, *It is?* but I didn't.

"And it makes me think I should work very hard never to let myself forget my melancholy again," she added.

"Well, forgetting can be a form of protection."

"Or a path directly to denial."

I knew all about that, but there was something much bigger going on here than Kaye's winter blues, though I knew that blues on their own could be debilitating. I didn't want to steer her wrong. In fact, I didn't know her well enough to want to steer her in any direction at all, but I had one idea.

"Have you talked to Dr. Powder about how you feel?" I suggested. "He's a wonderful listener."

She frowned and shook her head. "No, I'm afraid not." She looked around the woods. There wasn't another soul in sight, not even a bear. Nevertheless, she lowered her voice, "The Millers don't believe in doctors."

"Oh."

In a few months, if things went as I hoped and Kaye and I became actual friends, not just amicable fellow dog walkers, I would tell her that her family was being dumb. Okay, well, maybe I wouldn't use that word specifically, but I'd do what I could to convince her that doctors were sometimes necessary.

We weren't there yet, but I couldn't stop myself from speaking the next question that came to me.

"Why?" I asked.

"They don't trust them. They think they can handle everything by themselves. To be fair, they've done pretty well so far. Camille isn't a terrible nurse."

"Is she trained?"

Kaye shrugged. "She reads books."

I nodded. "Well, if there ever comes a time when you or someone in your family needs serious medical help, I hope you call or go see Dr. Powder. He's very good, and he can be trusted."

I did trust him, but I couldn't rightly attest to his medical abilities.

He was unquestionably the best doctor around, for miles and miles. Being the only one will give you that superlative.

This time I was sure that tears filled her eyes as she looked at me again.

"What is it, Kaye?" I asked.

Almost violently, she wiped away the tears and sniffed once. She forced a smile. "It's just so good to talk to someone . . . else. You know? Not a Miller or . . ."

"You can talk to me anytime. I'm either downtown or at the shed. Look for my truck and you'll find me nearby. Anytime, Kaye."

She nodded.

The rumble of an engine caught our attention. We hadn't been walking for very long, I thought, but that was Warren's truck coming this way.

"Oh, shoot," Kaye said.

"I can take you home if you want to keep walking. It's no bother at all."

She lifted her eyebrows briefly as if that sounded like a great idea but then she shook her head and wiped her fingers over her cheeks again, seemingly just for good measure. "No, I'd better go with him."

The truck came to a stop next to us. Warren put it in park and then hopped out and came around.

"You're Beth," he said as he extended his hand.

"I am. Nice to meet you, Warren." We shook.

"I should have gotten my lazy butt out of the truck and introduced myself earlier. Apologies if I was rude."

"Not at all."

Warren was handsome in a shaggy sort of way. He was trim, but his shoulders were wide, and his arms were clearly muscular under his plaid jacket. His dark hair was slightly too long and unbrushed. His teeth were crooked but made for an appealing smile. His beard was short, more two-day stubble than anything.

He looked at Kaye. "I'm sorry to cut your time short, darlin'. Pops called for me at the bar and needs me to get home."

"I could bring Kaye home later," I offered. I meant it sincerely, but I also wanted to see how he would react.

He didn't miss a beat. "Oh, that's all right. My mom needs Kaye's help with the bread. Today is bread day. There's plenty to do around the house. Thank you, though."

Kaye smiled apologetically and nodded. "It *is* bread day."

"Okay, well, see you both tomorrow, right?"

"The Death Walk? We wouldn't miss it for the world, unless we were dead, of course." Warren laughed.

Kaye and I smiled. Some version of that joke had been heard around town all month.

He seemed like an okay guy, but I couldn't shake the impression that my time with Kaye had given me. Was it something about Warren or his family that was bothering Kaye, or was it just the seasonal blues she spoke about? I would make an effort to find her tomorrow and see if she seemed better. I suddenly looked forward to meeting the rest of Warren's family, just to see what they were like.

They hopped into the truck. I noticed how Finn sat between Kaye and Warren, and then I noticed how Warren didn't even look at the dog. He didn't seem bothered by him, but he didn't acknowledge him either, not with a "Hey, boy" or a quick scratch behind the ears. Finn didn't seem bothered by Warren, either. He didn't seem anything by Warren.

These were observations I would never have made before I'd been put in charge of finding homes for Elijah's dogs.

Gus and I watched them drive away. We were only about a quarter mile from the shed. We could see it, could see the blue sky above.

I was pretty sure Gus felt as much disappointment that Finn was gone as I did that Kaye was. I hoped we'd get the chance to walk the dogs, or just hang out, again soon.

"It's okay, boy," I said.

He looked at me as if he'd believe me for now, but I should probably do better at making sure he got to visit with Finn. I laughed at his expression. "I'll work on it. I promise."

I lifted my face toward the sky. The sun wasn't shining from above even as it was closer to the horizon, but it was light outside, and the brightness was comforting underneath my eyelids. My face was cool but not cold. I'd been thawing out over the past few weeks. I opened my eyes and peered down the road, thinking that maybe Kaye was doing the same.

I heard a sound that might have been a twig snapping in the woods behind us. I turned quickly and looked out into the trees. I also sniffed but didn't smell anything, including the ripe scent I'd noticed with the wild animals.

I didn't see anything, either.

But I felt something. "Hello?"

The hair stood up on the back of my neck. I was sure someone was out there. So was Gus. I had hold of his leash as he focused his concentration toward where the noise must have come from, wanting to explore but knowing he couldn't unless I let him. The woods were thick, almost impossible to travel through quickly. They made for easy hiding places.

Someone was out there, I was sure, but that didn't mean it was someone being sneaky. It just meant that they didn't want to show themselves. Around here, that could be for reasons that had nothing to do with me specifically.

"Hello?" I said one more time, again to no avail. I muttered to myself, "I know you're out there."

Gus looked up at me.

"No. Come on, let's get back to the shed."

I kept watch behind us as we made our way, but no one emerged from the woods. Once inside, I locked the door, checked it twice, then slipped a chair under the knob.

Two

I was awake before anyone else, or so it seemed. I hadn't slept well anyway; though very little of what had kept my mind spinning had to do with the presence I'd felt in the woods the day before. In fact, I'd concluded that if there had been someone there, they were just walking through; it happened around here. They'd simply moved on. Much like Kaye forgetting her annual melancholy, I did not want to dwell on being concerned that someone might have been watching me.

"Good morning, boy," I said to Gus, who'd slept much better than I had.

He perked up quickly and panted his response. He was fond of mornings and had given me a new positive perspective. A new day, ah the possibilities.

It was only about 5:30, but I got ready and then took Gus out front. In a couple hours, this small downtown would be very busy, but for now it was still quiet and cold. The sun rose at about 4:00 A.M. this time of year, but cloud cover had kept colors muted and shadowy today. I hoped it would turn into a nice morning with no rain—but even if it did rain, the "show would go on" according to what Gril had said a few days earlier.

It was also because of Gus that I'd discovered the solitary early mornings outside. Even in a small town, peace and quiet isn't always easy to find. I savored the new moments in nature I'd found with Gus as he did his morning things across the road in a small patch of woods, and I kept vigil next to the Benedict House's front door.

This morning, I caught sight of Benny leaving the bar. She was bundled up and appeared to be taking out the garbage. I spotted Gus and made sure he had his eyes on me as I hurried over to the other leg of the downtown buildings.

"Can I help?" I asked. "Let me take one of those."

"Much appreciated. What are you doing . . . ?" She spotted Gus across the way. "Oh, that makes sense."

I took one of the two trash bags she was carrying. "The better question is what are *you* doing up so early?"

"Getting ready for the day," she said. "I'm in charge of refreshments."

We made our way to the end of the buildings, where a Dumpster for all the downtown garbage was located.

"No rest for the weary?" I asked.

"I'd say." She sighed.

We lifted the Dumpster lid and tossed the bags inside. After the lid dropped, I took a good look at her. She was visibly tired.

"What time did you close last night?"

With her hands on her hips, she looked out at Gus, who seemed to be chasing something small through the leftover snow. The trees were thick enough over there that things hadn't melted to mud quite yet, and some of the rodents had come out of their winter hiding. Gus never caught anything, but he sure enjoyed the chase.

"I finally got done at around two," Benny said.

"Benny. Why so late?"

She set off walking back toward the buildings. "Had a customer who wouldn't leave."

"You're the boss. You can kick them out."

She shook her head. "No, this one needed some time. I didn't have the heart."

"Who was it? Or is that bartender-patient privilege?" I lightly bumped shoulders with her, just so she knew I was kidding.

She laughed once. "Do you know Cyrus Oliphant?"

"Nope. Never heard of him."

"He's . . . well, he doesn't come around here much, sticks with his family out there." She nodded westerly, as if to indicate the woods on the other side of the downtown buildings. "He was visibly upset, and I was . . . I guess I was worried he was too upset. I wanted him to calm down. He's not much of a drinker, but I managed to get him to nurse a beer long enough that I didn't think he'd drive home either too angry or drunk."

"That was good of you."

She shook her head. "It was nothing."

"Nothing except your sleep. What was he upset about?"

"I still don't know. He wouldn't tell me. He just fumed, held on to his glass too damn tight. I realized he'd come down off whatever ledge he was on when I didn't see smoke coming from his ears anymore and his fingers weren't white from gripping the beer. I got him to laugh—some stupid joke." She chewed on the inside of her mouth. "Just part of the job, I suppose."

It was and it wasn't. Benny had every right to shut the bar down at the posted time, but she wasn't one to kick out someone who might need to be there, or maybe get away from something or someone.

"You're a good friend, Benny," I said.

She waved it off. "Don't even know Cyrus that well."

I heard a *but* in there. I didn't push it. "What can I do to help you? Take a nap. I'll get stuff put together."

"No thank you. The sun is somewhere out there. I'd hate to waste it on a nap." She smiled wearily at me. "You'll like today, Beth. You'll get to see and meet lots more folks."

"Maybe even Cyrus Oliphant."

"Maybe."

Gus bounded up to the boardwalk and greeted Benny with wet (but not muddy, thank goodness) paws and a big smile.

Benny returned the greeting. "You are the best dog ever," she said as she rubbed his neck, both sides at once just like he liked. When they finished their hellos, she turned toward the door. "See you later."

"Yeah. Call me if you need anything. I'll be there"—I nodded at the Benedict House—"until it's time."

"Thank you. See you soon."

I raced Gus back to the Benedict House. He won and was even sitting by the door by the time I got there. I hoped he'd burned off enough energy for a few hours at least.

He and I made our way inside. I cleaned off his paws with one of the towels I kept behind the reception desk, and then we went to find Viola. I didn't see her in the kitchen, dining room, or her office, so I assumed she was still in her room.

I stood outside her door and listened. I thought I heard water running. I tapped on the door lightly.

"Beth?" she said a moment later. "Come on in."

We were the only ones there at the moment. Though the Benedict House was a halfway house for nonviolent female felons, no "clients" had been around for months.

I opened the door. Her bed was made, the room squared away. At one time I'd asked if she'd served in the military. She hadn't. She was a neat freak, though: liked corners tight, no knickknacks anywhere.

"You are up early." She leaned out of the bathroom holding a toothbrush.

"I'm not the only one," I said. "I just saw your sister, and your bed's made. I haven't made my bed yet."

"Benny's in charge of refreshments."

"She told me." I didn't mention the dark circles under Benny's eyes. "What are your responsibilities today?"

She finished brushing her teeth. "Whatever Gril tells me to do. Most years I've just set out to knock on the doors of people who didn't show up."

"Found any dead ones?"

"Just once."

I hadn't expected that answer. "Who?"

"Believe it or not, the remains still haven't been identified. I came upon them as I was making my way out to the old Wilson cabin. The Wilsons, Molly and Darrin, died a long time ago now. They hadn't had the energy to make it downtown that day but they were okay. The remains were about a half a mile from their place." She came out of the bathroom as she was pulling her hair back into a ponytail.

"That's not good."

She shrugged. "As you know, it happens out here." She frowned as if she thought maybe she had too casual a tone. "People do enjoy seeing each other again."

I pulled out a chair that had been tucked into a small, mostly unused desk and sat down. The desk in her office was Viola's preferred working space. "I've heard about it for months."

"Someone will be missing. That's a given. Only one time in all the years I've done the walk has someone we were looking for been found dead, though. Mostly, people forget or just don't want to bother. It drives Gril crazy. He thinks that every able-bodied person should care enough about the community to at least let everyone know they're okay."

"People are private. No one liked having the census man here."

"This is different. Nothing is being recorded for posterity. We just want to make sure you're alive. We don't want to write down what you're up to."

The census man's visit hadn't gone well, but she was right, the Death Walk was nothing like that sort of inquiry.

"Will we all help search?" I asked.

"Depends on who's missing."

Viola was dressed for the day in her typical jeans and long-sleeved T-shirt. Her ever-present gun had already been holstered around her waist even as she'd brushed her teeth and fixed her hair.

"Should we help Benny with the coffee or run over to the restaurant to help with the donuts?"

"The donuts are muffins this year, and they'll be coming from Toshco. The fryer at the restaurant went on the fritz yesterday, so we had to punt. Fortunately, someone was over in Juneau, and they could gather the muffins before they hopped on the ferry. We can help Benny with the coffee."

I'd come to recognize that though they might not be the heartbeat of the community, Viola and Benny certainly kept the blood flowing in the right directions. Gril and Donner were key figures, too. Everyone had their place, but Gril and Donner were trusted and good lawmen. Growing up with my grandfather taught me the value in having those sorts of people leading a town.

"Tex coming?" Viola asked.

"No, he and the girls are traveling in the lower forty-eight for a couple of weeks. This is the girls' first time out of Brayn."

Tex, my . . . something like a boyfriend, and his daughters lived in a Tlingit community about half an hour away from Benedict. We'd had a great time getting to know each other, but I still wasn't sure where the relationship was headed. I missed him, though, and wished he was here. I'd tried not to be "moony" over him, but I'd certainly had a few moments when I'd thought, *Goodness, this man makes me feel squishy inside.*

"He invite you?"

I laughed. "Yes, actually, he did. And I would have loved to spend that kind of time with them, except I didn't want to miss today, and . . ."

Viola gave me a long look. "You're not ready to go back down there yet?"

I sighed and nodded. "I'm just not ready."

"Then it's good you didn't go. Did Tex understand?"

"Yes." I squinted at her. "I like him a lot, Viola, and I adore the girls, but we aren't talking marriage or anything."

"I have two things to say about that."

"Okay?"

"One, yet. And two, marriage . . . it's not like it used to be. No one here is going to judge anything, Beth. You know that?"

"Like if we live together?" I thought the whole world had re-laxed its judgment on most of those types of things.

"Well, sure. But I'm trying to say something else. Marriage out here is a commitment to take care of each other."

"Isn't that what all marriages are?"

"Yes, but out here that particular vow is tested even more. I know you like him—shoot, maybe even love him. He's a good man, there's no doubt, but when you live with people, locked together over a winter, you need to make damn sure you're good with their company."

"You and I did all right this winter."

"This is a big place. Hell, Beth, even Benny and I couldn't live together long-term. All's I'm saying is you need to know yourself, and you need to know if you want that kind of—marriage or even just living together—company. That's all."

I nodded. I heard what she was saying, and I wondered if she was trying to scare me away from Tex. But I quickly realized that wasn't it. Viola was talking about herself. Not only could she not live with her sister, but she also wasn't meant to live in a tight space with anyone. As the notion seemed to come clear in my mind, I watched as she stuck out her elbows a couple times, testing her own space.

I smiled. "Thanks, Viola."

"You're welcome."

All this talk about marriage and living in close quarters with peo-ple had brought something else to the front of my mind. "Do you know Kaye Miller?"

She sent me a strange, questioning look but then normalized. "Sure. Why?"

"She got Finn, one of Elijah's dogs. She and I have spent a few dog walks together. I thought we'd get a good long one yesterday, but her husband, Warren, picked her up and cut it short. I just wonder about them."

Viola shook her head slowly. "There's a lot about that family."

When she didn't continue, I said, "I'm listening."

"Too much to nutshell it for you now but maybe later."

"Well, now I'm very curious."

Viola gave me a half smile. "If anyone should know that the people in Benedict are made of more layers than they appear to be, it is you."

"They have secrets?"

"Everyone has secrets."

With that, Viola grabbed her coat and Indiana Jones fedora and led the way out of her room. Gus and I looked at each other and then followed behind. I couldn't wait to hear more, but for now, there was plenty to do.

Benny's coffee maker was working triple time. Carafes had been filled, and Styrofoam cups had been appropriated from Toshco just like the muffins. A month or so ago, I'd finally met the young couple Nancy and Lucas Nowiki, who ran the Costco-supplied local store.

The Nowikis dropped off the provisions and then grabbed a clipboard that hung on the wall next to the bar door. They marked off their names and told Benny they had to get back to the store. Since everyone would be coming into town for the Walk, the place would be busy.

"It's just a clipboard with names and a column to check them off?" I asked as I inspected it, looking for my name and then making a mark.

"Yep," Benny said.

My thriller-writing mind immediately created a murderous scenario. It was obvious. Someone could kill someone and then mark their victim's name off. If people weren't paying attention, no one would know.

"Doesn't seem super thorough," I commented.

"It's worked so far," Benny said and went back inside the bar to gather something else.

I looked around, watching people make their way to the square. Five hundred souls wasn't a large population, but when everyone came together at the same time in the town square, it made a pretty big group. Everyone seemed to know what to do. First, each person found their name on the clipboard, then they gathered coffee and muffins. I didn't see anyone turn and leave after they got their breakfast. Everyone milled around, talking, laughing. I knew there was more to come.

Benny and Viola had the coffee table under control. I felt more in the way than helpful, so Gus and I walked around, saying hello to people I knew, introducing myself to others. I looked for more of Elijah's dogs but didn't see any, not even Finn. I'd never been a social person, but something inside me enjoyed everything about this morning. It wasn't raining. Everyone I talked to was glad to be there, maybe just glad to be alive on this Death Walk day.

I understood why it was so important, why emerging from the dark, cold winter with good cheer could make a difference to everyone.

From a distance, I watched Gril make his way to Viola, pulling her away from the coffee table with an urgency to his actions. Benny seemed fine on her own, so I didn't rush back to help her. I spotted Orin, a friend and our librarian, standing at the edge of the crowd.

He was the spitting image of a younger Willie Nelson—complete with an ever-present aroma of weed, which he used to help with the pain from an old back injury. He'd spent some time doing secret government work, things I could only imagine filed away under *Special Operations*. He wasn't built for battle, though. Instead, it was his eidetic brain that had attracted government higher-ups and given him security clearance I would never comprehend.

He was looking at a piece of paper, a megaphone tucked under one arm. I approached slowly in case he was trying to focus on something.

He looked up and smiled. "Beth, Gus. Hello." He tucked the paper into his pocket and gave Gus a scratch behind the ears.

"Hey, am I interrupting?"

"Not at all. Did you check off your name?"

"I did." I nodded at the giant mouthpiece under his arm. "Are you the one in charge?"

"Until Gril takes the power from me." He patted the megaphone. "So have you met some more of our lovely community?"

"I have. I can't get over the atmosphere. It's jovial."

"That's the way it's been every year since I've been here. It's good to survive, I guess."

"Yes, it is."

Orin's gaze shifted to where most people had entered the square, from the end of the buildings. His easy smile fell quickly into a concerned frown. "Uh-oh."

I followed his eyes and saw Finn at first, though not Kaye or Warren. I assumed the older woman with a stern face was Camille, Kaye's mother-in-law. The three men who were with Camille looked sort of like Warren, though all of them, including the older one, wore much longer beards.

"The Miller family?" I asked.

"Yep."

"Why did you *uh-oh*?"

"Look at the other group arriving at the same time."

The Millers were clumped close together, just like another group of five who seemed to be purposefully keeping a distance from the Miller group.

"Okay. Who's that?" I asked.

"That's the Oliphants."

"As in Cyrus Oliphant?" I asked, remembering Benny's late-night customer.

"That's one of them. They are . . . quite a bunch—and not friendly with the Millers. In fact, it's a real feud."

"Oh." I observed the two groups again, but again, the crowd made everything difficult to see. I was mostly hoping to spot Kaye, Finn, or Warren, but I didn't. "What happened?"

"Rumor has it that it started because of a girl."

"A story as old as time." I narrowed my eyes as I tried again to watch everyone, but there were just too many people.

"True." Orin nodded. "Each family has its own place, 'compound' they call them. They are geographically next door to each other, but from one you can't see the other. For a long time, they got away with harassing each other without repercussions. Gril changed all that, and they've been forced to keep their noses somewhat cleaner since he got to town."

I could not picture Kaye being a part of such a thing. I didn't know any of the rest of them well enough to have an opinion.

"Excuse me, Beth, I need to grab the clipboard and ask Gril a question before I get this rolling."

I returned the nod and told Gus to stay with me as Orin walked toward the police chief, who was now standing in front of the Benedict House with Viola. Their conversation seemed serious, though I had no way to determine if it was about the feuding families who'd just arrived.

I looked back toward the crowd. I could no longer spot the Millers or the Oliphants, but the entire atmosphere was still positive and lively.

"Hey, Gus." I petted his head. "Should we go find Finn?"

I was pretty sure Gus knew Finn's name. He smiled bigger at the mention of it.

I couldn't spot the dog immediately as I scanned the crowd again, but I did see that Benny was handing out coffees as quickly as she could. Maybe she needed our help now.

I took a step in her direction, but something stopped me. It was the same sensation I'd had the day before, and it made the hair stand up on the back of my neck again.

I turned around quickly, looking toward that patch of woods, but literally no one was behind me. Everyone was in front, milling around the town square.

Not only were there wild animals in the woods, but three domesticated horses also roamed around town. I hadn't seen them during the winter, but I had spotted them just last week, trotting down the road as if they were happy to be out again, too. They weren't behind me, either.

I put my hand on the back of my neck as I continued to search the woods and still saw no one.

"Mom?" I asked quietly.

If there was anyone I might pick up vibes on, it would be Mill Rivers, my mother. Was she back? Was she watching and following me? She would know that she didn't need to be covert with me. Wouldn't she? But there were a lot of people close by; covertness would be in order this morning.

A part of me had felt some dread for this day because of her. What if someone found her body out there amid the thawing tundra? I could only hope that if she was indeed found, she'd be alive and well. I hoped that if it was her I was sensing, she'd show herself soon.

Gus whined next to me.

"It's okay," I said distractedly.

"Beth?" a voice said from behind me.

I jumped. Orin had returned, the clipboard under his arm as he now held the megaphone.

"What are you looking at?" he asked.

"Nothing."

He looked at the woods for a moment and then shrugged. "Okay, then. Here we go." He lifted the megaphone. "All right, everybody, gather around."

I stayed close but stepped to the side to give him enough room so that people didn't think I was part of the official crew.

"If anyone hasn't signed in, please let me know now." Orin held up the clipboard. No one moved toward him or raised their hand.

After another moment, Orin continued, "Okay, it looks like we've got four unaccounted for. That's not as many as usual, but we need to find them. Ready? All right, Donner will check on the Abacos— that's two on the list. Gril will run up to Old Al's place, though I bet he just forgot this was today. Let's hope." Orin looked toward a specific area of the crowd. "Miller's really not here?"

That got my attention. I strained to search for the Millers.

One of the younger men stepped forward. "We haven't seen him since yesterday." He looked toward the Oliphant group suspiciously. "In fact, we're beginning to be worried that he hasn't come home."

I looked even harder, trying to spot Kaye, but I didn't see her, either.

"Thanks, Luther. Did you tell Gril?" Orin asked just as Gril started to make his way toward the Miller contingent.

Luther shook his head. "We are worried, sure, but Warren's also been known to take off for a day or two. We just can't be certain nothing happened to him, and today's the day to let you know." Again, he gave the Oliphant group a suspicious glare.

The Oliphants seemed none too happy, all with their arms crossed in front of them.

I stepped closer, still looking for Kaye but also wanting to be a witness to whatever happened next.

"Step back, Beth," Viola said in my ear. "They'll be fine, but there's no need to get in the middle of those two factions."

"Factions?" I was surprised she'd found her way to me. "That sounds even more serious than a feud."

"It is, but Gril can handle it."

"Have you seen Kaye Miller?" I asked her.

"I'm not sure. Why?"

Everyone's attention was on Gril and Donner as they approached the families. I hurried next to Orin and grabbed the clipboard. He was watching the goings-on, too, so he didn't protest or even really pay me much attention.

I scanned the alphabetical list, stopping at the Millers. There was Kaye, a check mark next to her name. Warren's name, right above hers, was not checked. I returned the board to Orin and then moved back over to Viola.

"Is she marked off?" Viola asked.

"Well, there's a check mark there, but it would be pretty easy for someone else to do that."

"Anyone seen Warren Miller over the last couple days?" Orin asked through the megaphone.

"Saw him a week ago at the mercantile," a voice said from the crowd.

"A week?" Orin asked. "Are you sure?"

"One hundred percent."

"Anyone seen him any more recently than that?"

"I saw him yesterday early afternoon," I spoke up. "He picked up Kaye and Finn from a dog walk."

"Okay, Beth saw him yesterday early afternoon. Kaye, are you here?"

"She ran back to the house," the older Miller woman, Camille, offered.

Orin looked at the clipboard, at the same spot I'd been inspecting, I presumed.

"I haven't seen Kaye this morning," I said to Orin.

"I thought I did," he said to me, though he did sound unsure, then he lifted the megaphone again. "Kaye was here, right?"

The Millers nodded that yes, she had been. Then one of the Oliphants stepped away from his group.

"I saw Kaye this morning." He bit his bottom lip as if he was working to keep himself from saying anything more.

"Thank you, Cyrus," Orin said.

I focused on him. It was impossible to see if he was as tired as Benny seemed. He just reminded me of most of the men all around—a little scruffy, dressed in warm clothes that seemed a little worn, though he also sported what seemed like a very fresh black eye.

"But it wasn't here," Cyrus continued.

"Where was it?" Orin asked. The question seemed abrupt coming through the megaphone. Orin lowered it.

Gril walked over to Cyrus and the two of them spoke privately.

Once they were finished, Gril turned around to face the crowd. His voice was loud enough to be heard by everyone. "All right. I'll be checking out the Millers' place. I'll send Orin up to Old Al's. Donner will check out the Abacos. Anyone else we need to be concerned about? If anyone isn't feeling well, Dr. Powder is available inside the bar. The ferry is back on schedule if anyone needs to get to Juneau today. Any questions?"

He was diffusing a spark in the air before it grew into something uncontrollable. Something wasn't right about Warren and Kaye not being there, but even Gril couldn't know how wrong it might turn out to be. Of course, it could all be nothing, too.

"I have a question," a woman's voice said from the crowd. She stepped around a few people and toward Gril.

"Hey, Tressa, what's up?" Gril asked.

I'd met her before. She was a local pottery expert and had hosted pottery classes at her cabin. I'd attended one, but the craft hadn't stuck with me. I remembered her being soft-spoken and eternally patient.

"Gril, is someone staying in the community center? Sleeping there?" she asked.

"Not that I'm aware of. Have you seen something?"

"I have. I stopped by there early this morning to see if anyone has signed up for a class I've got scheduled for next week. Normally, I don't stop by so early, but when I got there today, I saw a sleeping bag and pillow on the floor, shoved up against the wall. I didn't think anything of it at first, but it stuck with me, and I wonder if it was supposed to be there. If someone needed shelter, I'm glad they had it, but with wondering where Warren is, well, I thought maybe I should bring it up now."

"Glad you did," Gril said. "Anyone here know anything about that? No one's in trouble. I'd just like to know if there's someone out there needing shelter. I can help with that."

No one spoke up. If someone had been staying there, they might volunteer the information in front of everyone, but I thought they'd probably prefer to approach Gril later. He was thinking along the same lines.

"Okay, just come talk to me if you need to," he said. "I'll head out to the Millers' in a few. Anything else, anyone?"

He turned to Orin, and they sent each other a silent look that Orin punctuated with a nod.

The crowd was uncertain what to do. The main part of the event was over, but the majority of folks seemed in no hurry to leave. Rumbles of conversation built again. I stepped away from Viola and jogged over to Gril, Gus right at my heel.

"Gril, can I come with you out to the Millers'?"

"No, you cannot."

"Okay, I get it. Then I need to tell you what Kaye said to me yesterday."

He stopped and gave me his full attention.

I told him about our brief walk with the dogs and how she'd mentioned a yearly melancholy. I told him she asked me if I'd ever felt like running away.

"It could all be nothing, but I thought I should let you know," I said.

"I'm glad you did. They're probably fine, but today's the day that I have to get eyes on everyone."

"Kaye and Warren would understand the importance?"

"Yes, they would."

"I hope you find them."

"I will." He turned and continued on his way.

Gus and I hurried to Orin. "I'll come with you to Old Al's. Gus could use a good hike."

"It's not an easy hike," he said, but he didn't tell me we couldn't go.

"I'll be okay. Gus will definitely be okay."

"Why do you want to go?"

"Burn off some energy."

Orin shrugged. "Fine with me. I could use the company."

A ring sounded from somewhere. It was unusual to hear the sound of a phone outside around here. How had it found a signal?

"What's that?" I asked, looking around.

"Excuse me a minute, Beth," Orin said as he put his hand into his coat pocket and hurried across the way, to a spot behind a tree.

I watched him, my mouth agape. Did he have a special phone? What was it, a satellite phone?

I'd wondered if Orin was still "on assignment," or at least consulting.

"I think I just got my answer," I said to Gus, who whined agreeably back to me.

Three

It wasn't the toughest hike I'd done, but it wasn't easy, either. I was in better shape than when I first arrived in Alaska, but still had some work to do.

We'd taken Orin's truck to a spot past the airport. I didn't know there were homes beyond there, but Orin informed me there were, indeed, a few of them, set up on a rocky ridge with amazing views of the ocean.

"And someone named Old Al lives up on a rocky ridge?" I asked as Gus and I set out, following close behind Orin.

At least it wasn't muddy—all the rocks made for less mud and surprisingly better stability.

"He's lived here for about fifty years," Orin answered. "He's ninety-four."

"What?" My heart rate and breathing had already sped up. "How does he get up and down this?"

"Not as well as he used to."

"Okay."

"In fact, he doesn't get down from here much at all anymore. He orders supplies and Randy gets the things up to him, or neighbors pitch in."

"I can't imagine," I said, picturing Randy, the owner of the mercantile, trudging up the side of the hill with supplies. In fact, I couldn't see many people making such a trip.

Orin continued, "I talked to Randy right before we left. He said that Al ordered enough to get him through the winter and none of the neighbors had come by to order anything extra."

"Through the whole winter?"

"That's what Randy said."

"That might not be good."

"It might not, but Al is determined to live his life his way. More power to him."

"Sure," I said.

That had been something I'd struggled with, the not-uncommon lack of fear many people out here had about their own safety. I'd been told that there were those who moved out here because of the isolated and independent lifestyle. I needed to respect that more, not be so judgmental. If someone chose not to be prepared or to remove themselves so far from civilization that they couldn't get help immediately, I had to accept that they were making their own choices, living their own lives.

Still, it gave me pause: shouldn't ninety-four-year-olds be in places where they wouldn't fall down rocky ridges, where they could get medical attention quickly?

"He's ninety-four, Beth. If we come upon his body, he had a good, long life."

"I hear you," I said.

Gus handled the terrain much better than sure-footed Orin or me. The strong, young husky was jogging ahead of us and then coming back, only to do the same thing again and again. He was having a great time.

We'd been walking for about thirty minutes when we came to the top of the ridge. Once the ground flattened out some, I put my hands on my hips, savored my warm muscles, and let my breathing do its thing as I glanced at a cabin tucked amid some tall spruces.

"Look." Orin turned and pointed behind us.

I turned, too. "Oh. Wow."

The expansive view of the ocean—on a clear day, how lucky was that—was breathtaking. It reached all the way to the end of the world.

"You can see why he likes it up here," Orin said.

"I can, but ninety-four . . ."

Orin shrugged. "Not many people get that many years."

I hadn't asked him about the phone call. I'd wanted to, and I sensed we were close enough friends that I could ask and not be offended when he told me it was none of my business. But as we'd set out, I remembered the strangest thing: I had never been to Orin's house. He hadn't invited me. Anywhere else, it might have seemed odd that I hadn't been to his home, but here it seemed like just another aspect of Benedict life. Our friendship had taken place mostly inside his library and the *Petition* shed. It was a close kinship. He knew who I was, along with Gril, Viola, Benny, Donner, and Tex.

I shouldn't be nosy about the call, and he had every right to keep it to himself even though I was sure he knew I was deeply curious. How could I not be?

I turned again and looked back at the house, reminding myself that ninety-four-year-olds could live wherever they wanted to—it wasn't anyone's business but their own.

"This is spectacular," I said.

"It is. Come on, let's check on Al."

I followed Orin to the cabin door. "How long has he been called 'Old' Al?"

"As long as I've been here, so at least seven or so years." Orin knocked on the door. "Al, you in there? It's Orin." No answer. "I'm coming in." He looked at me. "Give me a minute. If he shoots, two targets would be easier to hit."

"Okay," I said, my eyes wide. "If you get shot, I'm going to be very unhappy."

In fact, he'd been stabbed once in my presence, and it had been awful. He'd recovered well, though.

"His aim is pretty bad," Orin said before he pushed on the handle and then the door. "Al?" He looked back at me. "No bad smells. That's a good sign."

"Uh-huh. Don't get shot." I held on to Gus's collar as the dog sat anxiously at my side.

"Just give me another minute." Orin disappeared into the darkness of the front room. "Al? You here?"

From the outside, the cabin didn't appear to be very large, though it was deeper than I'd originally gauged. I leaned and scanned. It wasn't tidy, but it was neat, the many stacks of things seemingly organized. The front room was made up of the living and cooking spaces. Two wood-burning stoves, one each on one side. I didn't see a fireplace, but those stoves probably warmed the space well enough.

There was nothing modern about the home. All the furniture and shelves were wood planks somehow secured together. A couple of lawn chairs were folded against the wall near a side table.

The stacks of things ranged from magazines to tools to food—I saw ten boxes of saltine crackers.

"Beth, come on back," Orin called from a hallway I could barely see off the back of the kitchen area.

"Come on, Gus," I said.

I squinted through the front room and short hallway but was able to see much better once we were directly outside Al's bedroom. Simple fabric remnant curtains were spread open, letting in plenty of light. Al was there, sitting up on his bed. His eyes were closed but he was breathing. I could see his narrow chest rise and fall with quiet snores. His white hair was a mess, and his even whiter beard appeared to be only a week or so old.

"What's going on?" I asked.

"He's okay, but he's been stuck here for a few days," Orin said. "He was awake just a second ago."

As if on cue, Al's eyes opened, and he cleared his throat.

"What's . . . ? Hello, Orin. Yes, I said hello to you already. What's going on?"

Orin crouched next to the bed. "Hey, Al, this is my friend Beth. We're here to get you some help."

"I don't need help."

"I'm afraid you do. We're going to get you to town."

I had no idea, other than maybe carrying him, how we were going to do such a thing.

"No, Orin, you're not. Let me be." Al looked at Orin, his blue eyes runny and pleading. "Let me be, Orin."

"I'm afraid I can't, Al." Orin patted the man's arm.

Al fell asleep again.

"Oh dear," I said. "What do we do?"

Orin thought for a moment. "You or I will go get some help. Do you want to stay with him or go?"

Honestly, I didn't want to be the one in the cabin if Al died, and indications were that that outcome was a distinct possibility. I could take the exact path Orin and I had taken, and I'd be fine. Probably. That had been the first time I'd walked it, and I knew enough about this wilderness to have a healthy fear of it. But I would have Gus with me—maybe that would be protection enough. Maybe not.

"I'll stay. Gus and I will stay. I'll try to get some fluids in Al," I finally said.

"Good plan."

Orin stood. He petted Gus on the way out of the room. "Take care of them."

Gus smiled up at him.

I walked Orin to the door and then watched him disappear down over the ridge. I was alone with Gus and an old man who could die any minute.

I rummaged around the kitchen and found some cans of soup. I'd never used a wood-burning stove, but I managed to get a fire started in one of the bellies and a pot on top to warm the liquid. I took things one step at a time and tried not to look at my watch. It had taken us about half an hour to climb the ridge. Orin would probably be back in an hour, an hour and a half at the most, with help.

I wished I'd asked what he meant by getting help. Was he getting people to carry Al down the mountain or was there a helicopter somewhere?

As I stirred the pot and it began to steam, I glanced at the time. It had only been fifteen minutes.

Al was asleep again when I took the soup into his room. I nudged his arm gently. "Al, you need to eat something."

It took a couple of nudges to get him to open his eyes. "Who in the hell are you?"

"My name is Beth. I came up here with Orin. He's gone to get you some help. I have soup. You need to eat."

"I don't want to eat. Why won't everyone just leave me alone?"

His eyes were pleading again. I knew what he was trying to tell me, and I knew that neither I nor Orin could have just walked away from him.

I sighed and put the spoon back into the bowl. He didn't seem to be hard of hearing, but I raised my voice just a little in case.

"That's a fine question," I began. "But I have to look at it this way. If we found you alive, you are meant to still be alive. You just didn't die quick enough."

"Hogwash. I'll die when I'll die."

I smiled and lifted the spoon. "Let's not make it today, okay?"

"Who *are* you?"

I lowered the spoon again. "I'm fairly new in town."

Oh, what the hell, I thought. "I came here to hide from a man who kidnapped me and held me in his van for three days. I'm a thriller writer, but I've never managed to write something as terrifying as what I actually lived. I'm working on it, though." Speaking that aloud did something to my insides—released something weighing them down. It was wonderful.

Al blinked at me. "Really?"

"Yeah, and lots has happened since then. Want to hear the story?" I held the spoon up.

"Not if you're going to feed me. Give me that damn bowl." He reached shaky hands toward me.

I grabbed a towel and made him a combination bib and placemat. I set the bowl on his lap.

"Tell me," he said.

"I'll tell you some of it with every bite you take."

Al laughed a second later. "Attagirl. Stick to your guns. Always." He took a bite. "Give me something."

As he downed spoonfuls of the soup, I told him the story I'd only begun so he would pay attention to me. That had worked, but now I'd committed myself to speaking much more aloud than I'd shared with anyone else. Maybe a part of me thought he wouldn't live long enough to tell my secrets to anyone else, but whatever was motivating me, my words seemed to bring Old Al back from however close he'd been to that final precipice. The details of what had and what hadn't happened to me in the van, of my father leaving when I was a kid, of my mother's obsession, and of how much I still missed my grandfather. Al's attention became rapt as he downed the soup and I kept sharing.

It passed through my mind that Leia was going to be impressed by my ability to say the words without breaking down. In fact, at one point I began to feel great about it, freer, maybe even a tiny bit giddy, though I reined that part in. Al didn't need to witness me giggle and shake out my arms—though, that's what I had a notion to do, giggle a little and shake it off.

Finishing his second bowl of soup, Al said, "Goodness, now that's a lot of life for someone so young."

I hesitated. "Well, sometimes it does feel like a pattern, like I'm someone who gets 'left' a lot. But when I say that it sounds like I'm feeling sorry for myself, and you know what, Al? I'm here and alive and doing just fine, so I should not ever feel sorry for myself."

"Don't be silly. You're no different than any of us. We all get left behind in one way or another. Or we die and do the leaving. That's the way it's supposed to work. And if we feel sorry for ourselves every now and then, well, that's normal, too."

I smiled at this man, who now didn't seem anywhere near death. "Want more soup?"

"No, thank you. I'm full, but I do feel better. I'm glad you made me eat."

"You're welcome." I set the bowl on the side table. "Tell me your story, and let me warn you, anything you say might very well be used in an upcoming book I write."

"Understood. Okay, well, I was born in California back in 1925. Can you even imagine what life was like back then?"

"Sure. It was between the two big wars, and the Industrial Revolution was in full swing. What do you remember from your childhood?"

"I remember playing outside. I had brothers and sisters, all gone now, and we were always outside. My parents were schoolteachers. We had food, we had disciplined love and care, but we also had the outdoors. I loved it so much that I slept out there. I grew up on the east side of the state, and then one day, I went west and saw the ocean." Al shook his head. "I fell in love with her right then and there."

"The ocean?"

"Yes, ma'am. Never has there been a love stronger or longer lasting for me."

"Interesting. Were you ever married? Did you have kids?"

Al nodded and fell into thought. "I loved my Dina, and our girl Sasha, but they died when Sasha was only four. They got sick. It was probably a flu or something, but no one ever confirmed anything. When they were gone, I had to get out of California. I came here."

I'd heard a similar story a few times now. "How old were you?"

"Thirty-two."

"You've been here since then?"

"Yes, and I wouldn't have been happier anywhere else."

"By yourself?"

"I had my memories."

"But no one has ever lived with you since you moved here?"

"Nope."

"Wow."

"You think sixty years is a long time?"

"I do."

"It's not. It goes quickly. Make sure you are living your life for you first, Beth. If you don't, you'll have regrets. Everyone is bound to have a few, but don't make a pile of 'em. It sounds to me like you might have figured some of that out already."

"And you don't regret being alone?" I asked, though once the words were out, the question felt impertinent.

"I'm not alone. Yes, I live alone, but I have the wild animals; I have neighbors far enough away not to be annoying. I can go into town. Well, not as easily as I used to be able to, but in nicer weather, I can manage it."

"Did you used to go to town more?"

"Sure. I used to work at the bar that was there before this one. The earlier one burned to the ground along with everything else downtown, except the Benedict House."

"That's where I live."

"Yeah? Have you committed crimes, too?"

"Nope. When I was searching for a place to run and hide, I accidentally booked a room with Viola. She was happy to take my money."

Al chuckled. "Sounds like Viola. She doing okay?"

"She's great, as far as I know."

"She's a peach, that one," he said fondly.

"She's been a great landlord."

Al nodded and then reached to pet Gus. The dog had been resting his head on the bed.

"I've had a dog or two over the years. They make for great company, but I was worried I couldn't take as good care of them as I used to. I can't go for long walks anymore."

"How about a small dog?"

Al chuckled again. It was an endearing sound, almost cartoonish. "My days are numbered, Beth. It doesn't seem fair to do that to any size animal."

"You seem like you're doing much better after the soup. Maybe you were just hungry or dehydrated."

"I probably was." He sent me a sly, knowing smile.

"Well, let's hope you have longer than you think."

A boom of thunder startled us. Gus barked once and then hurried out of the bedroom to investigate.

"I'll be right back," I said to Al as I followed Gus.

Once over the initial boom, no one, even Gus, was too bothered by the rainstorm. We were all used to them.

However, the weather could mean that Al's rescue would be somehow delayed. I opened the front door and was greeted by dark clouds and heavy rain. I couldn't see beyond the storm—the breathtaking ocean views were hidden, the world now shrunken and gloomy.

It would either pass quickly or not, but at least we were sheltered. By my calculation Orin should have returned by now. He was probably waiting for things to calm down.

I closed the door, and Gus and I returned to Al.

"Love the rain," he said with a smile as we came into his room.

"I do, too, but that probably means that Orin will be a little longer. Can I fix you anything else to eat?" I paused. "Do you have a deck of cards?"

"Do I have a deck of cards?" he said with a conniving smile. "Check the end table next to the couch."

I left the bedroom again, Gus remaining with Al. I was trying hard not to look bothered by the storm. I wasn't overly worried, but there were unknowns. I'd dealt with lots of them for almost a whole year now. There was no way to reach anyone, and even after living that way, the disconnection sometimes made me anxious.

I opened the end table drawer and found at least twenty decks of cards inside, organized by box colors. I picked a blue deck adorned with the Eiffel Tower and took them back to Al's room.

We started with go fish, just so I could get my card mojo back, and then moved on to gin rummy and finally five-card stud. Al was a much better card player than I was, no matter what the game.

Another hour passed. I made him more soup, this time also

opening a can of pears and pouring them in another bowl. His appetite seemed fine.

It rained on and off the whole time, with brief reprieves but no sunshine. Al finally said he was "plumb tuckered out" and he'd like to nap a bit.

Gus and I left him alone and went back to the front room where we could watch the outside through a thin pane of glass that served as a picture window. During a pause in the storm, we stepped outside. It was cold but not miserable, and I was so enamored by the scent of wet pine that all I really wanted to do was stand there and sniff.

But then the sensation I'd first had the day before came over me. Was someone out there watching? I scanned the entire area, but surely no one was riding out the storms in the woods. I didn't see anyone. I put my hand on the back of my neck again. The hair was on end.

What was going on?

"Come on," I said to Gus. "Let's get back inside."

I hesitated, though, as I heard the rumble of an engine. I couldn't immediately place from which direction it was coming. A second later I was rewarded with an answer. Gril rode an ATV up and over the ridge. A trailer that someone could lie down and ride in was hitched behind. Once the getup had cleared the ridge, Donner appeared on another ATV, this one without a trailer.

The cavalry had arrived.

"Where's Orin?" I asked as Gril disembarked and turned the key to the squat machine.

"I have no idea," Gril answered, none too happily if I was reading his tone correctly.

I looked back and forth between him and Donner. "What does that mean?"

"How's Al?" Gril asked.

"Resting, doing better. I got some food in him. Where's Orin?"

Gril said something unintelligible and then made his way into the cabin. I looked at Donner.

"Let's get Al taken care of, Beth," he said.

Gus and I followed the men inside.

Al didn't like the fuss. This was no surprise to anyone, but he wasn't given any choice. He was coming down the mountain and spending at least a few days with Dr. Powder. Gril had decided. He wasn't in the mood to argue.

Once the men got Al up, he needed assistance walking for a few steps, but was able to make it on his own after that, though slowly.

The rig on the back of the ATV looked homemade but sturdy. Al lay down on the bed, inside some thick sleeping bags, and Gril and Donner secured him with ties. They made him wear a helmet and also bundled his head into the sleeping bag.

Donner and I watched as Gril maneuvered over the ridge and slowly down the rocks. The sky had mostly cleared by the time Donner and I hopped onto the other ATV. Gus walked by our side as we took the slope just as slowly as Gril.

"What's going on, Donner?" I asked. "Did something happen to Orin?"

"He left a message for Gril, said that Al needed help, but then we couldn't track him down after that. The message was left about two hours ago, and Gril was fit to be tied that Orin hadn't done a better job to try to find us. Orin didn't answer the library phone, and he wasn't at his house."

"That's weird," I said. "I . . . I thought I saw him talking on a phone near downtown today. He might have a satellite phone."

It seemed important enough to let Donner know about the phone, but I did feel a small wave of disloyalty, maybe like I was telling on Orin.

"We know. Gril has that number, too, but Orin wasn't answering it, either."

"That's weird," I said again. "Do you think something happened to him?"

"I doubt it, but Gril sure would have liked to learn about Al in a timelier manner, and he is now worried about Orin."

"But you're not?"

"A little, but this can happen. You know how communication is out here."

"I do. Should you and I stop by Orin's house again on the way in or does Gril need help?"

"No. Gril needs my help but not with Al."

I thought for a moment. "Warren Miller?"

"Well, we're more interested in his wife, Kaye."

"What's going on?"

I held on tight as Donner maneuvered the ATV over a particularly unruly clump of rocks. I remembered them from the walk up and was glad I was on the vehicle on the way down.

"She signed in this morning but left quickly, as far as we can understand. When Gril went out to the Miller house, neither Warren nor Kaye was there."

"Wait, did anyone truly see Kaye at the Walk this morning?"

Donner shrugged. "Not sure yet."

"No sign of Warren either?"

"Nope. Some of the family said they were sure at least that Kaye would be back this evening, but Gril has some suspicions. We're heading out there again once we get Al situated."

Now I wondered if I'd been ignoring something because I was glad to have a home for Finn, willing to just listen to the part of my gut that told me Kaye was a good person but not keying in on something else I should have.

I didn't even know exactly where they lived.

"I know Kaye," I said.

"Okay."

"I know the dog. Finn. Want me to come with you?" I said.

Donner laughed. "Beth, knowing the dog doesn't mean you should be involved. I'm sorry about that."

I frowned behind him. He had a point, but I didn't know how to explain to him how seriously I took the mandate of taking care of Elijah's dogs. I'd seen the folders before Elijah had disappeared. My mother had asked me specifically to make sure the dogs were okay if, in fact, Elijah didn't return. She had been immediately besotted by all of Elijah's animals—though I later wondered if it was actually Elijah, aka Hugh Givens, she was besotted with. No matter. I took my role as dog re-homer seriously.

But it was my rekindled concern for Kaye that made me really want to go. Our time together the day before had left me feeling concerned about her. I hadn't seen her this morning, and I'd wanted to. Had she really been at the Walk? What about her mention of sometimes wanting to run away?

"Okay," I finally said.

"I can tell you don't mean it, but I would recommend you staying out of Gril's way on this one. He's not in a good mood about any of it."

"I hear you."

"Good."

I looked at Gus walking next to us. I wasn't about to ignore any of Elijah's dogs, no matter what kind of mood Gril was in, and I was becoming increasingly concerned about Kaye. Where was she? Was she okay? I held on tight to Donner and thought about what to do next.

Four

pulled open the Benedict House's front door. Viola was inside, standing behind the old counter that was used back when the place was an inn. She appeared to have been waiting for me.

"Beth, I need to talk to you." She came around and absentmindedly greeted Gus as he trotted to her.

"Okay."

"We have a new temporary resident today."

"Uh-oh. Bad shape?"

"No, in fact, not bad at all, but . . . he's a he."

"You're in charge of a male felon this time?"

Viola nodded, concern pulling at her features. "This is the first time, and I know that might make you nervous. I don't want you to be uncomfortable, but I've got no choice but to keep him here for at least a week or so."

I nodded, trying to keep a neutral expression. "What did he do?" I didn't want her to see how nervous it made me. I'd put the notion in my head that since all the felons who stayed at the Benedict House were female, none of them could be like my abductor. It was a stretch in logic I'd used to make myself feel more secure, and something I didn't feel I could let go of. In fact, a male resident might bother me enough to stay at the *Petition* shed for a while. "Is he violent?"

"His name is Chaz and he's from Fairbanks. He embezzled money from one of the oil companies. Well, he tried to. There were no weapons, not violent." She paused to let those important words sink in. They did and I nodded her on. "It was a federal crime and he's shifty. He was in prison for a while but released to a house in Anchorage. He ran away. They caught him and gave him the choice of going back to prison or coming here."

"He doesn't sound dangerous." I sounded more hopeful than certain.

"I don't think he is." She smiled briefly, though it seemed forced. "Well, not in a brutal way."

"What way, then?"

Viola's shoulders relaxed. "He's a charmer."

"Oh." I smiled, too, feeling real relief now. "I think I can control myself. I'll try to, at least."

"Yes, but I wanted you to have a heads-up."

"Thanks."

Viola relaxed even more. "He's also a better cook than we've had in some time. He made dinner. Left you a plate in the fridge."

"That's great," I said. "Thank you."

I realized she had, indeed, been waiting for me to come home. I appreciated her concern. She knew the story of my days with Walker and that men I didn't know made me extra vigilant.

Viola didn't take violent female clients, and I accepted that the powers that be wouldn't send her a dangerous male client, either.

We heard footsteps trotting down the far stairway. Viola turned and I peered around her, more curious than I'd been in a long time to meet a new resident.

My first reaction when seeing Chaz was to smile because, well, he was smiling, too. My second reaction was to laugh, because it simply wasn't humanly possible to be that good-looking. Was it?

Probably just over six feet tall, it was obvious that he worked out. His wide chest, muscled arms, trim waist, and flex-while-you-walk thighs were the first clues.

His smile shone brightly with perfect teeth and his brown eyes twinkled as he approached.

His skin was dark, his hair short—too short to do anything like fall over one side of his forehead or wave with the wind—thank goodness for small mercies. Having fabulous hair on top of everything else would be unfair.

"You must be Beth," he said as he stopped in front of us and extended a hand.

To top everything off, he had a slight British accent. Or maybe that was Australian.

"I am," I said as I extended my hand, too. "You must be Chaz."

"Guilty." He smiled at Viola and then back at me. "In so many ways." He winked.

On a less confident person, his act might have felt forced. But in the few seconds I'd been in Chaz's company, I'd sensed he was one hundred percent genuine, and though my life's experiences had put me way past having my head turned in such a way, I could see how this man could accomplish pretty much whatever he set his mind to with a smile and a wink, if he found the right people to be appropriately receptive. There were many such folks.

"I made you some dinner," Chaz said when we released the shake. "Shall I warm it up for you?"

"I can warm it. Thanks, though."

"Viola made me taste everything to prove I hadn't poisoned anything."

"How distrusting of her." I looked at her as she rolled her eyes. In fact, it was what she always did. When the guests cooked, they also tasted everything first. This was nothing new.

"Come on, let's get you fed." Viola walked around me and Chaz and led the way into the dining room.

Chaz swept his hand for me to lead the way. I nodded and did exactly that.

* * *

"Goodness, you are a really good cook," I said as I took a bite from the plate he had put in front of me. He had insisted on doing the warming preparations.

"Kind of."

"Is this chicken parm?" I asked as I took another bite. It was delicious, even reheated. My appetite had been insatiable when I'd first moved to Alaska. It was more under control now, but my hunger was still more noticeable than it had ever been before Travis Walker.

"Yes, ma'am. Tomorrow, I'm thinking tri-tip if Viola can get her hands on some beef."

"Well," I said in between chews, "don't call me late for dinner."

Chaz smiled but then frowned when he saw Viola's unamused expression.

We sat around the table together. They watched me eat, and I didn't mind the attention—the food was delicious. I could tell Viola felt the need to be there, but not because she thought I might be taken in by Chaz's charms. Though she'd said he wasn't violent, she clearly didn't trust him. She didn't trust any of the clients at first.

"Have you heard anything from Orin in the last few hours?" I asked her.

"No, why?"

"He and I went up to check on Old Al, but Gril and Donner came up to get me and Al after Orin left to get help. Orin seems to have disappeared."

"I should have asked earlier—is Al okay?"

"He's . . . I think so. He's spending some time with Dr. Powder. I don't think he'd eaten for a few days. I got some food in him, and he seemed to perk up. He told me his days were numbered."

"He is ninety-four, so that's probably true. But damn, he doesn't need to rush it along," Viola said.

"Are you two friends?" I asked.

Chaz lifted an eyebrow and looked at Viola. The expression on his face was complete interest. If she looked at him, she'd think he cared more about her than anyone else on the planet. Yes, he was very good at . . . charming.

"He was like a father figure when Benny and I first came to Benedict."

I nodded, looking at her expectantly.

"He worked at the original bar in town." Viola paused. Then she smiled and fell into thought. "When Benny and I disembarked from the ferry that day a hundred or so years ago—we were kids *and* stowaways—we went into the bar because that's the sort of place we knew about. Our parents spent all their time back in Juneau in bars before they were killed in a car accident. He saw us, two ragamuffins, and took us under his wing. He let us stay in the back room for a while, made sure we had food. We found our own place a few months later, but Al was always there for us if we needed him."

"We talked about you briefly, but he didn't tell me any of that." I'd put my fork down.

Viola shook her head. "We were kids, selfish, and when we got a small taste of independence, we just kind of went with it. Al, who had treated us like his own, got forgotten for a while. He was always good to us, even when we were rotten to him, bratty and ungrateful like kids can be. We made amends at some point, but things were never the same."

"Well, it's not too late, if you want to see him," I said. "I really think he's in better shape than he wants to acknowledge. He'll be at Dr. Powder's if you're inclined to check on him."

Viola nodded. "That's a good idea."

"Oh yes," Chaz added. "You have a chance to make something better. It's a rare opportunity."

This time both Viola and I shot him questioning glances.

He cleared his throat and smiled at me again. "I also made cake!"

"I'm not one to turn away any sort of cake," I said. I lifted my fork and got back to work on the chicken Parmesan.

After dinner, I settled in my room to take notes for a potential new story, keeping the other one on my mind's back burner. I'd been disappointed that Donner wouldn't let me go with him to check on Kaye, but meeting Chaz had given me something else to think about.

I wrote a quick email to Tex, inquiring if he and the girls were enjoying their trip. I shared some events from the day, telling him that I'd learned about a local feud but wished for details. He knew about Kaye and Finn, so I told him those details, too, letting him know my concerns. I ended the note with *XOXO* but not the word *love*. Not yet, though there had been moments . . . I shook myself out of my thoughts. Even if I did have time for romance, I wasn't sure it was a good idea. Benedict was certainly my home—but only for now. Right?

I'd have to send the email the next day when I got to the shed. There wasn't enough signal at the Benedict House to do much of anything but catch a random and unreliable call every now and then. I was just about to pull up an old sitcom I'd downloaded on my laptop when Viola knocked on the door.

"Phone call for you. It's Donner," she said.

I joined her in the hallway. "Really?"

The Benedict House had a landline, which though rare around Benedict, wasn't as uncommon as a good cell signal. I'd used mine to make a few calls, mostly to and from Tex, but I didn't think Donner had ever called me. I was immediately worried about both Orin and Al.

"Yes, ma'am," Viola said.

Sock-footed, I hurried down the hall toward her office, and Gus followed behind.

"Donner?" I said as I picked up the phone.

"Hey, Beth. Listen, we're at the bar. I'm calling from Benny's phone in her back room."

"Okay. We?"

"Gril, me, and the Miller family. I . . . Well, Kaye hasn't come home, and Warren is still missing, too. We asked the rest of the family to come into town—get them out of their comfort zone, you know?"

"I do know."

Asking a group of people to meet Gril and Donner at the bar was probably equivalent to asking them to come down to the station.

The official police offices were housed in a cabin, but I knew the heater had been on the fritz lately. It was June, but nights were still pretty chilly around Benedict.

"You mentioned you know Kaye, talked to her yesterday?"

"Yes. Well, we took the dogs for a walk together. We've done that a few times now."

"I don't know her well and have no idea who her friends might be. I wonder if you could come over. Gril and I won't even mind if you interject a comment or question. We need to find Kaye and Warren, and we're not getting anywhere very quickly."

"Absolutely," I said. "I'll be there in a few."

"Good. Thanks."

"How about Orin? Al?" I asked quickly before he hung up.

"Al's doing well. We still can't find Orin, either. But, Beth, Orin does things—I don't know, he has been known to disappear for a day or two."

Despite Donner's unworried tone, my heart sank a little. It was more than the fact that Orin had disappeared. He'd left me with Al without any indication he wouldn't be back. He would have said something to me if he'd known he wasn't going to return, I was sure of it. Even something ambiguous. I'd just have to hope he'd show up soon.

"I'm on my way," I said.

"What's up?" Viola asked from the doorway to her office as I placed the handset onto the cradle.

"Kaye and Warren Miller are missing, or haven't come home, or something. The Millers are at the bar now, came in for questioning, I guess. Since I saw Kaye yesterday, Donner wants me to come over."

"Why?"

I shook my head. "I'm not exactly sure, but . . . maybe Kaye doesn't have many friends? Maybe they don't believe something the Millers are saying and think I can help clear up some timing maybe."

"Okay. Well, that's . . . yeah, I don't know anything about Kaye's friends, either."

"Al's okay, but they haven't found Orin yet."

"Orin will be fine," Viola said confidently.

I wished I was as sure.

Viola continued, "I think it's okay that you're going over there, but you need to stay out of the fray, if there is indeed a fray."

"What do you mean?"

"The Oliphants and the Millers. I've seen fisticuffs, guns drawn, knives thrown. Neither family is particularly even-keeled."

"I don't think the Oliphants are at the bar, and I've never seen Kaye behave unreasonably."

Viola bit her bottom lip. "She came here from the lower forty-eight, and I think she was escaping something bad down there, so bad maybe the feud is easier. I don't know the story or the details, but just be careful."

I nodded. "Okay. You really don't seem worried about Orin."

"Well, honestly, I'm always worried about Orin, but he knows what he's doing even if the rest of us aren't in on it."

"Got it." I took a deep breath. "I'll let you know how it goes." I looked at Gus. "Stay with Viola." He seemed agreeable.

Viola stepped away from the doorway. I went to my room, threw on some shoes, a hat, and a coat, and made my way to the bar.

Five

I t wasn't terribly crowded, but it was unusually smoky. Benny didn't allow smoking, so my first concern was about the smell. Was something on fire?

My eyes zeroed in on an ashtray on the bar where a cigar had been snuffed out, a thin smoke trail still lingering above. There was no indication who'd been smoking it, but I didn't think it was Benny, Gril, or Donner. My eyes found Benny's. She still looked tired as she frowned curiously at me. I would have bet she'd wanted to close early tonight.

It was rare that I was in the bar this late, past my self-imposed ten-thirty bedtime. It was somewhat rare that anyone was here this late. The environment was too unpredictable; most folks were under the protection of their own roofs by now.

Benny's attention was quickly redirected to everyone else. She watched them all with a suspicious gaze.

I made sure the door closed behind me and then took in the group.

Gril and Donner sat in chairs by the bar, both of them turned to face the other people who were also sitting or leaning on tables that had been brought together into the middle of the small space. None of the booths around the perimeter were occupied.

I recognized some of the people from this morning's event, but I didn't know who was who. Benny waved me over to her. I joined her just as Gril was trying to get all the others to quiet down and stop talking all at once.

"What are you doing here so late?" Benny asked me quietly.

"Donner called me."

She gave me a concerned frown. Keeping her voice low, she asked, "That was you he called? Why?"

I shrugged. "I saw Kaye yesterday? I'm not exactly sure."

"Okay. Heads up, though. These are some unhappy people."

"The Miller family?"

"Yep." Benny nodded toward the eldest man, who had one hip resting on the corner of a table closest to the dying cigar. "That's Ike. He's the family's patriarch, but they are governed pretty equally by the matriarch, too."

"Okay."

"Ike's wife is Camille, and the two sons here are Luther and Craig." She nodded respectively.

Ike, with his gray hair and long gray beard, was big and solid, reminding me of a weathered tree trunk. His wife, Camille, sat in a chair next to him. Her dark hair was pulled up into a severe bun, and her lips were pursed tightly in an expression that told me she wasn't in the mood to suffer fools this evening, probably ever. And if I could read it correctly, she thought pretty much everyone was a fool.

Luther and Craig, also sitting in chairs, both had their arms crossed in front of themselves, their eyes angry. Luther favored his mother with a long face and thin lips. Craig looked more like their father, reminding me of a less roughened tree trunk, though gray was already showing at his temples.

"You all, there was no sign of either Kaye or Warren at the Oliphants'. None," Gril said, as if he'd already said the same thing a number of times. He was tired.

The three Miller men were working hard to keep their mouths pinched tightly shut. They all looked toward Camille, who spoke with an even tone.

"Well, again, Gril, that's hard to believe," she said.

"Camille, I looked everywhere."

"Did you have a warrant?"

"I did not, but I didn't let that stop me from opening doors or searching every corner. They weren't anywhere."

"You know Warren is the third son and Kaye is Warren's wife?" Benny said to me.

I nodded. "Yes. When did they get married?"

"Ten years ago, I think."

I nodded again.

"Who is sleeping in the community center?" Camille asked.

"We don't know yet, but we'll be checking it throughout the night," Gril said.

"Put up a camera," Luther added.

Gril sighed. "You all know it's not that easy." He looked around. "Sure, we might get a camera up to record things, but the power at the center isn't trustworthy, and there is zero internet access there. We don't have any sort of feed that we could watch remotely. You all know this, but you also know I'll figure out who it is, and if that person has something to do with Warren and Kaye. Now, you need to answer my questions so I can be as thorough as I need to. Stop deflecting."

"That can't be good. They're deflecting," I muttered to Benny.

"Yes, big time. They've been annoying as hell, and they sure behave like they've got something to hide. They keep insisting Kaye and/or Warren is at the Oliphants' but won't really tell Gril and Donner why."

"Why not?" I asked.

"I can't understand yet."

"What do you know about the feud?"

"Too much to share right here, but it's been ugly, and that's only the parts we've all seen—remnants of fights, black eyes, swollen lips." She lowered her voice even more. "When Cyrus was here last night, he didn't have that black eye yet."

"Feud or in-family fighting?"

"Everyone thinks it's families fighting each other, but, and this probably won't surprise you, no one fesses up to anything. Running into things happens a lot with them."

"Kaye?" I asked, wondering if she'd been physically abused.

Benny shook her head. "I've never seen her injured. Never. Gril would have put a stop to that if he'd seen it."

I turned my attention back to the group. Even though Benny had immediately said that she'd never seen Kaye injured, a new anger simmered under my skin. Had this group done something to Warren and Kaye, their own people? I gritted my teeth and tried to watch them all at once.

The members of the Miller family looked at one another. I sensed they were either about to stand up and leave or remain and not say another word.

"Look," Ike finally said, breaking a silence that went on a beat too long. He glanced at Camille who seemed to silently tell him to shut up. He shook his head once at her and continued, "Warren and Kaye were fine as of about a week ago. Nobody sensed anything was wrong, but Warren started leaving the house at night about then. He was always home in the morning."

"Did anyone ask what he was doing?" Gril asked.

"Sure, but none of us got an answer." Ike looked at the others, who, in turn, nodded their agreement, though Camille took her time.

"Okay, well, thanks for that information, Ike. I appreciate knowing it. Did Kaye go with him?"

"No." Camille's voice was sharp and quick, like a knife.

"Something happened, though, and I bet someone here has an idea what it was." Gril sighed and rubbed his hand over his scraggly beard. "Look, let's go with this question. To any of your knowledge, has Kaye ever just up and left for any extended length of time? Hell, even overnight?"

Once again, the family members all looked at one another, but didn't immediately respond.

"This is frustrating," I muttered to Benny.

Gril slammed his hand down hard on the bar, startling us all and filling the air with a boom followed by the oddly pleasant sound of glass tinkling somewhere.

"You're upset that I haven't found your family members, but none of you are being up-front with me. How can I find them if you're not talking?" Gril bellowed. "I need to do my job, but you can't expect it to be done right if you won't tell me anything."

"Gril," Ike said calmly. "We are certain that the Oliphants had something to do with their disappearance. You just need to keep asking them. Be forceful with them; search their place more deeply."

Gril leveled his gaze. "Why? What happened?"

"Nothing," Ike said, sounding exactly like he was lying. "It's just the same old stuff over and over again. The 'feud,' as everyone in town calls it."

"Come on, Ike," Gril said. "Why would Kaye and Warren be in the middle of this more than any of the rest of you?"

Luther stood slowly, as if he wasn't so sure he wanted to do it. But when he was upright, he looked at his parents. "Gril has to know. We have to tell him."

"We keep our business private." Camille spat the words with gritted teeth. "Gril just has to trust us to know that we know what we're talking about. The Oliphants are up to something."

"Maybe, Ma, but right now we need to spill some things," Luther said. He looked away from his parents and took a step toward Gril and Donner. "They had a fight. About a week ago, Warren caught Kaye over at the Oliphants. He thought she was cheating on him with Cyrus Oliphant. He blew up at her, and then he left overnight. He's been a mess since then. She left yesterday morning, took the dog with her, and then didn't come home when the dog did."

He'd rushed the words, probably wanting to get them out before one of his family members physically stopped him.

"Uh-oh," Benny said. I guessed she hadn't told Gril about her late customer the night before.

I wanted to ask her for details, but too much was happening at once.

"Goddammit, Luther, sit down!" Ike stood and yelled.

"Hang on." Gril stood, too. "You sit down, Ike. Why you think I don't deserve the truth is beyond my comprehension."

Wow, I thought. If what Luther said was true, this was only going to add even more fuel to a fiery feud.

"Is that why Cyrus Oliphant has a black eye?" Gril asked Luther.

Luther shrugged unconvincingly. "I can't tell you why he has a black eye. Ask him, and while you're at it, ask him if he knows where Kaye went and why she was there at his house last week. None of us know those truths, I promise. He said today that he saw her this morning. You went and talked to him."

"Thank you, Luther." Gril looked at the others. "Yes, Cyrus did say that he saw Kaye this morning. I will only tell you that when I talked to him about it, he told me he wasn't sure but he thought maybe he saw her out walking."

"Horseshit, Gril!" Ike said. "He's the one you need to be questioning further."

Gril nodded at Ike though he kept his expression firm. "I will. It would have been helpful to have this information sooner, though. Now, is there anything else you can tell me? I want to find them. I'm on your side here."

"You've always been on the Oliphants' side," Camille said.

Gril cocked his head at her. "When I say I'm on your side, I mean I'm on the side of everyone in this community, and I will bring those who break the law to justice, no matter what their last name is."

Ike gave Luther a look that was somehow even sterner than the one he'd just been giving him. Luther backed up and sat back down. Ike leaned on the corner of the table again.

"That's all we know," Ike told Gril. "We're pretty sure Cyrus Oliphant knows what's what, though. We do suspect an affair, though it's not something we want to spread around. Got it?"

Gril glared at Ike. "I'll talk to Cyrus again. This information helps. It does. I'll get more out of him." He turned to Luther. "Thank you."

Ike frowned and nodded at Gril, though anger at their dirty laundry being aired still showed in his expression.

I hadn't known anything about Kaye's family, and we'd never met at her house. She'd preferred downtown or at the *Petition* shed.

"I saw them both yesterday . . ." I said, interjecting, just like Donner told me I could. "Yesterday morning. Warren dropped Kaye off so we could walk the dogs together." I'd put together the time frame enough to know that there was a good chance that I was the last person to see her before—whatever happened to her. I was ready for someone to turn that around on me and surprised when they didn't.

"You're the one who gave her the dog," Luther said as everyone's eyes fell upon me.

"Yes. I'm Beth."

Camille stood. "You're the girl with the scar."

"I am." I took off my hat, displaying the thing people had come to know me by. I'd discovered that whatever mystique came with my reputation deflated quickly the second I showed the scar and scraggly haircut.

"Kaye said she sometimes goes on walks with you," Camille said.

"That's true."

"You weren't with her two days ago?"

"No, ma'am. We walked the dogs yesterday, briefly. Warren picked her up, said that his father"—I nodded toward Ike—"needed him and that you"—I nodded at Camille—"needed her for bread day."

"Yesterday wasn't bread day," she said to me. "And Warren didn't pick her up from the house." Camille looked at the others, who nodded. "She left on her own. If what you're saying is true, they met away from the house before he brought her out to you."

"What I'm saying is true," I said.

Camille continued, "She said she walked the dogs with you at least three times a week."

Well, of course, this was news. My gut told me not to share with her family that Kaye and I hadn't really had that many encounters over time, but Gril and Donner needed to know. I'd tell them later.

"I've been busy lately." I shrugged. I didn't want to expose Kaye's lies to them like this. "I haven't seen her for a while, though. I'm not exactly sure when the last time was."

I was. I had it written on my calendar.

Camille frowned at me like she didn't like what I was saying, but she didn't argue. She fell into thought and then turned back to Gril. For the first time, her tone wasn't lined with anger and frustration. "Find them, Chief, please."

"I will," Gril said.

He would.

"Anything else I need to know?" he asked. "Anything?"

I looked at Benny. She shook her head and mouthed, "Later."

You could feel it in the air, the diffusion of their anger mingled with the secret they'd been carrying. Sure, they were upset at Luther for sharing something so private, but they knew how important that information was going to be to Gril, even if they hadn't wanted to acknowledge it beforehand. Having observed my grandfather in the same sorts of situations, I still didn't understand why keeping a family secret was more important than the truth, but I knew that sometimes it just was.

The Millers cleared out shortly thereafter, leaving the rest of us with our own weariness. Nevertheless, Gril turned to me before Benny could speak up. "Why are you here, Beth?"

I had kind of been under the impression that he knew about Donner's call, but since that hadn't been the case, I wasn't sure what to say.

"I called her, Gril," Donner jumped in. "I knew about the dog connection, and I remembered Beth saying she saw Kaye, but I didn't remember or know all the details."

Gril nodded. "Well, that actually seemed to work." He looked at me. "You haven't been walking the dogs three times a week?"

"No. Before yesterday, I hadn't seen Kaye in a month or so. I've got the exact date written on my calendar, but I didn't bring it with me."

"Well, she was going somewhere all those times she said she was with you. I doubt we'd know about those times if you hadn't come over." He looked at Donner. "Good call."

Donner continued, "I don't know if Cyrus and Kaye were seeing each other romantically or not. But I've asked around, and I think Beth might have been one of the last ones, other than Kaye's family, to have had confirmed eyes on her."

"What else can you tell me about your visit with Kaye?" Gril asked me. "You told me about her running away comment, but was there more? Did she bring up Cyrus Oliphant to you?"

"No, not once. We don't know each other well, but . . . I think we might end up friends. We got along and just clicked every time we were together, but I still don't know her well. I wish I did. We haven't been walking the dogs three times a week. Only about five times since January. I'd never heard of the Oliphants until the Walk this morning."

"Yeah, Kaye was lying," Donner said.

"Or they're lying about what she said," Gril added.

At this juncture, it seemed impossible to know for sure, but I put my money on the fact that Kaye had done the lying.

"Gril," Benny said. "Cyrus was here last night. Kept me open late."

"Oh?"

She nodded. "He was upset."

She had everyone's attention, but Gril said, "Details?"

"I wish I could give you something solid, but it was mostly him crying in his beer, almost literally. He was wound up, angry, upset. I just kept him here to get him to calm down. We didn't talk about much of anything important, but he managed to relax some. He didn't say one word about Kaye, the Millers, or even his own family, just . . . cursing about 'those greedy assholes' and such. I even asked him who the assholes were, but he didn't answer."

"But he said 'greedy'?" Gril asked. "Did he talk more about money?"

She shook her head and frowned. "I don't think so. Shoot, more than anything, I just kept trying to change the subject, lighten things up. But, Gril, he didn't have the black eye last night. That was new."

"I figured," Gril said. "When I talked to him . . . well, I think he only spoke up about seeing Kaye this morning to get the Millers' attention, see what they'd do. When I talked to him, he really wasn't sure about seeing her."

"He's lying, too?" Benny asked.

Gril lifted his eyebrows. "They're all probably lying in one way or another, but I suppose it's my job to suss out some truth somewhere. I searched both the Millers' and the Oliphants' houses today and didn't find Warren or Kaye or evidence that something might have happened to either of them. We didn't get all the information we need tonight. They'd never tell us everything they know, but at least we know who specifically the Millers suspect—Cyrus—and their reasoning, which could be wrong or right," Gril said.

"How was Kaye and Warren's marriage?" I asked.

Gril and Donner shared a questioning look.

"No problems that we've been made aware of," Gril said.

"Like Camille said, I bet they take care of their problems on their own," I said.

"That's probably true," Gril said. "Except this time around the Millers need my help, which means they've probably exhausted their methods of inquiry."

"Cyrus's black eye," Donner said.

"I'm surprised it wasn't worse," Gril added.

I knitted my eyebrows. "Could Orin, Warren, and Kaye somehow be together right now?"

"I don't know of any connection," Donner said.

"Me either." Gril zipped up his coat. "I'm headed over to the community center before I call it a night. We'll get after it again early. Thank you, Benny and Beth. See you in the morning, Donner."

We told him good night and watched him leave. There was no twenty-four-hour team in Benedict other than him and Donner. I'd seen Gril go for days with little sleep, but hoped this would all be solved by tomorrow.

"Call me if you need me tonight," Donner said. "I'll pay attention to my phone."

Gril had been gone for no longer than it took for me to come back around the bar to head back home too, when there was a *crack* and a *boom* and the front window of the bar shattered.

We all reflexively ducked and then looked at one another in wide-eyed shock.

"Someone just shot out the window!" Benny exclaimed.

"Get behind the bar, both of you," Donner said as he made his way out the front door.

"Beth, get back here," Benny said when I hadn't moved.

I finally forced my frozen legs to take me behind the bar.

"Donner? Gril?" I asked weakly.

"They'll be okay," Benny said.

I really hoped she was right.

Six

"No one got hurt." Viola was holding my arms and looking into my wide eyes. My stomach was sick and churning. "Everybody's okay."

Dr. Powder was on the way.

Cold fear spiderwebbed through me. We were all okay. No one had been shot. Gril had returned and then left again with Donner. The window was shattered and now a bullet was lodged in the bar's back wall, but no one had been hurt.

The shooter hadn't been caught, though. If anyone knew who'd done the shooting, they hadn't told me. My nerves were frayed and fried to a crisp.

Benny had tried to liquor me up, but I couldn't swallow anything other than water. I was sitting on the bed in the back room, which was conveniently the place where Dr. Powder saw people sometimes. Viola and Benny were by my side.

Finally, the doctor came through the door. He stood inside a moment and looked at me, his brow furrowed.

"Vi, Benny, give us the room, please," he finally said, his calm and confident voice working a tiny bit of magic. Now I knew I was going to feel better soon.

"I can't stop shaking," I said when it was just the two of us.

"I see that."

Slowly and purposefully, Dr. Powder scooted a chair to where he could face me.

"I'm afraid my heart's going to explode or something." I'd never felt such fear in my life, even when I'd been in Travis's van. I'd experienced moments when I'd just wanted to die and get it over with and times filled with fear but never anything like this frenetic uncontrollable quavering throughout my body.

Dr. Powder shook his head. "No, that's not going to happen."

He wore a stethoscope around his neck. He tucked in the earpieces and then put the circular monitor up to my chest. He listened for a minute and then leaned back, taking the ends from his ears. "Your heart is fine, Beth. It won't explode. I promise."

I was oddly aware enough to think that if it did explode, I'd be dead and unable to hold him to his promise. The thought made me laugh once.

Dr. Powder smiled. "It's not a hollow promise, my dear. You're going to be okay. Is there any chance you could take a deep breath? We could work on it together, or you can do it on your own."

Benny and Viola had been trying to get me to breathe deeply, but there was something about the way the doctor spoke that made me feel like I could actually do it.

I nodded and then took a deep, shuddering breath. I let it out.

"That's it." He folded his hands on his lap. He smiled bigger. "I have a funny story to tell you. It's about that dog you gave us."

Dr. Powder and his wife, Lynny, had taken one of Elijah's dogs. Her name was Jill and she'd been the smallest member of the sled team.

"Jill is the sweetest dog we've ever known. She's like having a nurse around. You know how sometimes we get calls or visitors in the middle of the night?"

I nodded, still shakily but feeling some calm work its way through my veins.

"Well, she hears our visitors long before they ring the bell. Must be able to hear vehicles when they turn down our road. She woke us up the other night, put her paw right here"—he pointed at his shoulder—"because we let her in the bed even though we know we shouldn't. And I was able to pull the door open just as the patient was reaching for the doorbell button. Mavis, the patient, jumped and said the scare from me opening the door cleared up the heartburn she thought might be a heart attack."

I laughed again with a bit more humor this time.

"We love that little dog. If Elijah comes back, I'll arm wrestle him for her."

I took another breath. This time the air moved in and out evenly, not shakily at all.

"There. See, you're fine."

"I think I am. I don't even know what happened, Dr. Powder. I know no one got hurt. Why did my body do what it did?"

"The gunshot scared you. Do you have any sort of PTSD from guns or bombs? Were you in the military?"

"No." I shook my head and remembered telling Kaye that if she ever needed a doctor, Dr. Powder was good at what he did and that she should never hesitate to go to him. However, I still hadn't told him who I was, what had happened to me. Since more people than just Gril now knew, maybe he'd heard some of the details. He hadn't pushed me to tell him more, though, and the timing hadn't seemed appropriate for me to go into it deeper. I had a small urge to do it right then, but it still didn't feel quite right.

"Our bodies just sometimes do things. The noise, a bullet in your vicinity, these are scary things. Even if you didn't think you were frightened, even if you know you're okay, our bodies can make their own decisions sometimes not to behave exactly like we want them to. It's normal, Beth."

I breathed again. In out in out—yes, that was becoming familiar. I'd heard what he was saying before. They were things I already knew but hadn't gotten an immediate handle on when that bullet had done what it had done. "Thank you, Doc."

"You are welcome. Now, what else can I do for you?"

"I think I'm okay," I said after I thought about it for a good few seconds. Yes, I was going to be fine.

"Excellent. Go drink some warm milk and then get some rest. That will be the best medicine tonight."

I nodded.

Dr. Powder looked at me for a long moment. His eyes transformed—from somewhat worried to certain. He had no doubt that I was going to be fine. I hoped he was right. Finally, he nodded and then stood and left the room, leaving the door open.

"Better?" Viola asked as she leaned in only a few seconds later. "Did he give you anything?"

"I'm good," I said. "Warm milk."

"Righto. We can do that."

My legs were no longer shaky, but they did feel heavy from the adrenaline release that was now happening. I stood and joined Viola, and we made our way out of the bar. Benny was examining the bullet stuck in the wall to the right of all the bottles. A few inches to the left and glass would have been shattered, booze spilled.

"You okay?" She took a step toward us.

"I'm fine," I said. "I'm sorry. Everyone's okay and I lost it."

"You've been through some things," Benny said. "You're going to be fine. I know it."

I smiled at her. How had these women, these two sisters, become like family in just under a year? When I'd first come to Benedict, I'd been told that friendships were formed quickly out here. You had to learn who you could rely on and who you couldn't, because at any moment, you might need each other. Those comments had been about the weather, the environment, but now I knew they were meant for more than just that. This community leaned upon and needed one another, like one big common organism. I'd never felt anything like it before, and suddenly, I relished it.

I blinked away some tears of gratitude. "Gril and Donner?"

"They took off for the Millers' and Oliphants'," Benny said.

"That makes sense," I said.

"Kind of." Benny shrugged. "Sure, it seems like it could have been someone from one of those families, but stuff happens, and bullets do fly out here. It might not have been them at all. We'll see."

"Did you tell Viola about what went on tonight?" I asked Benny.

"All the gritty details."

I looked at Viola. "What do you make of . . . all of it?"

She shook her head. "I don't know what to make of it. My first inclination would be to think that the Oliphants are involved with Kaye and Warren missing, but they're *both* missing, which means they just might have gone off somewhere together." She looked at her sister. "The timing of a bullet coming through the window is odd, but Benny's right; that can happen out here."

"At night? People don't really hunt in the dark, do they?" I asked.

"Well, I'm not saying it was a hunter, but folks have guns and sometimes they're stupid with them. I wish that weren't the case, but it is." She paused. "Beth, no one got hurt from that bullet. There are many things going on right now, but about the bullet, all's well that ends well. I know that might be a tough idea to swallow, but close calls are more common out here—of all kinds."

I looked at her. "I'm jumping to conclusions?"

She smiled wearily. "No, you're trying to make sense of things that might not make sense yet. It's what you do. I know that. It's fine, but so are you. All of us are fine."

I nodded. "I get it."

"Ready to go home?" Viola asked.

"So ready."

As we left, Benny locked the door behind us. She hadn't looked as tired as she had earlier, which made me think she'd probably felt her own rush of adrenaline, as it followed a good dose of fear. I hoped she'd be able to finally get some rest. I'd lost track of time, but it felt late. Pure exhaustion came over me as we walked through the cold, dark night the short distance to the Benedict House. Home.

Gus was right inside the front door to greet us. I hadn't let him sleep in my bed with me like Dr. Powder had allowed Jill, but it had been tempting.

Plus, Gus liked his bed. However, tonight he sat up on his cushion and waited to curl up and rest until I told him good night.

I didn't even need the warm milk to fall asleep.

Seven

Someone was singing. No, maybe that was just a band. Jazz? There was music or the beat of music coming from somewhere. *Okay, if there was a consistent beat, it must not be jazz,* my weary mind put together.

I pulled a pillow over my head.

The noise wasn't muted much.

I lifted the pillow. "What the hell?"

I sat up and gathered my bearings. It was almost eight, a couple hours after I usually woke, and Gus was already up. But it had been a late night, and I'd hoped to sleep in a little, maybe even until nine. It wasn't meant to be.

"Need to go outside?" I asked Gus.

He whined in the affirmative. The music continued.

"Chaz?" I wondered as I looked toward the doorway.

There was no other explanation for the male voice I thought I heard mingling with the beat, but I couldn't understand how I could even hear anything. If he was in the kitchen or dining room, it was down the other hallway of the building.

I got out of bed, brushed my teeth, splashed water on my face, and covered my hair with a cap.

The second Gus and I stepped into the hallway, the voice ramped up. It wasn't Chaz's voice but someone *had* turned up a song to very loud.

"Disco?" I asked. "Bee Gees?"

Gus was too curious to head outside first, so we made our way to the kitchen. Chaz was cooking up a storm as an old boom box sat on a dining table, blaring out "Stayin' Alive." I found the power button and pushed it. The blessed silence allowed my ears to relax.

Chaz looked up from the stovetop. "Good morning, Beth, Gus! How are you two today?"

"We're good. The music was a bit loud, though."

"Oh. I'm so sorry. I'm such an early bird; I forget that some people sleep in. Come eat. I'm making . . . everything."

It appeared he was telling the truth. There was food all over the kitchen area. Viola must have snuck in some shopping at some point. "Where's Viola?"

"I have no idea. I've been awake in my room, starving for a few hours. I came down and knocked on her door about half an hour ago, but no answer. She told me I'm not allowed to leave without checking with her first, but I wasn't sure if she meant my room or the building. I figured she wouldn't mind if I cooked. I'll ask for forgiveness if that's the case."

"We'll be right back." With Gus at my heel, I left the dining room and traveled down the other hall. Viola's office was empty. I knocked on her room door and received no answer. It was locked. She always left it unlocked if she was inside—though that wasn't something she told everyone.

I couldn't remember if she'd mentioned to me that she had something to do this morning, but it wasn't completely unusual for her to be away. It was a tiny bit odd, considering Chaz had just arrived, but not totally out of character. There was no cell phone to call.

We passed the kitchen again, Chaz now singing without the aid of the boom box. As I let Gus outside, I surveyed the downtown, but there was no sign of Viola anywhere. It was still early enough to be very quiet. The morning was biting cold. Even Gus, who relished the cold, hurried through his morning constitutionals, and we quickly made our way back to the dining room.

"Are you hungry?" Chaz asked.

I thought for a moment. "I am."

"Excellent. Have a seat, and I'll fill a plate. I'll bring two forks and take a taste, so you know I haven't poisoned anything."

"I accept your offer."

It wasn't long before a plate, overflowing with every sort of breakfast food you could think of, was in front of me, and then another plate appeared with baked goods. Eggs, bacon, ham, sausage, more eggs. Then cinnamon rolls, orange rolls, biscuits . . .

I looked at Chaz as he took bites of all the items. I asked, "How in the world did you do all this?"

"I've been working for hours. It's what I do." He shrugged. "Eat up."

I started with the scrambled eggs. They were the fluffiest eggs I'd ever eaten. I tried some of the other items, just small bites. Even I wasn't going to be able to eat everything, but I certainly wanted a taste of it all. "Where did you learn to cook?"

He sat across from me, watching me with a satisfied smile. "It's a hobby, something to do when I'm not working. I don't like television, I despise movies, and books drive me crazy."

I suppressed my own smile. He and I were as opposite as we could be. He sure could cook, though.

"I enjoy listening to music—disco in case you didn't notice—but cooking relaxes me and gives me something to do while I'm listening."

"You're in good shape," I said. "If I ate like this every day, I'd have to buy bigger sizes."

Chaz laughed. "I work out just so I can eat more than a normal human should, but I also give most of my food away." He paused. "Even in prison, I cooked."

"Did that make you . . . popular? Safer?"

Chaz sighed. "My incarceration was pretty cushy as incarcerations go, but yes, my cooking kept me very valuable to everyone. Most prisoners lose weight when they're behind bars. The warden told me that our facility was doing the opposite and the powers that be were curious about what we were doing. They kept shopping for the food, so I kept cooking."

"How long were you in prison?"

"Less than a full year. I did not manage to steal the money, so it was just attempted theft. I sure tried, though."

"You'd have served more time if you'd succeeded."

"Not if I'd gotten away. I had a pretty good plan. I just messed up toward the end, got too impatient."

"Well, if you need to make an honest living, I'm sure you could do it with food. You could own a restaurant. I don't know how it wouldn't be successful."

"I've thought about it." He paused and looked at me as if he was trying to read something in me. I tried to send him back the least judgmental nod I could muster. He continued, "I'm not sure I'm meant to make an honest living. Some people aren't, you know?"

I chewed a piece of bacon. "You aren't violent. You can be reformed."

Chaz laughed again. I tried not to smile, but I liked his laugh.

"Maybe I don't want to be reformed. I like me just the way I am."

"I like me just the way I am, too," I said. "Although, I'm working on being better."

"What part of you do you want to be better?"

I shook my head quickly. "Nothing specific. Just always want to be better."

"Well, with all due respect, that's a slogan for a coffee mug, not a real way to live. I think you should live the most authentic life you can. Be you. Whatever that means."

"Well, that sounds like a slogan, too. With all due respect back, Chaz, I heartily disagree. However, you being here is not a bad thing in my book."

"Glad to hear it." He lifted his coffee mug.

I lifted mine and we clinked gently.

I heard the front door open and stood from the table. Gus and I peered out to see Viola removing her boots.

"Vi?" I said. "Chaz made break . . ."

She looked at me. Her eyes were rimmed in red, and a frown pulled hard at her mouth.

"Oh no. What's wrong?" I hurried to her, putting my hand on her arm.

She stood tall and took a deep breath. "I have some terrible news, Beth."

I swallowed hard, feeling the fear I'd grappled with the night before start to find its way through my veins again. "What?"

"Come sit down."

I was frozen in place as she walked past me. She turned back. "Come on, Beth. To my office."

I unstuck my legs and followed her into her office. When we walked past the dining room, somewhere in the back of my mind I heard Chaz say something. When neither of us answered, he followed behind me and stood in the doorway of Viola's office as she and I sat, her in her chair, me in the one across from her. Gus was next to me on alert because of the serious nature of whatever was going on. Viola didn't ask Chaz to leave.

With her hands folded together on the desk in front of her, she sighed. "There's no easy way to say this, Beth. They found Kaye. She's dead."

I hadn't known what she was going to tell me, but I'd pondered the possibilities on the short walk from the front door to her office. I'd thought maybe she had bad news about Orin, which would have broken me apart. The bad news being about Kaye wasn't much better, but as much as I would not want to admit it, I felt a tiny bit of relief—only for an instant. Then the severity of the moment truly hit. My heart sank, my stomach turned. My world became tunnel-visioned. I was glad I was sitting down.

I managed to croak out some words. "What happened? Where?"

"Down by the creek back behind the community center. Blunt force trauma to the head with a rock." Viola closed her eyes for a moment, then opened them again. "The rock was still there."

"Murder?" I asked.

"It sure looks that way."

"Oh, Viola." My mind searched around for something—an answer, an explanation—but there wasn't anything readily available. "What about Warren? Did they find him?"

"Not yet." She shook her head again.

"Oh no."

Kaye was dead. It couldn't be true. Murdered? No one would murder Kaye, would they?

"Oh, Viola," I said as tears began to fall down my cheeks.

She let me cry for a few moments. She didn't have any real answers and she was upset, too. I excused myself to my room, telling her I just needed some time.

I sat on the edge of the bed and let the emotions work through me. Gus tried to comfort me, but I was distracted. I squeezed my eyes tight and tried to wrap my mind around what might have happened. No one knew much yet. Viola admitted to having been told only the obvious details. If Gril or Donner had a theory about what happened, or any specific suspects, they hadn't shared that information with her.

It was devastating. I felt the weight of it. Once some of the initial shock wore off, though, and with Gus's nudging, I began to feel something else.

I wanted to know what happened. No, I needed to know what happened.

I put myself together and went back to Viola's office. She and Chaz were both still there in the middle of a low-key, quiet conversation.

"Hey," Viola said when I appeared in the doorway. "Any better?"

I nodded. "I guess I just needed some time to process it."

"Understandable."

"I'm sorry for your loss, both of you," Chaz said.

"Thanks, Chaz," Viola said before she turned her attention back to me. "What do you need, Beth? Can I help with anything?"

"I'm heading into the *Petition*," I said. "Work would be good. I think Gus should stay with you today."

I didn't think I could give him the attention he deserved. That probably wouldn't have bothered him, but it would have made me feel irresponsible when I knew he'd be happier with Viola.

In fact, it was normal that Gus sometimes stayed at the Benedict House when I went to the shed. I took him with me most of the time, but the shed was small. He enjoyed having the entire Benedict House to roam and Viola, and now Chaz too, to hang out with.

"Gus and I will be fine today," she said. "Gril asked me to keep an eye on you, though. Sure you don't want to stick around here today?"

"I'm okay. Really."

"I know, but it's some terrible news."

"Yes, it is." I paused. "Anything else you can tell me? Does Gril have anything?"

"Not that I'm aware of."

I nodded. Viola might keep details to herself, particularly since Chaz was there, but I didn't sense she was holding anything back.

"I'll check in later."

Viola studied me for a long moment. "Good plan. Be careful out there."

"I will be."

Chaz gave me a weak smile. I returned it. As I walked away from Viola's office again, I was aware enough to sense that things were going as well as could be expected regarding Viola's first male client. I'd come upon a number of conversations taking place in her office with previous Benedict House tenants, and I'd been left with a similar impression after each one. The meetings were calm and cordial. Though I'd heard Viola raise her voice—even threaten to shoot a client or two—never had one of those moments happened during a meeting in her office. I wondered if she set parameters or if that's just the way things went. I'd ask her at some point.

I loaded up my backpack with notebooks and my laptop and swung it over my shoulder before I headed to my truck. Gus walked me to the door and gave me his normal send-off. I responded with a few extra moments of ear scratching. "Thanks for being there for me, buddy."

He whined as if it was no problem at all.

Outside, it had warmed slightly from bitter cold, and I was greeted with a cloudy sky. In less of a hurry than Gus and I had been earlier, I glanced around downtown as I made my way to the small parking area at the end of the Benedict House. Other than boards over the bar's window, there was no further evidence of what had happened the night before. I watched a couple people walk into the mercantile, but they didn't notice me. If they saw the boards over the window, they weren't bothered by them.

A wave of lingering concern about the shot through the window ran through me, but it moved along quickly. I remembered my fear, but it wasn't settling in again. I wasn't ashamed, but in the light of the day, it did seem like an overreaction. Again, no one had gotten hurt. I hadn't thought to ask Viola if she'd heard anything about it from Gril.

Even if it hadn't been because of the bullet through the window, someone *had* gotten hurt—killed. Kaye. I'd been with her two days earlier. We'd walked the dogs. And now she was gone. I hadn't known her well, but her death was devastating, and I felt the weight of it.

Gripping my truck handle, I looked back toward the quiet downtown again. There was nothing ominous about this place, nothing immediately frightening, but if anyone knew about layers of evil, it was me. Who had killed Kaye and why?

I hopped in the old but reliable vehicle and headed away from downtown. This time, I turned right when I usually turned left, steering in the direction of the community center.

Set in the woods down a well-traveled but unpaved road, the squat but long warehouse-like building served as a catchall for a variety of different classes and events. There were even workout machines in a back room.

As I pulled into the gravel parking lot, there was no indication that I was anywhere near a crime scene. In fact, gauging by the number of vehicles—mostly trucks—in the lot, there was some sort of class in session inside. How far away from the building had Kaye been found?

I hadn't asked Viola where they'd taken her body, but since the weather was clear, it had probably been put on one of the Harvington's planes and transported to Juneau.

I parked the truck on the edge of the crowded lot and stepped out toward the berm above the creek that ran along and away from the back of the community center. It wasn't quite a river, but it was bigger than a Missouri creek. I'd heard it called "the center creek," so that's how I thought of it. From what I'd seen, the water in it always ran fast enough to be intimidating.

I looked all around and into the woods, which got thicker farther away from the building. I didn't immediately spot anything that stood out. Finally, about fifty feet downstream, I thought that maybe some ground had been disturbed. I was doubtful because, again, there was nothing cordoned off, but something wasn't right over there. I climbed down the berm and tromped along—temperatures were still cold enough, at least at night, that the earth next to the water was mostly solid under my feet rather than a muddy mess.

I'd been correct. The area I'd spotted had been disturbed and in no small way. The top of the berm had caved some, and rocks were obviously misplaced. I stopped a good six feet from the disruption and inspected it as closely as I could from that distance. It was as if I flipped a switch, and my old skills came right back. If this was, indeed, the spot where Kaye's body had been, why was it not more protected?

The answer came to me quickly, and it was twofold: Gril and Donner had done what they needed to do to investigate the scene. Protecting any space out here long-term was next to impossible. They might have a pop-up somewhere that they could maneuver enough to cover some of the area, but any big wind (and we had quite a few of those) would take it down. They'd had to do what they could, gather possible evidence, and get out of there.

But I could sometimes see things in ways other people couldn't. I had an uncanny knack for visually calculating distances and what could and couldn't happen in the spaces that were available. I could see the numbers that made up the angles.

I hadn't known it was a rare thing until my grandfather had noticed and then cultivated it. In fact, he'd told me I could have been a talented mathematician, but I'd only laughed. I hadn't gone to college and hadn't had any desire to work with numbers, no matter that they seemed to appear in my head naturally and I never struggled with them. Words had always been much more appealing.

I looked over to where I was pretty sure Kaye had been found, and suddenly I could envision her, the angle of her. It was all obvious.

She'd been prone, her head toward the creek, her body at about a thirty-degree angle. With that understanding and the knowledge that she'd been hit over the head with a rock (that was now gone from what I could discern), I could even guess where she might have been standing when she was hit. My eyes moved up the berm to the edge and landed exactly where it looked as if feet had come over the side.

I brought my gaze back down and toward the ground along the creek bed. I took a few steps closer and inspected the berm's wall. Small toe indentations. She'd come over the berm headfirst—no somersault maneuver involved.

I saw something else and stepped even closer to the creek. There was a handprint next to the edge of the water. This told me how she'd probably landed. It had been a rough, body-slamming fall. There was no blood anywhere that I could see, reinforcing my idea that if there had been any there, the elements had already washed it away—and the elements were currently calm.

Had Gril seen the handprint? I didn't have any way to take a picture, but I'd ask him as soon as I could. I hoped he had. I hoped he'd photographed it. Clearly, he hadn't taken any sort of plaster impression, which is what my grandfather would have wanted to do.

As I pondered the scene a little more, I decided that I didn't think Kaye had been in a hurry and running from someone. If she'd come off the berm at a high speed, all the angles would have been different. I could visualize all the scenarios.

I was pretty sure Kaye had been moving slowly or standing still when her body went over, which meant she wasn't being chased—at least that she was aware of.

Either someone snuck up on her or someone she wasn't afraid of was with her. I didn't see any indication of another person near where I thought her body had been, but again, with the elements and the fast water, that might not have been currently obvious.

"What happened, Kaye?" I said aloud.

When there was no answer, I turned and hiked back toward the community center, then climbed back up from the creek bed. The land had been cleared of trees for a good distance when the building was built. I remembered Viola telling me that the company who came in to take the trees overdid it but then donated the lumber to Tex's tribe. The woods had long begun their encroachment and were wild and unruly, thick and dark even in the brightest of light. There was so much beauty in this land, but it was also intimidating.

Something moved among the trees. When I realized it was a mama moose and a calf, I smiled and took a small step closer to better see the baby.

I hadn't had enough of these moments in Benedict. I'd seen plenty of animals from a distance and some closer up, but as this was my first "spring" in town, I hoped for more moments watching the babies get their legs underneath them.

I thought about Kaye, alone out here except for her killer. I wished I—someone—had been there for her.

I hopped out of the truck again. I thought about Old Al's solitary existence and how he claimed it wasn't solitary at all. At that moment, as I watched the moose and heard the calf's bleating, I understood my new friend and his peaceful happiness in a way I didn't think I could have grasped even a few days earlier.

Even with the tragedy of Kaye's murder, I realized something else. For the first time in my life, I was feeling all of life's moments, living them. I wasn't just paying bills and thinking about the errands I needed to get done. Is this what happened to people after they were here a while? Did the idea of living any other way suddenly feel so much less like living and more like just surviving that Benedict became the only home imaginable?

The calf bleated again, and the mama suspiciously snorted through her nose at me. I shook myself out of the reverie.

Then, I shook my head at myself and looked back at where I'd been. Okay yes, the woods were gaining on the open ground, but there was still some cleared space. Could someone have snuck up on Kaye? Possibly.

I looked across the creek from where I thought she'd been, squinting hard but knowing there was no nearby way to get over to the other side where the animals were, where the woods really got thick. I didn't know where those woods led or if someone lived in there. Chances were good that someone had made a home somewhere in there.

"Damn," I said out loud. Had someone thrown the rock from across the creek? It would have been quite a trick, but it could have been done. I needed to see where that rock had landed. I needed to know the location and depth of the injury to Kaye's skull.

I hoped Gril would tell me. With a mission in mind, I hurried back to the truck. I wanted to find the police chief, but as I put the key into the ignition, I remembered the question about someone bedding down in the community center. Since I was already there and it wouldn't be a risk of being alone inside now, I decided to take a quick look.

Only a couple steps through the door, though, I realized I'd picked a terrible time to be curious.

I recognized the members of the Miller family that I'd seen in the bar the night before, but there were many other people in the main gathering space. They all looked at me as I came through the door. This wasn't a class. This was a meeting that included lots of visible weapons and unhappy tones.

Ike Miller had been the one speaking as I entered. Camille was seated in a chair by his side. Ike fell silent and looked at me.

"I'm so sorry for interrupting," I said. "I didn't know . . ." I turned to leave again.

"Beth, right?" Ike asked.

He'd just learned my name the night before.

"Yes." I turned again.

"Did you need something at the center?" Ike asked. "We're here without previously scheduling it, so if we're in your way, you just need to let us know. We'll go."

His eyes were red, and his face seemed stained from tears, as were the other members of the family. But there was more anger than sadness in the air. It was palpable and thick.

"No, I . . ." I didn't want to stay, but I also didn't want to behave as if they scared me. "I'm so sorry about Kaye. So very sorry."

"Thank you," Camille said.

"We're devastated," Ike said. Rumbles of agreement filled the room. "But that's not why you're here, and we don't want to be in anyone's way."

"No. Honestly, I was just going to see if I could understand who might have been sleeping here. Does anyone know yet?"

"Not to our knowledge," Ike said. "And no one's found Warren. We're here to . . . We're trying to figure out what to do next."

I steeled myself as best I could. I was one hundred percent intimidated. This was a large group of mourning and angry people who wanted answers, and they were used to going after them themselves from what I'd heard. But Ike wasn't being anything but friendly.

"Gril will figure it out," I said.

Tears fell from Camille's eyes, but she didn't say anything. My heart squeezed for her, for all of them.

"We hope he does," Ike said with zero confidence.

I nodded. They certainly didn't need to hear any more words of wisdom from me. I hoped they made the right choices about what they were going to do, but I had doubts. I wanted to stay and listen in. I wanted to understand the family and their relationship with Kaye. I wanted to eavesdrop, but this wasn't my place. I wasn't ready to be a part of anything that appeared to support them—not until I understood their feud with the Oliphants and what that might mean to the town, Kaye's murder, and Warren's disappearance.

I tried not to be too abrupt. I nodded sympathetically to Camille and then looked over the crowd, my eyes landing on Ike again. "I'm so, so sorry. I hope Warren is found soon."

"Thank you, Beth," Ike said.

I turned and left the building, hurrying to my truck and then, finally, the police station.

Eight

Donner was the only one there. He was standing behind his desk and talking on the station's landline phone.

"Yes, ma'am. I am sure of it. Thank you for the call. I'll have Gril get back to you. Sure." He hung up the phone. "Beth? What's up?"

"Where's Gril?"

Donner squinted and shook his head once. "I'm not sure exactly, but I think he's trying to find a killer."

I took a deep breath and nodded, telling myself to cool my jets a little. "I know. I'm sorry, Donner. Do you have any pictures from the scene?"

Donner squinted at me again. "Beth?"

"I know, but . . . Gril would probably let me see them if I asked him."

"Then you should wait and ask him."

"You know I can see things others don't always see."

"I doubt that's the case this time, Beth. He and I were thorough, and it was all very cut-and-dried."

"I didn't mean to imply that you weren't thorough." I knew Gril and Donner were great at their jobs, but even Gril had told me I had a special sort of vision, and I'd helped him before. "I might be able to help. Maybe not, but maybe."

Donner rubbed the back of his neck. "Okay, I know. It's been a morning." He paused. "This is shaky ground. You were one of the last to see Kaye alive, but Gril did mention he'd probably ask you to look at these. I'd like for him to be here when you do, but none of us think you're a killer." He was convincing himself. "Okay, they're on my computer. Come over here. We want to catch whoever did this as soon as possible."

I stepped around the desk and took a seat in his chair. I steeled myself. For all my talk, this was going to be emotional.

"Did you see any helpful footprints? Did you notice the handprint near the water?" I asked before I focused on the screen.

"We didn't see any helpful footprints, but we did see the handprint." He clicked to a picture of the handprint taken with a tape measure next to it. An adjacent picture was a close-up of Kaye's hand, not in the print but clearly muddy, and at a glance, the probable match to the print. "We have no plaster here, but Gril was going to try to round some up, even though we think we were already too late to get a clear impression."

"Okay."

I inspected each gruesome picture closely. I held a wave of sadness and frustration at bay—my grandfather would have called it being professional. I'd deal with the emotions later.

Kaye had been hit on the left side of her head, but, as I'd suspected, her body had been found facedown as though she'd fallen that way, not as though she'd fallen sideways and then hit her head. But it was, at best, only a guess.

You don't know what you don't know.

I studied the pictures of the rock, bloody but only slightly. Kaye's head had bled but it had been located so close to the creek bed that I hadn't seen blood. It had probably washed away by the time I'd been at the scene.

The rock was about the size of a softball and roundish but naturally jagged.

"It was three feet from Kaye?" I asked, confirming the measurement I saw on a picture that also displayed a measuring tape.

"Yes." Donner sighed. "Since there were no other footprints, we've surmised that the killer might have crossed the creek to kill Kaye and then again to run away. However, we didn't find any good prints on the other side, either. Too many prints of all kinds. Unreliable."

"Crossed the creek? Wouldn't that have been pretty difficult? The water is pretty fast out there right now."

"I know, but it's one of the possibilities. Maybe they crossed before she got there and then hid under the lip of the berm."

"Could someone have thrown the rock across the creek and hit her?"

"That would take quite an aim, but we considered it," Donner said. "We're hoping the ME can help us understand if she was hit close up or from a distance."

"How long had she been there? Who discovered her?"

"We currently can't pinpoint her time of death any closer than sometime between yesterday and last night, probably not much later than around midnight," Donner said. "We might not have found her for a long time, but Ruke was at the community center and decided to have a look at the creek to check its depth. That creek's been known to flood and word is that we have some noticeably warmer temperatures coming in a week or so."

I hadn't seen Ruke, a local Tlingit man and the person I'd purchased my truck from, for months. I didn't remember seeing him at the Walk the day before.

"He didn't run down and make a mess of the scene?"

"No. He said he thought about it, wanted to pull her out of there, but he could tell he was seeing a dead body and he knew enough to just gather Gril. Drove straight to his house and woke him up."

"What time?"

"About five this morning."

"So she was most likely killed after the Millers were at the bar?"

"That is our best guess. We have the ME in Juneau getting us something more accurate, hopefully today."

"The Harvingtons flew her over?"

Donner nodded. "Yes."

"Does Gril suspect any of the Millers?"

"Yes. He suspects them all, as well as the Oliphants. He would love to find Warren. Right now, he's banking on it being something to do with the continual fighting between the families, but he doesn't want to overlook something because of that notion."

"Any indication who shot at the bar last night?"

"No. In fact, Gril doesn't think it was any of the Millers or Oliphants, but he doesn't have a line on exactly what happened."

I turned in his chair and looked at him. "Tell me more about the feud."

"I don't know much. Gril hasn't been here much longer than I have, but he's tried to understand it. I find it all ridiculous. A bunch of people who need to grow up and get on with living life without the need to think about revenge all the time."

"Revenge? Not just nastiness but real and ugly revenge?"

"They live out where months could pass without anyone seeing either of the families. Gril makes an effort to stop by every now and then just so they know someone is paying attention." He shook his head. "It all started with a murder . . ."

"I thought Orin said it was a girl."

"Well, rumor does have it that a girl might have been involved."

"How?"

"It was Ike's brother who was killed. At the time, he and the patriarch of the Oliphant clan were probably interested in the same young woman. Jealousy, that sort of thing." He lifted his eyebrows. "I'd all but forgotten who the girl was, but Gril reminded me last night."

"Who?"

"Well, there were a couple rumors that maybe it was Viola."

"My Viola?"

"One and the same."

"Ike's brother was potentially killed by an Oliphant because they both had their eyes on Viola?"

Donner nodded. "I don't know anything for certain, and as the years have gone by, everyone's quit talking about it, but they've stayed mad. That's pretty much all I know."

"Huh. I'll have to ask Viola about it."

"And then maybe tell me the rest of the story."

I nodded. I'd been distracted by Donner's story, and it all suddenly felt like a million years ago and like it couldn't have anything to do with Kaye. I needed to see if I could catch anything unusual in these pictures.

I turned my attention back to the computer screen. "Donner, this feels personal, not random or sudden at all."

"Most things are personal around here," Donner said.

"Good point. I walked in on a gathering of the Millers at the community center."

"Lots of people?"

"Yes."

Donner nodded and then grabbed his jacket.

"Where are you going?" I asked, thinking maybe I should have told him about the gathering sooner, but his answer surprised me.

"If their place is empty, I might have a chance to look around even deeper. Gril might already be doing exactly that."

"Can I come with you?"

"No, Beth, you cannot."

"I . . . I can make sure the dog is being taken care of."

"Beth."

"I'll just follow you in my truck if you don't let me come with you."

Donner was in a hurry, which helped convince him quickly. "Will you stay in my truck until I tell you to come out?"

"Yes," I said, not even sounding a little bit like I was lying, which I was.

"All right. Let's go. We might run into Gril, though. Just be low-key. Got it?"

"Absolutely."

But before we could go anywhere, the police station door was flung open. A man with a fresh cut at the corner of his mouth that perfectly matched the black eye he'd recently received came in, bringing with him a mix of anger and fear that immediately felt way too familiar to me.

Nine

Cyrus?" Donner asked. "What happened?"

I had seen him around, even before yesterday morning's gathering. But before the Walk, I hadn't known this was Cyrus Oliphant, the man Luther spoke about last night, the man who'd allegedly been seeing Kaye, and had been Benny's late-night customer. He wore a firearm in a holster around his waist just like Viola did, but on him it seemed more threatening. Blood from the cut on his mouth dripped down his chin.

"Where's the chief?" Cyrus asked, his gaze glassy and wild. He swiped the back of his hand over his chin.

Donner stood straighter. "Sit down, Cyrus. Remove the gun." He held out his hand.

Cyrus neither wanted to sit nor remove his weapon, but Donner's tone didn't leave room for argument. As Cyrus unbuckled, I scooted to the bathroom and moistened a paper towel, then grabbed a bottle of water from the small fridge Gril kept in the main room. I delivered them both to Cyrus just after he and Donner took seats. He took them from me but just held on to them. I didn't think he really noticed I was there until after we all sat down and the gun had been placed on the desk behind Donner. It wasn't until then that he spared me a quick but questioning glance.

"Cyrus, I thought Gril was headed out to your place this morning. Have you checked for him there?" Donner said.

"I haven't been home since yesterday. The Millers . . . and I just heard that Kaye was killed. That can't be true. Is that true?"

"Where have you been?"

"Here and there. Kaye . . ."

Donner shook his head and pointed at his own mouth. "That could use a stitch or two. Want me to call Powder?"

"No, I'll be fine." With a somewhat more controlled tone, Cyrus asked, "Is it true?"

I recalled now that I'd seen him in the mercantile, maybe even at the bar once or twice. He'd made an impression. He reminded me of the farm boys back home, big and beefy and also striking with short curly dark hair and bright blue eyes. Unlike most of the men around here, he didn't wear a beard or any facial hair at all. It appeared that he shaved every day, except maybe this morning.

I remembered something else I'd noticed about him. He seemed like a loner. I'd never witnessed him with anyone else, just shopping alone at the mercantile or, now apparently, drinking alone on a stool at the bar. I'd never heard him speak until now. His voice was deep and big, rich and smooth, even as he was so upset.

"Tell me what's going on, Cyrus. What happened to your eye and your lip?"

"Tell me about Kaye," Cyrus said. "Donner. Please."

Donner shook his head again slowly. "Not until you tell me where you've been. Why haven't you been home?"

Cyrus looked down at the ground. "I haven't been home since right before the Walk yesterday morning."

"Why?"

"The Millers are after me, Donner. They think . . . doesn't matter what they think. I've been hiding."

"It does matter. Why were you hiding? Where?"

"Just in the woods." He only answered one of the questions.

"Have you been the one sleeping in the community center?"

Cyrus's eyes opened wide. "Not last night."

"But you were the one sleeping there?"

Cyrus shook his head. "I wasn't there the night before the Walk. Over the last few weeks I've slept there a time or two, but someone else was there before me. I saw the sleeping bag, too."

"Hang on. Why? You left your house yesterday morning. Why were you sleeping in the community center over the last few weeks?"

Cyrus shrugged. "To get away from the house, Donner. Winter was too much with . . . You know how it goes. It can get claustrophobic. I'm not the only one who does it. Folks need to get away. The community center is shelter."

Donner squinted as if this was news to him. It was news to me. I wondered if Gril knew.

"Who else does that? Who else has been there recently?" Donner asked.

"I don't know."

"Okay. Why were *you* sleeping there?"

Cyrus's gaze went to me, truly focusing for the first time. Then he turned back to Donner. "Just stuff. You know how it goes."

Donner knew he wasn't going to get a better answer. "Where were you last night from about eleven on?"

"At the airport. It was still open. I was just hanging out, fell asleep in my truck there, too."

The only good internet spots were at the airport and the library. Lots of folks spent lots of time in those two places, but overnight?

I figured that Donner was not only wondering if Cyrus could have killed Kaye, but if maybe he'd been the person to shoot out the window of the bar. Between asking the Harvingtons if Cyrus had been around the airport and checking Cyrus's weapon, Donner would be able to come to a pretty good conclusion if Cyrus was telling the truth about his whereabouts last night.

"Donner," Cyrus continued. "Please tell me about Kaye. Please."

Donner took a deep breath and then let it out. "We found her body this morning up by the creek behind the community center."

Cyrus's eyes filled with tears, but he blinked them away.

"Her body? What happened to her?" he asked.

"Best we can determine, she was killed, hit in the head with a rock."

Cyrus's expression twisted into shocked sadness. "God no, not Kaye."

"What's going on, Cyrus? Were you and Kaye friends?"

Cyrus shook his head, and then his expression that had been so pained a moment ago became sharp with anger as he stood. "I need to go, Donner."

"Hang on there, Cy. You're not going anywhere yet. Have a seat. Tell me who did that to your lip and your eye."

"You can't stop me."

"In fact, I can, Cyrus. I can arrest you. Do you really want that?" Donner stood, too.

"You're not going to arrest me." Cyrus turned and took a step toward the door, not asking for his gun back.

Donner was around his desk quickly and grabbed the other man's arm, twisting it behind his back.

"Cyrus," Donner said, "last chance. Sit down, or I will arrest you."

Cyrus breathed hard, like someone who was building up to something, but he seemed to think better of it quickly. "All right, all right. I'll sit down. Let go, Donner. Come on. We go back, don't we?"

Donner guided Cyrus back to the chair. There were no holding cells in Benedict. I'd seen Gril handcuff people to a desk or a pipe along the wall, but if Cyrus fought and if Donner really wanted him to stay, I wasn't sure what he'd have to resort to.

I hoped it didn't come to that.

When Cyrus was finally in the chair again, I released a breath I'd been holding.

Donner picked up the phone and dialed a number. "Gril, I've got Cyrus Oliphant here in the station. I'd like for you to join us. All right. We'll be right here." Donner hung up the phone.

I would have bet real money that Donner hadn't actually reached

Gril, but it had been a good act, and he probably knew Gril would be on his way back at some point anyway. Cyrus didn't appear doubtful.

Donner looked at me. "You can go now, Beth."

I was momentarily stunned but bit back an argument. I was disappointed—I had so many more questions—but it only made sense.

"Go, Beth," he said more sternly.

I blinked out of my dismay. I couldn't think of anything I could say to convince him I should stay. Reluctantly, I stood and left the building.

I stopped on the front porch for a long moment, wondering if I could eavesdrop. The station might only be a converted cabin in the woods, but the door was thick, and the windows were covered.

Was Donner okay in there? Should I let Viola know what was going on? Should I try to find Gril?

I decided that Donner was fine, and I needed to remember that it wasn't my job to question local suspects. My grandfather had let me in on a few interrogations, and Gril had let me be there one time, but those were extenuating circumstances, not the way things were supposed to be.

Maybe I'd gotten a little carried away. Or maybe there were other things I could do.

I'd been excited to go with Donner out to the Miller place before Cyrus had barreled in. Maybe I'd head out there, but I wouldn't go inside. If they'd returned home, I could check on the dog, ask if they wanted to keep him or if I needed to find him another home. It was probably too soon after Kaye's death to ask such questions, but it seemed important.

I just had to figure out where they lived.

The road away from the police station took me right by Toshco. Someone there would surely know how to get to the Millers'. However, as I pulled into the small parking lot, I had another thought, and I detoured around to Elijah's properties behind the store. When I'd told Gril that I'd find homes for all the dogs and that I knew about the files

Elijah had left behind, the police chief had given me keys to the place. He'd even told me I could move in if I wanted to.

The place—home and barn—was fine, but I had no desire to leave the Benedict House. I enjoyed Viola's company. I liked having only one room to be responsible for. Besides, I held out hope that Elijah would come back someday. If I read Gril correctly, I might be the only one who thought that was a real possibility.

People come and go out here, Beth. Most folks know when enough is enough. I suspect Elijah was at that point, he'd said.

The thought of checking on the dog had jogged something in my memory that I'd read in Finn's file. It wouldn't hurt to look over it again.

I unlocked and opened the barn door. I'd cleaned the place after the dogs had been relocated, and a faint whiff of pine-scented cleaner still hung in the air, mixing with the mustiness of a closed-up space. The individual dog stalls were empty now. Two of Elijah's sleds still filled the area at the end of the barn. Gril said we didn't have to do anything with them until we figured out what would happen to the property. And who knew when that would be.

I made my way to the desk where Elijah kept the files on the dogs. I had put them back exactly as I'd found them. I thumbed to Finn's file and set it on the now-pristine desktop.

The notes on Finn had been about Kaye. She had been the person listed for Finn, but Elijah had written more, and now I wondered if I was remembering some type of warning. The instructions had been typed out:

```
Kaye Miller loves Finn, and though Finn loves
most people equally, he has a special place
in his heart for Kaye. I am worried about the
other Millers and their reaction to adding
Finn to their family, so make sure Kaye is
comfortable with taking him and that her
family won't disapprove.
```

There *was* more. Sure, I'd read all of this before, but it hadn't meant much of anything after Kaye had so enthusiastically agreed to take Finn. Now, I was seeing this next part in a whole new light.

```
Do not let Finn or any of the dogs go to the
Oliphants. They don't treat their dogs like
family, and I can't abide that. One of them
might try to convince you they need one. Cyrus
Oliphant seems to like the dog, and I've come
upon him and Kaye together a few times now.
They both seem friendly to Finn, but still,
the Oliphants cannot have any of the dogs.
Period. The end.
```

"The Oliphants weren't fit for any of the dogs," I said to myself. "Where did you come upon them together, Elijah?"

There was one more note:

```
Last resort for Finn—Orin. When I say last
resort, I just mean if Kaye can't or won't
take him. Orin and Finn would be great
together, but Orin sometimes has too much
going on to care for animals. At least that's
what he told me. Still, he loves Finn, and
Finn loves him. I'm sure.
```

That part made me think about Orin again. He was still missing, too. I hoped we'd hear from him soon.

Other than phone numbers for both Kaye and Orin, that was all that was in the file.

I closed it and put it back in the drawer. Though it might seem untimely and inappropriate so soon after Kaye's body was found, now I was absolutely going to check on the dog.

I locked the barn, then ran in to Toshco. I found one of the owners, Nancy, and asked her if she knew where the Millers lived. She was too busy stocking industrial-sized packages of napkins to think to ask me why I wanted to know.

"You mean the compound?" she said.

I nodded.

She gave me precise directions, and I set out. I decided I was going to get Finn back from them. I hoped I could charm my way in, but I doubted it would be that easy.

I was up for the challenge.

Ten

Rules got broken out here. All the time, in fact. Sometimes it was by necessity, but many times, it was just because "you can."

I'd heard about a beautiful house out past Dr. Powder's place that was purposefully hidden by well-positioned foliage. The place was off all grids. Bottom line, the owners didn't want to pay taxes, so they remained hidden. Visitors needed a password to be welcomed inside. Very cloak-and-dagger but an accepted way of life out here.

I'd asked Gril about it, and he'd only shrugged, not saying one word. Later, I heard that the family who owned the property had paid for a new landing strip at the small airport a few years back, which might have been why the secret was so well-kept.

Tex's adoption of his two girls had been anything but legal, but even after all the circumstances were brought to light with state officials, nothing was done about it. A part of me liked that sometimes it just made sense to leave well enough alone, but another part of me worried that too many things could fall between the cracks.

Sometimes it's just about the caliber of the person, Beth, Gril had said. If the folks involved have good intentions, well, maybe we should just go with it.

I understood completely, and Tex was a great father. Why would anyone in their right mind mess up that situation for those two girls, no matter what the law said?

I slowed the truck as I came up on the outside edge of the Millers' property. A bent chain-link fence covered in signs told me I was there. The gist of the signs was that I would be shot dead if I came onto the property unwelcomed, and pretty much everybody was on that unwelcome list.

I was just stubborn enough to take the chance. The Millers had met me and probably decided I wasn't any sort of threat. If they were home they might not shoot me right away.

I turned onto the gravel driveway in a break of the fence. Rolling along, I still hadn't spotted a house, but I noticed more of the same sorts of signs attached to trees along the way.

I'd had no idea that Kaye lived in a place like this, in what felt like a fortress made by paranoid people. I'd left her a phone message about Finn on a cell phone that probably didn't get reception in this neck of the woods. She'd called me later.

If I had known about her circumstances, would I have still let Finn go with her? Probably. Elijah's file had guided my every move with the dogs, and Kaye and I had hit it off or at least felt immediately comfortable with each other. At least that's what I'd perceived.

The number of signs only increased the farther I traveled. But I wasn't sneaking up on the Millers. I didn't have a weapon. It would all be fine.

When I came upon the house, I understood why I'd heard it called a compound.

The main structure had begun its life as a small cabin, but, as Kaye had mentioned, other clunky pieces had been added on over time. The mismatched structures made up two legs of buildings as well as a back structure that was taller than everything else.

Here in the woods, anything could happen, and anything could probably be hidden. This sight only reinforced that idea. I suspected that no one had inspected any of this, no renovations had been approved.

I swallowed a hard gulp and got out of the truck. There were other vehicles around, but what I thought was the main parking square was vacant except for some sunken tire tracks.

I heard a bark from inside the house and knew immediately it was Finn. He didn't sound like he was in distress, just as if he was announcing my arrival.

I thought all places like this had lots of dogs. Kaye had told me that Finn would be the only one in the home but that a few outdoor cats kept the rodent population down. And Elijah hadn't said anything about other dogs in his file. I was now surprised there weren't more dogs around.

"Hey, boy," I said through the front door. It was closed, but he was directly on the other side.

I knocked. There was no doorbell, no camera. I remembered what Gril had said when the Millers had requested a camera on the community center about unreliable electricity and no internet access to monitor a feed.

I turned the knob, unsurprised to find it unlocked (who in their right mind would open this door uninvited?), and the door kind of opened on its own. I didn't have to push hard at all. Finn was going crazy. Finally, I pushed it wide and held a hand up in a halt instruction.

All of Elijah's dogs had been trained to sit and quiet down with that signal. Finn did so immediately.

"Ike? Camille?" I called. "I'm in the house. The door was unlocked, and Finn was barking. It's just me. Beth."

The inside of this main structure wasn't as disorganized as the outside of the place made me think it would be. It was cozy, the couch and chairs welcoming and all covered with winterscape-decorated blankets and quilts. A large-screen television took up the front part of the room. It was impossible to miss the foil-wrapped antenna taped to the back of the television and sticking up in the air. I would be surprised if even that helped get a signal.

A well-used dog bed filled the corner of the front room. I looked at Finn. He had no idea that Kaye was gone. At some point, he'd miss her, but for the moment, he looked perfect. He was in good shape and obviously taken care of.

"Hello?" I said into the unknown.

Still no one answered.

I wanted to explore, to look in all the crannies and crevices of the crazy house, but I also didn't want to be shot dead. I knew that searching was a terrible idea. Even what I was already doing was unwise and also illegal.

"Okay, I'm just going to look around this room a little," I told the dog, who whined in support.

Survivalist magazines were stacked on one end table and a bag with yarn and an in-progress crochet project on the other. An empty, stained, plain white ceramic coffee mug sat next to the crochet. There wasn't much to the room. It was a gathering spot but not for anything suspicious. I didn't see weapons anywhere.

I went back to Finn, who was still sitting, though his tail was sweeping the floor enthusiastically.

"Okay, boy, you seem fine. Are you okay?"

He smiled at me again.

"I'll come back when they're home, but I'm not worried about you. Should I be?"

Wouldn't the world be a much better place if animals could talk?

I heard a distant rumble of truck engines. Quickly, I told Finn goodbye and exited the house. I took a seat on the front porch and waited.

I fully expected to see the Miller family coming this way. I wondered how many vehicles were attached to all the noise.

But it turned out it wasn't the Millers after all.

I'd been a little worried before, but when I realized that the men stepping out of the two trucks that parked next to mine weren't Millers, I thought it might be time to be downright afraid.

Eleven

Hello?" one of the men said.

I stood. "Hi."

"Who are you?"

"Beth Rivers," I said, putting my hands on my hips. I hoped they didn't notice my trembling limbs. "And you are?"

"Blair, and this is my son, Kingston Oliphant," the older of the two said, pointing at himself first.

"Well, nice to meet you."

"Do you live here?"

"I do not. I came to check on the dog."

"What? Why?"

I looked back at the house and then back at the men. "I'm the one who helped find homes for the dogs when Elijah left."

Blair nodded. "You mean when he up and abandoned them?"

He had a point, but I didn't comment. I just tried to look unbothered and tough. I doubt I pulled it off.

"How's the dog?" Blair asked.

I thought I might have heard a gentler tone this time.

"I don't know. No one answered the door. I assume no one is home. I'm waiting for them to get back."

Blair and Kingston looked at where I'd thought the main parking area was located. They said something to each other.

"It doesn't look like they *are* home." Blair returned his attention to me.

I wanted to ask what they were doing there. I wanted to know if they knew Cyrus was in the police station probably at this very moment. But I knew better than to ask any of those things.

"Do you want me to relay any message?" I asked, hopefully still sounding unbothered but helpful this time.

Blair cracked a smile, but it wasn't friendly. "No, that's all right. We like to deliver our own messages."

"Okay," I said.

"How come we don't know you?" Kingston spoke up. He looked nothing like Cyrus, who I assumed was his brother. Kingston was heavy but not muscular, and a dark beard covered his face. His eyes were blue but not as striking as Cyrus's.

I shook my head. "I've lived here for about a year. I live with Viola."

"Oh! You're the one with the scar."

"That's me."

"Can we see it?" Kingston asked.

"King, that's not polite," Blair said, crossing his arms in front of himself, leering at me curiously.

Kingston took his father's pose as some sort of challenge. He stepped closer to me. "Whaddaya say?" he asked. "Take it off, take it off."

I'd willingly shown my scar to just about every person I'd met in Benedict. If anyone had asked to see it, they had been curious but not creepy.

I stood on the porch and crossed my own arms in front of myself. They were going to have to come up there and rip the hat off my head before I'd show them my scar. I was not going to kowtow to these two idiots.

The face-off lasted a good thirty seconds to a minute before Blair laughed once and then uncrossed his arms. He smacked Kingston on the arm and said, "Let's go, son. We'll take care of this later."

Kingston seemed surprised by his father's behavior, like he was hurt to be missing a chance to bully a girl, someone who probably weighed at least a hundred pounds less than he did.

I didn't take my eyes off him.

After Blair got into his truck, Kingston stood there a moment and glared at me. He balled his fists at his side in a challenge I was more than ready to accept.

Don't flinch; don't flinch no matter what he does, I told myself.

Kingston didn't make a move toward me, which was probably better news for me than him, but I was still fuming. When Blair had his truck turned around, he leaned out his window and hit his car door with the palm of his hand.

"Let's go, son," he said.

Finally, Kingston got into his truck and followed his father off the property that none of us should have been trespassing on.

Once they were out of sight, I crumpled into a heap on the porch, the rush of adrenaline now dissipating and turning me into momentary mush.

My throat tightened and tears fell down my cheeks. I knew this emotion wasn't only because of the Oliphants and their behavior. My body wasn't willing to ever let me be bullied again. I would rather be killed than held captive, physically or in any other way.

Literally, I would have rather died than show those men they could have any sort of control over me.

This was probably something I needed to talk to my therapist about.

I wiped my face and stood again. What was I going to do about Finn? Was I just going to sit there and wait for the Millers to return? It seemed like the best idea.

But I no longer wanted to be out there in those still cold woods away from civilization. In fact, it was so far away from civilization that no one for miles could hear me scream.

The urge to do what I did next was almost as strong as the stubbornness that had probably just made me a family of enemies.

I opened the door.

"Come on, boy," I said.

I left a note on the door saying that the dog had been out when I'd gotten there so I took him with me back to the Benedict House. The Millers probably wouldn't believe the lie, but I didn't much care. I wasn't leaving Finn with people I didn't trust, and at that moment, I didn't think I could trust most of the Millers or any of the Oliphants.

I didn't care if it made any of them mad. I was mad, too. I had a right to be.

Finn hopped in my truck, and I drove us out of there.

Twelve

Hello!" Chaz said as Finn trotted toward him.

He and Viola had been walking toward the stairway at the end of the hallway. They'd turned when I came in.

The dog was happy to greet Chaz and Viola, even if Viola did look at him, and then me, curiously.

"I'll figure it out," I said to her. "I . . It's a long story."

Viola had been more than welcoming to Gus when I'd brought him home. She adored him, but I didn't think she'd want two dogs around permanently.

Gus peeked his head out from Viola's office door.

I saw his eyebrows rise in happiness to see Finn.

"It's okay," Viola said as she petted both dogs when they greeted each other. "For now."

"Thanks," I said.

"May I walk them?" Chaz asked her. "It would be a great way to get some exercise."

Viola was immediately skeptical.

"Where am I going to go?" he asked. "I can't swim."

If I hadn't witnessed people manage disappearing acts from this land with ocean on one side and untamed wild mountains on the other, I would have thought her skepticism overboard.

"Okay," Viola finally said. "We have two main roads. You may walk the dogs next to those roads only. That's for your own good too, you know. You'd never make it out here."

"Oh, I hear you, and I don't even want to try to run away, I promise, but I'm very excited about walking the dogs. Leashes?"

Viola gathered two leashes from her office, and Chaz ran up to his room to put on a thicker sweatshirt and a jacket. We stood outside the front door as Viola pointed out the obvious intersection of the main roads.

I realized I trusted Chaz more than I had the Millers or the Oliphants, and I hoped my intuition wasn't off track as we watched the felon and the dogs head out toward the road.

"This might be interesting," I said.

"I hope it will be good for all of them. Those three weren't meant to be stuck all day behind closed doors."

"How *is* Chaz?" I asked. "How's his . . . reformation coming?"

"He's somewhat remorseful but mostly because he got caught, and he knows he could have done what he'd planned on doing without getting caught. He got impatient."

"He said something like that to me."

"Right. Well, I've got to get him to understand that he needs to never try to do what he did again. Honestly, I'm not sure if I can pull it off. He's smart and he had a good plan. He might end up a successful criminal one day, but that's a rare breed. I think it's more likely he'll end up in prison again. And that's a shame. He's a good guy."

"And an amazing cook."

"No kidding."

"So, Viola, the Millers might come looking for Finn. I'd like to make sure they're going to take care of him before I give him back."

"You took the dog from the Millers?" she asked.

"I did it when they weren't home and immediately after having something of a showdown with the Oliphants on the Miller property."

"You've been busy."

"That's one way to put it."

"Well, I won't let anyone take the dog, I promise. And no one's going to challenge me, even a Miller or an Oliphant."

It was good to have friends in high places, and Viola was in one of the highest.

"Thank you."

"However, I'd recommend you stay away from those groups for a while. Someone killed Kaye, and Gril needs to get that figured out, hopefully without an innocent bystander getting in the way."

"Do you have a suspect in mind?"

"I have a few." She frowned. "But I really don't think it was her husband, Warren."

"Tell me about him. I don't know much, and the Millers think Kaye and I spent a lot of time together with the dogs."

"They do?"

I nodded. "She was with Cyrus Oliphant more than I think either of them shared with anyone."

Viola whistled. "This isn't good."

"Orin said he thought their feud began with a girl. Has anyone seen Orin?" I asked. I didn't want to tell her that Donner had mentioned her name. Not yet. Viola didn't like people talking behind her back, and I never wanted to give the impression, even as a misunderstanding, that I didn't *have* her back.

"Not that I know of."

"I keep thinking we need to be worried about him. Do you know if Gril has called one of Orin's superiors or bosses?"

"I don't know, but it's too soon to be too worried. Let's give it a few more days and then I'll push Gril to do something."

"Okay," I said uncertainly.

"What else did he tell you about the feud?"

"Not one thing."

"Want to hear the story?"

"I do."

"Coffee. And Chaz made a cake. Let's go in. I think they'll be okay." Viola looked toward the road. We couldn't see Chaz or the dogs any longer.

Viola was good at understanding people. I could tell she was piling on some extra hope that she hadn't misjudged one this time.

I made the coffee while she cut us each a piece of cake.

The coffee was good, but the word that came to me as I took a bite of the lemon cake was *divine*.

"Remember how good Ellen was with bread?" I asked.

"Sure."

"Chaz is a hundred times more incredible with everything."

"I know. Surely, he could find a way to make an honest living."

"I guess he's got to want to."

Viola nodded.

For a few minutes, we enjoyed the food.

Finally, Viola nodded and sat back in her chair. "Warren is a good guy. He tried to get away from his family when he was younger, but he came back. They were so much wilder without him." Viola smiled sadly. "Before Gril got here, our local lawman wasn't full-time but came back and forth from Juneau. Anyway, his name was Lars. Lars had so much trouble with the Millers when Warren left the family that in the middle of a brutal winter, Lars trudged up to where Warren and Kaye had moved—a place near where you picked up Al—and begged him to go back to the family. He told Warren that there was no other way to prevent everybody killing one another. Warren told him he would only do that if his new-to-town wife, Kaye, agreed to go with him."

I thought about the position Kaye had been put in. It had to be difficult. I'm not sure I would have ever agreed to go—and now she was dead.

"How long ago?"

"Ten years or so, back when Kaye first got here," Viola said.

"And Kaye agreed? Wow."

"I know. I wouldn't have, but she was a nice person." Viola frowned sadly. "However, I will tell you this: from all indications, it was the best thing that ever happened to any of them, and Kaye really seemed happy, too, at least from what I could tell. I don't know the details, but Kaye came up here to escape a bad situation down in Montana, I believe. I think Warren placed an ad somewhere and Kaye answered it. No one judges those sorts of things, but it was a topic for a while, calling Kaye Warren's mail-order bride and such. Shoot, even ten years ago, folks were internet dating. She took the gossip in stride. She seemed to be doing well whenever I saw her."

"She never seemed unhappy when I was around her. Until a couple days ago, when she was a little down and used the word *melancholy*."

"From what I could see, she got along with all the Millers. And she and Warren, but mostly Kaye, kept everything between that family and the Oliphants defused. A little. Sure, the families still didn't like each other, but Kaye somehow managed to keep everyone in their own corners for the most part. I don't know why. It was as if their anger at each other just wasn't as important after Warren and Kaye moved back into the Miller compound. I talked to Gril about it a few times over the years. He told me they all still 'hated' each other, but Kaye . . . somehow smoothed the waters some. He thought maybe all their anger was just sticking around because neither family ever wanted to show weakness or be the one to give in and make peace."

"Wow, how did she do that?"

Viola shook her head. "He didn't really know, but he was glad to have her there."

"Boy, I sure don't sense any peace between the two families now."

"Something must have happened."

"Could Warren have killed Kaye because she was seeing Cyrus?"

Viola laughed without humor. "Yes. Even Warren, the least violent of them all, still doesn't like the Oliphants. And a betrayal of the heart is never good. It's hard to imagine Warren as a murderer, though."

"Do you know Cyrus Oliphant?"

"Sure."

"I don't really know him, but I've seen him around. He appears to be a loner. Maybe he's soft-spoken, too. Maybe Kaye liked that in men. I saw him in a new light today."

"Oh? Where?"

I launched into the story about Cyrus's appearance at the police station. Viola nodded and took in the details of the brief moments I'd witnessed between Donner and Cyrus.

"Cyrus isn't quite as mellow as Warren, but of the Oliphants, he might be the most civil. I don't know, Beth. I can't believe Kaye was spending any time with any of the Oliphants. That would be considered disrespectful to any Miller. Even Kaye would have thought it was too risky."

"Maybe Cyrus told Donner what they were up to. Maybe it was innocent."

"I suppose we'll see."

My heart sank again for Kaye. She'd gotten herself into something she couldn't get out of. I'd hoped we would become closer with another month of good weather down the road. Had she had anyone to talk to? Would she have ever confided in me? We'd never have answers to these questions now.

"Tell me the story of the feud," I said.

Viola smiled wryly. "Would you be surprised to learn that I'm right in the middle of it?"

"I'd be shocked to my toes." I matched her smile and hoped she didn't hear the lie in my tone.

"Well, I have to begin by saying I was quite the looker when I was a girl."

"To me you're absolutely beautiful," I said. "I mean it."

Viola blinked. "Well. Thank you."

I nodded and sipped my coffee.

"Hang on." Viola stood from the table and made her way back to her office. She returned a couple minutes later. "Here, look at this."

It was a picture of teenage girls, probably from sometime in the sixties. Both girls wore bell-bottom jeans. One of them had a crocheted peace-sign sweater and the other a tie-dyed long-sleeved T-shirt.

Viola pointed to the girl in the peace-sign sweater. "That's me." She pointed to the other one. "That's Benny."

From what I could tell from this old full-color-but-faded picture, Viola and Benny had been drop-dead gorgeous teenage girls, both with long, wavy blond hair and perfect smiles.

"What happened, right?" Viola asked.

"No." I looked at her and then at the picture again. "I can still see it. I didn't before you showed me the picture, but that girl is still here."

"Yes, she is, and she's shocked every time she looks in a mirror now." Viola laughed. "Benny's gained more weight than I have. I like to remind her of that."

I laughed, too. "I imagine she doesn't care."

"Could not care less."

"You look very happy in this picture."

"Yes, we were happy. We had shelter, jobs, food. We were no longer living with abusive, drunken parents. We loved Benedict. Still do," Viola said as she looked at the picture again. She brought her eyes back up to me. "You know we all have our secrets here, don't you? You're not the only one."

"I've heard that a time or two."

"Well, I'm about to tell you my secret, Beth. And you're the first person I've admitted it to, though some people have probably figured out the truth."

"I'm ready."

"It's big."

I cleared my throat. "I'm extra ready."

"Back when I was just a little older than this girl right here"— she pointed at the picture that was on the table now—"I killed a man. It wasn't accidental. I meant to kill him, and I did it."

I gulped. "I won't tell" were the first words that came to me.

Viola laughed again. "Don't care if you do. I'll deny it to the rest of the world until the day I die. And there's no evidence, so no one can do anything about it. Besides, he needed killing."

"Well, I've heard that a time or two as well." I was thinking about my mother. When Viola didn't speak again immediately, I said, "Does it feel good to admit it?"

She smiled sadly. "No, but it doesn't hurt like it used to, either. I'd never felt the urge to kill before, and I haven't since. I had no choice. If I hadn't killed him, he would have killed me—or worse."

"Self-defense."

"Yes, but . . . well, let me start at the beginning."

"Please." I grabbed the coffee pot I'd set in the middle of the table and refilled both our mugs. "Okay. Now we're both ready."

Viola nodded. "I'm the same age as Ike Miller and Zevon Oliphant, who was Blair's younger brother. We all ran around together, if you will. We went to school." She nodded toward where the one-building, all-grades school was located. "It was different, though. School was less important back then, which wasn't good. But there you are. We all did the bare minimum education-wise, then worked or played like only stupid teenagers are apt to do.

"The generation before, Garrett Miller and Omer Oliphant were running the show out in those woods. They didn't like each other, but the best I can tell you is that the dislike all stemmed from them both being bullies and just not wanting to get along and not wanting to share their woods with anyone else. The families have lived out where their places are since forever as far as I know. They always claimed they liked their privacy, but as time went on, we all could see that neither group wanted to be told what to do about much of anything, and they resented any sort of rules or any social norms. The men liked the control of their own families.

"Anyway, there's only a small number of kids around the same age out here at any time. The Miller and Oliphant kids might have had to obey their fathers when they were home, but away from those places, they could have friends, even between the families." Viola sighed as she fell into thought for a moment. She looked up at me. "For a long time, no one in our group really dated anyone. We were kids, but kids turn into teenagers. There were others, though their names aren't important to the story. There were about ten of us who stuck together through thick and thin. For a long time, it was wonderful. And then one day it wasn't. One day, Ike Miller decided he wanted more from me than just a friendship, and he tried to force himself on me."

"Oh, Viola, I'm sorry."

She took a deep breath and let it out. "I'm not making excuses for him because it was the wrong thing to do, but he truly didn't know better. Believe it or not, his father, Garrett, who is long dead now, was worse than any of them living out there in that cabin and unwelcoming to everyone. He was a terror, and we all knew it. We all tried to support Ike in that. He wanted me and probably did what he'd seen his own father do to his mother. We were in the woods. He didn't get away with it. I kneed him in the balls and then ran away. In the fray, his truck key fell out of his pocket. I took it and drove back to town, figuring he could damn well come and get that truck and apologize to me before I gave him back the key."

"Did you tell anyone?"

Viola smiled sadly and shook her head. "Who was I supposed to tell? Benny couldn't have done anything about it. We had less law enforcement than we did when Lars got Warren to move back home."

"Al," I said. "You could have told Al."

"No, I couldn't have," Viola said. "Beth, I promise you there was no one I could tell. But you have to remember, Ike didn't get away with it. I escaped." She looked at me. "You lived through worse, and you escaped, too. I can imagine the enormity of your escape because I know how it felt to get away from Ike that day."

I nodded but didn't speak. This wasn't about me.

"Anyway, Ike's truck did disappear from where I'd parked it, and I saw him driving it the next day, but I still had the key I'd taken. I figured he was too embarrassed to demand it back from me and just used another key. I was okay with that. Our friends saw a change in the way both Ike and I started to act. Anger and discomfort and embarrassment were all mixed together with a bunch of unruly teenage hormones. It was weird. Pretty soon, they all probably thought we had a simple spat or something. That's when things went from bad to worse.

"Zevon Oliphant also had a thing for me, but it wasn't something I even knew about until after everything with Ike. When things got uncomfortable because of Ike, Zevon started hanging around just me more, acting all sweet on me. I was irritated by the whole lot of them. One day I told Zevon to just leave me alone. I was ready to dump them all, except Benny of course. I didn't need the hassle."

When she paused, I asked, "So Zevon Oliphant . . ?"

Viola licked her lips, swallowed hard, and nodded. "He followed me out to the woods one day. He was . . . more violent, used more brute strength against me than Ike had. He knocked me to the ground and pinned me, tried the same thing Ike had tried but he was even more . . . insistent. I was terrified. I yelled for him to stop, but there was no one around to hear us. He told me that he'd heard that Ike liked me and that it would be wrong for me to ever be with a Miller. I should always choose an Oliphant. Beth, again, I promise you, this attitude, probably his exact words, all came from something he'd heard his own horrible father do or say. I told him I didn't like Ike, and I was so angry I told him I didn't like him that way, either. Well, his ego wasn't ready for that. I mean, I remember seeing his expression change, like I'd slapped him with my hand not hurt him with my words. The last thing he said to me was, 'If I can't have you, no one can.' He growled like an animal and put his hands around my neck."

"Oh, Viola," I said and put my hand over hers on the table. I realized another reason I might have been so drawn to her and why I hadn't left the Benedict House even after I learned it was a halfway house. Why Viola had become family to me so quickly.

We shared a similar horror, and our intuitions knew it.

"For a split second I thought I might get him to calm down. Maybe if I didn't fight back, maybe if I could talk him through whatever this rage was. But no, I was smart enough—and I want you to know that I've never regretted coming to this conclusion—to know that he was going to rape me or kill me, Beth. Or both. I could see it in his eyes. He was lost to the rage. I had no choice. I've always worn some sort of weapon on me, and back then it was a knife. I was able to grab it from the sheath at my side, and I stabbed him when I was just about to fall unconscious from being choked. He was dead less than a minute later."

Even if he hadn't planned on killing her, too, I was hard pressed to think she hadn't done the right thing.

"I remember rolling and stepping away from his body as clear as if it happened yesterday. I threw the knife in the river, went home, and cleaned up. And no one ever even thought it was me."

"Oh, Viola, I'm so, so sorry."

She shook her head. I saw the pain in her eyes but also the resolve. "I had no choice."

"No, you didn't. But how did that cause a feud between the families?"

"I'd been carrying around Ike's truck key in my pocket. It fell out, probably as I grabbed my knife, right there next to Zevon's body. At first everyone thought Ike Miller killed Zevon Oliphant. Ike claimed to have lost the key a while before, and he had an alibi during the time of the murder—he was helping pick strawberries. Lots of people saw him. Well, none of the Oliphants saw him, but eventually, somehow word got around that Zevon had taken some girl out to the woods with him, but no one knew who, even though my name might have come up a couple of times. The only hint of substantial proof would have been if Ike had told everyone I had his truck key. If he'd done that, I would have exposed him for what he'd done. Everyone knew Zevon probably got what he deserved, and the Oliphants never wanted to believe anything but that it was Ike who'd killed Zevon."

I nodded. "Has Ike been blackmailing you?"

"I'd never let him do that. I waited for him to come talk to me and threaten me, but he never did. The Oliphants never believed the strawberry-picking story, and he never did anything to point the blame at me. No one was ever convicted for Zevon's murder. Shoot, I don't think anyone even investigated it."

"Wow."

Viola took a sip of the quickly cooling coffee. "The families never liked each other before all that, but that's what turned their dislike into a feud—one where they bad-mouth each other and probably destroy each other's property when they can get away with it, but no one else died. Until now."

I took a sip of my coffee, too. "That's incredible, Viola."

"It's terrible. I wish I could have done to Zevon what I'd done to Ike, just given him a good knee and left him, but there was no way. Either I was going to die, or he was going to have to. I still remember that feeling of knowing there was no choice in matter."

"I know that feeling, too."

"I bet you do."

"I'm sorry you went through it."

Viola smiled sadly. "I'm sorry when anyone goes through it. This world." She patted her gun. "I wish I didn't feel like I needed to carry this."

I understood even more why she thought she should, though I'd never considered carrying one myself. Donner had offered to teach me how to shoot and so had Tex, but I hadn't taken lessons from either of them yet.

I sighed. "I'm glad you're here, and I'm glad you're okay."

"Same." Viola smiled and then her eyes transformed again. She had said she'd come to terms with what she'd done, but speaking aloud about it had been painful to her. I hoped the pain would pass. "Back to the present. I wonder if something was going on between Kaye and Cyrus. If it was, I can tell you those families will only fight more. They are already jealous."

"Hopefully Cyrus tells Donner the truth, and that defuses things."

"The sooner the better."

The sound of the front door opening caught our attention. Viola and I stood to check out the commotion.

Chaz was back with the dogs. Smiles all around.

"That was incredible," he said. "I'll do it again later if that's okay."

Viola shrugged. "That's probably fine."

They were all a little muddy but not too bad, and they were all happy. I couldn't help but smile back.

"We had some of your cake. It was so good," I said.

"I know. Wait until I bake you one of my famous Boston cream pies."

"I look forward to it."

Viola sent me a secretive smile before she went with Chaz to attend to both dogs. I offered to help, but they told me they could handle things.

Her smile communicated to me that we weren't to speak of what she'd just shared with me ever again.

I'd never tell.

Thirteen

was distracted as I drove the truck toward the *Petition* shed. My mind worked through the events of the last few days, playing moments like the dog walk with Kaye over and over again. Had I missed something? I didn't think that anything I'd witnessed offered up any sort of clue as to who killed Kaye. I hadn't immediately liked Warren, but Viola didn't think he could have killed Kaye—unless she and Cyrus were . . . what? Romantically involved? Walking the dog? Kaye hadn't ever mentioned Cyrus to me, but even Elijah had come upon them together.

I wondered if the Millers would come to town angry because I'd taken Finn, or if the Oliphants would look for another opportunity to intimidate me. I wasn't worried about either of those scenarios, but I did ponder when they might occur.

I didn't see anyone on the way, but that wasn't unusual. As I came around to park along the side of the shed, I glanced over toward the library. Cars filled the parking spaces, but I didn't spot Orin's truck. I wondered who had unlocked and opened the doors and if they were still there. Instead of stopping at the shed, I took the connecting road and pulled into an improvised parking space in the library's gravel lot.

As I made my way up the steps to the front door, a man came out of the building. I only glanced at him briefly and didn't immediately recognize him, though I registered that he wore black pants and a black sweatshirt with the hood pulled up and secured around his head.

As he took the few steps down, he muttered a quick "Hello, Beth" in a voice I didn't recognize.

I said hello, then turned to take a better look at who I'd just spoken to, but the man was headed around the building. I presumed he'd parked in one of the vehicles back there.

I climbed down the stairs and glanced toward where he'd gone. He was already out of earshot, and from the quick look I got at him, he didn't seem familiar. I could tell he was a man with a medium build who maybe walked with a small limp. I couldn't place him at all. Even with those two words, that brief greeting, he sounded as if he knew me. How? I didn't think I knew him.

Though there were only about ten vehicles, I lost sight of him amid them, but I didn't hear an engine start up. I waited to see if he would drive away, so I could get a better look. But after a full minute, no engine started. I couldn't see him any longer, and I didn't have the patience to try to track him down.

I shook off the moment, and took the steps back up into the library. It was busy inside, as it was most days. Some people were there with their laptops just for the internet access, some to find and read books. I spotted some books stacked tall and precariously on the corner of one of the tables. I thought about straightening the stack, but someone was seated nearby, and it might have been intrusive. I nodded at everyone—they all looked somewhat familiar—as I threaded my way to Orin's office. The door was open.

"Hi," I said.

"Hello, Beth," Ruke said from Orin's chair. A magazine was open before him on the desk.

"You got library duty, huh?"

Ruke shrugged. "Helping where I can, I suppose. Gril said someone needed to be here, and I was available."

"How did you get in?"

"Gril gave me a key."

Though he hadn't invited me, I sat in a chair on the other side of Orin's desk.

Ruke smiled, pushing the magazine aside and giving me his full attention. The truck I had purchased from him had been his sister's, but she had left to marry into another Tlingit tribe. The truck was old, beat up, very unattractive, and perfect. I loved it more than I'd loved any vehicle I'd ever owned.

"Has anyone heard from Orin?" I asked.

"Not that I know of. He'll be back. He's probably on assignment or something."

"I keep hearing that. Do you know what he does?"

Ruke smiled. "I don't even think Gril knows what he does. I'm guessing they're important things, though."

I had tried to imagine Orin in a covert operation, but couldn't make those pieces fit together, either. He'd told me they used him more for his brain than anything, so maybe he just had to go be smart somewhere.

"I'm worried about him, Ruke."

Ruke nodded. "He'll be fine. I think Gril is concerned but not worried. People are on the lookout for him, too. Gril told me he searched his home and there was no sign of foul play."

"Do you know where Orin lives?"

"Of course." Ruke raised his eyebrows. "You haven't seen his house?"

"No."

Ruke smiled. "It's quite the place. Have him give you a tour when he gets back. He's out in the east coordinate."

I'd heard where the house was located before, but I'd never even had occasion to drive by it, and, of course, I'd recently pondered how I'd never been inside it.

"How's your sister?" I asked.

"She's a mother now. I have the cutest niece in the world." He pulled out his wallet and showed me a picture of a tiny girl with a head full of out-of-control dark hair.

"She's beautiful!"

"I know. Thank you. How's the truck?" He slipped the picture back into his wallet.

I slanted my eyes at him. "Your sister doesn't want it back, does she?"

"No, she bought a brand-new one."

"That's good. I love the truck. It's been great."

"Glad to hear it."

Ruke laughed and smiled.

I paused and looked at him. We didn't know each other well but, hopefully, well enough. "You came upon Kaye's body?"

Ruke's expression changed quickly and he frowned, nodding slowly. "I did. It was quite the shock."

"Did you see anything suspicious?"

He lifted his eyebrows. "Other than a body? No, Beth, I didn't see anyone else around. I saw the bloody rock, but, no, nothing else."

He wasn't irritated exactly, but I heard the insinuation of irritation in his tone. His reputation was that he was a great guy, one of the kindest in town, but he probably thought I didn't need to be asking him what I was asking. He wasn't wrong.

"Sorry," I said.

He shook his head. "No, I apologize. I'm still bothered . . ."

"Of course."

He smiled again, though it wasn't a happy expression. "No, I didn't see anything that would help us understand what happened. I've recently gotten to know Kaye. I hadn't even met her until this winter, and she was a nice person."

"Where did you meet her?"

"She would walk her dog many of the same times I was checking my winter traps."

"Finn."

Ruke continued to smile sadly. "A good dog."

"Yes, I . . . I was the one who gave her the dog. I went and took him back from the Millers until I know if he'll be okay there."

Ruke sat up straighter. "Good for you." He paused. "Let me know if they give you any hassle."

I nodded, but I wondered what he'd do if they did. Maybe I didn't really want to know. "Thanks, Ruke. Was Kaye alone when you saw her?"

He nodded. "Just Kaye and Finn. Yes."

If she'd been spending time with Cyrus, it hadn't been where Ruke witnessed it. I was disappointed, if only for the possibility of there being another lead.

"Do you know much about the family? The feud between them and the Oliphants?"

"Not much. They all keep to themselves. It's not easy to get to know any of them. I enjoyed the brief conversations I had with Kaye, but that's all they were, brief. I found out she's been here for around ten years, and I only met her recently. No one from either family has ever come to me with an ailment."

Ruke wasn't a medicine man. The tribe had done away with such a title, but he did work with plants and herbs and other organic substances to create remedies. In fact, Dr. Powder had once given Viola some of Ruke's peppermint oil to help her upset stomach. It had worked.

I thought about Kaye's mention of the family's aversion to seeking out traditional medical assistance. They might not have even known about Ruke's mixtures. "Kaye did mention to me that Camille takes care of them. Kaye used the word *nurse*, but I don't think she's had any formal education."

Ruke nodded slowly. "Well, they seem to be okay. Until now, I haven't heard of anything tragic happening to any of them."

"I guess," I said, thinking he wouldn't be old enough to have been around when Zevon had been killed.

"I think we all wish we knew them better. We all wonder if we could have somehow helped Kaye, but if they want to keep people out, the rest of us certainly aren't going to barge our ways in. We're good at letting people live the way they want to live."

I nodded and thought again about Old Al. I hoped he was doing better.

"That's true." I paused. "May I leave a note for Orin?"

"Of course."

Ruke looked around for a piece of paper, but nothing was visible.

"I think he keeps a notebook in the top drawer," I said.

"I'm not sure I should be opening drawers."

"I think it's okay. I've only seen the notebook and pens and pencils in that one."

Warily, Ruke opened the top middle drawer of the desk. Once he realized there wasn't anything that seemed private inside, he gathered a pen and the yellow notepad I'd seen Orin use many times. He handed them both to me.

As I took the notepad and set it on my lap, an angle of light through the window behind Ruke bounced off the paper, allowing me to notice indentations in the page.

I thought maybe I saw the ghost of a phone number because the first three digits looked familiar. I wanted to know for sure. I didn't think twice, and I didn't ask Ruke; I simply tore off the top page, folded it, then stuck it in my bag. I sensed Ruke watching me but I didn't offer any explanation. I wasn't even sure what I'd say if he asked me what I was doing.

I scribbled something on the next page, asking Orin to call me or find me the second he got back. I ended the note with "I'm worried!" and handed everything back to Ruke.

"Okay," he said and gave me a sideways glance.

I smiled and stood. "Thanks, Ruke."

He looked at the notepad. "You're welcome."

I turned and left the office, retracing the path I'd taken coming in. I noticed the stack of books again, and since there wasn't anyone sitting near them now, I hurried over to straighten them or at least push them a little farther back from the edge.

But as I came upon them, I stopped in my tracks. The book at the top was one I'd written.

Standing next to the table, I looked around the library. Was anyone looking back? No. Everyone was doing whatever they'd come into the library to do, and it wasn't to watch me.

I lifted the top book. The next one was mine too, as were the following three. This was a stack of my books.

I looked around again. I recognized everyone there. I might not have known them, but they were library regulars, and I spent enough time in the library to find them familiar.

Orin knew my identity, but as far as I knew, no one else in here, including Ruke, had made the connection to Elizabeth Fairchild.

My author picture didn't look a thing like me now. Instead of short, choppy, white-blond hair, the photoshopped picture inside my books was a version of me wearing makeup, my long brown hair smooth but curled up at the ends. Every time I looked at it, it felt like I was either seeing a stranger or a friend I hadn't talked to in a long time.

Okay, maybe it wasn't crazy that a stack of my books sat on the corner of a table in a library. My books were popular, and I'd frequently heard from my readers that they wanted to read everything I'd written after experiencing only one book. But who put these on the corner of this library table? Nudged by my intuition, my mind went to the man who was leaving as I came in and his familiar tone. He'd called me Beth, not my author's name. Had he made the connection? Had someone told him? Why was I even tying the two events together? Simply, something in my gut told me to.

I took a deep breath and told myself to calm down. I'd told quite a few people in Benedict who I was—the connection wasn't a secret anymore, just something my friends didn't really talk about. Or did they? I hadn't asked them not to tell, but they'd all mentioned they wouldn't anyway. Still, things come up in conversations; things can be overheard.

Would I have recognized the man if I'd been paying better attention? Had he, for whatever reason, been the person to leave this stack? And why in the world would he have done that? And why would it bother me, send up a red flag?

I was turning this into something it probably wasn't. I was connecting dots that might not even be part of the same puzzle. I took another deep breath. I straightened the books, pushed them back from the corner, and left the library. I had plenty of other mysteries to work on. This one, if it even was one, would have to be put on a back burner. For now.

Fourteen

As I made my way to the truck and then back to the shed, I looked around but didn't see the man. I didn't spot anyone.

I unlocked the shed's door and hurried inside. Once I locked the door behind me, I didn't bother with my normal routine of turning up the furnace. I walked to the window and held up the piece of paper I'd torn from the notepad. It took just the right angle for me to make out the indented marks.

It was a number I knew very well. Orin had been the one to deliver it to me, telling me it was a parting gift from my mother right before she disappeared. It was the same number I had been looking at inside my own desk drawer just two days earlier.

Though Mom had left the number for me, Orin had been the one to track my father down in Mexico, where it seemed he had, at least at one time, run a restaurant.

Why was the number imprinted on Orin's notepad? Had he tried to call it recently? Had that been one of the last things he'd done before he'd gone off to . . . wherever? Was he in Mexico with my father?

With hands I didn't even know had begun shaking, I reached for a phone in my backpack. It was my last burner phone. I'd used it for months, thinking I'd buy more burners when I took a trip to Juneau. I hadn't taken that trip yet, and I didn't see that happening anytime soon. This burner was also the last number my mother had for me, so I kept hoping I'd hear from her, too.

I punched in the now-familiar digits, and the ringing began. I was going to give it ten rings before hanging up and forgetting about it again.

But it didn't ring ten times. This time, after ring six, another voice mail picked up. A male voice said, "Leave a message."

And then the beep.

I was speechless for a long moment. My initial thought was to hang up and maybe throw the phone like it was on fire or something, but I knew that was a strange reaction. I didn't recognize the voice. It had been decades since I'd heard my father speak, and I had no idea if this was him or not. The first voice mail message had been a programmed voice; this was a person.

"Call me," I said and then left my number.

I didn't have a voice mail option on my phone and coverage was so spotty out here that I might never know if someone tried to call me back.

I ended the call.

What was going on?

I felt left out, cut off, and disconnected. The people I wanted to talk to—my mom, Orin, my missing father—weren't where they could, or maybe would, talk to me. I didn't want to burden Viola with any of this.

I did know someone who would talk to me, or at least I hoped she would. She had yet to ignore me.

I placed a call to the detective working on my case in Missouri, Detective Majors. We hadn't spoken for a while, and though she'd always been positive that they'd catch Travis Walker, even her optimism had taken a hit by now.

"Beth?" she answered immediately.

"Hi, Detective Majors."

"Hello." A chair squeaked in the background.

I was glad I'd reached her at her desk. "How are you?"

"I'm fine. How are you?"

"I'm well, better all the time."

"I'm happy to hear that. I . . . I've got nothing new on Walker. I'm sorry. I wish I had some news, any news, at this point."

"I know you're working hard."

"Always."

"Detective Majors, have you heard anything about or from my mother?"

"No, nothing from her, either. Why? Have you heard from her?"

"I haven't. I . . . have you heard anything about my father?"

"Oh. Well, no, nothing. I haven't . . . We haven't been looking for him in any focused way, Beth. Why do you ask?"

I wasn't sure what to say. Orin had already told me that no law enforcement agency could compel him to say or do anything. He had friends in *very* high places.

But I needed to not feel so suddenly unmoored. It wouldn't hurt to share some things. Even Orin had said that much, though I hadn't mentioned him to Detective Majors before today.

"I have a friend up here. He might have tracked my dad to Mexico."

"Really? Tell me more." The chair squeaked again.

I looked at the phone number on the piece of paper. I couldn't understand what the ramifications could possibly be for sharing it with her, but I couldn't stop myself.

"All I have is a phone number."

"Give it to me," Detective Majors demanded.

In fact, I didn't think I'd ever heard such a tone from her. She'd been on my side since the beginning. She'd been the one to drive me to the airport when I left the hospital without being formally discharged. She was the only person who knew where I'd run to, where I'd gone to hide, until she called Gril and gave him a heads-up. She had been my first real support.

I gave her the number.

"Thank you, Beth. I'll see what I can find out."

"I don't know that it will lead to anything. I suspect that if it is my father, he's as shifty as I am about phone numbers."

"It's still something. More than we had a few minutes ago. Who knows?"

It could very well lead to Travis Walker but neither of us said that aloud.

It might even lead to my mother.

And, now it might lead to Orin, and that was the real reason I'd told her. Had he gotten himself into the middle of my mess? If so, why? Did he need to be rescued somehow? I doubted it, but I wasn't completely sure, and I didn't want to look back and think I should have done more. He could take care of himself, but of all the people I'd just thought about, he was the one I most wanted to find—even more than my parents.

Orin didn't deserve to suffer in any way on my behalf.

"I hope you find something good," I finally said.

"Me too. Anything else, Beth?"

"Nope. That's it. I look forward to hearing from you."

We disconnected the call, and then I called the number on the yellow pad once again. The voice mail picked up again, but I didn't leave a message this time.

I'd worked myself up into a tizzy, for valid reasons I thought, but I could sense that my emotions had spun into an uncontrollable funnel cloud before I could manage to rein them in. I wasn't thinking clearly, but at least I was aware of the randomly firing thoughts and emotions in my head.

I spent a few minutes breathing deeply and trying to tell myself to get a grip. When that didn't work, I fired up my laptop, moved it near the window where it could best pick up the library's internet, and reached out to my online therapist, Leia.

I was relieved when she answered immediately.

"Beth, he—oh, you look bothered. What's up?" she asked.

Just seeing her face made me feel better. I was so glad that she was available to talk.

And that's what we did—talk. Mostly, she listened and then inserted the appropriate helpful comments to get me through this. My emotional trauma was real, and she had figured out how to not only help me see it more clearly but also deal with it. Many times now, because of her help, I could work through a big wave of anxiety on my own, but sometimes I still needed to see her on the screen. This had been one of those times.

"I feel so much better," I said about a half an hour into our session.

"That's great, Beth. You're doing so well. It's good that you called the detective. You trust her, and it's a good reminder that you don't need to shoulder everything. Other people are working to help solve your mysteries. You aren't alone, and you've done everything you can to feel safe."

I nodded. "True."

Our conversation turned casual and we spoke for a few more minutes. She asked about Gus, and I asked about her ailing mother. My feelings and behavior were more under control. After scheduling a follow-up meeting for the next week, we said goodbye. I closed the laptop and leaned back in my chair. I took another deep breath. I felt it at the bottom of my lungs—I'd managed to calm down.

People who can easily relax don't know the gift they've been given. In my entire life, it hadn't been until I started talking to Leia that I had been able to make a breathing technique work, even in a small way.

As I sat in my chair feeling the weight of my still-relaxing muscles and the steady beat of my heart, the thoughts in my head didn't whir back to an unmanageable level, but something did occur to me: a phone number—but not the one I'd been dialing. It was a different one or at least the idea of a different one.

When I'd looked in Elijah's file for more information regarding what to do with Finn, I'd seen Orin's name. But I couldn't recall if there had been a phone number with it. I thought there had, and I hadn't given it any real attention. Whenever I called Orin, it was on the library landline. I'd programmed only a few numbers into this burner phone; the library's had been one of my favorites. But something in the back of my mind told me the number I'd seen in the file wasn't the same one I used.

I grabbed the burner and pushed the arrow to get to my favorites. I looked at the number I'd put in for Orin, but it wasn't identifiable by anything other than selecting *Orin*. Now I really had no idea if the number in the folder was the same number on my phone. I hadn't taken the time to check. If it wasn't, it might be a landline to his home or maybe the satellite phone I'd seen him with.

I wouldn't be able to focus on anything else until I checked that number—until I called that number just to see if he answered. I gathered my things. I'd heard the rain start falling on the shed's tin roof earlier, but it was coming down hard as I locked up and hurried to the truck. I glanced toward the library and saw nothing unusual—Orin's truck was still not in sight—before setting out for Elijah's place.

I parked in Toshco's lot and had to cover the distance to the barn on foot, my bag over my head just to keep the cap I wore somewhat dry. Nevertheless, I was well soaked by the time I got inside the barn. At the desk, I grabbed the file, then opened my burner phone. I had zero signal. I'd heard that folks called Toshco when they'd needed a tow and then someone there would find Elijah to give him the message.

I could just take the number back with me to the shed or the Benedict House and use the landline there, but I wondered if I could catch a signal anywhere nearby.

I held out my phone and glanced at the bars as I walked around. It seemed that there might be a signal coming through as I held the phone closer to the wall toward the house. I locked up the barn and ran up the stairs to the front door. I got slightly more drenched, but the signal was improving.

Even though I'd been given a key, I hadn't ever used the house as any sort of escape or a place to write. It was a comfortable, cozy place, but it hadn't appealed to my creative senses. I grabbed my keys from my pocket, found the right one, and turned it in the lock.

The signal bumped up significantly the second I stepped inside. While I dialed, I absentmindedly made my way to Elijah's couch.

"Hello?" Orin said after half of one ring.

"Orin, it's me, Beth," I said. "Are you okay?"

"Beth? How did you get this number? You're not supposed to have this number."

"I found it in Elijah's file for Finn. Are you okay?"

"I'm fine. Don't call me again."

The call was abruptly disconnected.

I held the phone and looked at it for a long moment. He was okay, or at least he said he was. It hadn't occurred to me that I might interfere with some mission. No, he wouldn't have answered if that were the case. *Would he?* The relief I felt at hearing his voice far outweighed any anxiety I had about bothering him. *You're supposed to bother people you care about if you're worried, right?*

Feeling somewhat better about Orin's well-being, I stood. There was no need for me to stay except to wait for the worst of the rain to pass. I'd looked around the house already, but I thought I'd give it another once-over.

But as I turned to step around a half wall that separated the front room from the kitchen, I heard a rustle and soft thuds coming from a short hallway that I knew led to the house's two small bedrooms.

I froze in place for a second and listened hard. I heard what sounded like a slide of a window opening. Had I thought about it, I probably should have just run from the house, but the noise made me think someone was escaping, and I wanted to know who it was. Who was in Elijah's house? Elijah? And was my mother with him?

"Elijah?" I called before I ran to the hallway and then stopped at the doorway of the first bedroom.

It appeared that someone had been sleeping in the bed recently. I was sure it had been made when I looked through the house a few months earlier, and it wasn't now. A few pieces of clothing had been thrown on its corner.

I bumped my shin hard on the bed as I darted around it to get to the now-open window.

"Ouch, ouch, ouch," I said as I leaned out the screenless window.

As with most everywhere around Benedict, there were thick woods behind Elijah's house. And it was still raining. The darkness was even darker and murkier, but I was pretty sure I caught sight of someone running through the trees.

They looked like they were dressed in black, but it could have just been the woods and the weather. I wasn't going to chase them and I was getting rained on, so I pulled myself back in the window. I looked around the bedroom again. There was no indication of who'd been here, but I now realized that all the clothes on the corner of the bed were black, too.

Had I'd just seen the man who'd said hello to me at the library? That might have just been a conclusion of convenience and timing. There were other possibilities, maybe many. Everyone knew this house was empty. Maybe it was being used the same way the community center was being used—at least according to Cyrus—as an available shelter.

Was it Warren I'd seen running away from the house?

I didn't think so. Warren was a bigger person. The person I saw in the woods was closer in shape and size to the man at the library.

Who was he?

Did he have something to do with me—or with Kaye's murder?

I needed to get ahold of Gril right away.

Fifteen

called Gril and told him what had happened at Elijah's. I told him about the man at the library and about the stack of books. I even told him about the shadow of a phone number I'd found on the piece of paper from Orin's desk. I told him I talked to Orin. He wasn't overly moved by anything but the fact that someone had been staying in Elijah's house—and he didn't know who it was. He hadn't found Warren, and I thought that's who he pegged as being the trespasser. He said he was heading over to Elijah's right before he ended the call.

And then I went home and crawled into bed. Gus lay on the floor next to me, and I pulled my quilt over my head. I was exhausted. Finn was with Viola, seeming to have taken a quick liking to her and her to him.

When I woke the next morning with a start, Gus was sitting up, looking at me expectantly, but not with any sort of urgency.

"Oh, I'm okay, boy. Did I worry you? I was just tired."

He moved next to the bed and I scratched his neck.

A knock sounded on the door.

"I'm awake. Viola?" I said as I sat up and Gus turned to the door. There was no hat nearby, so I tried to smooth my hair with my hand.

Viola opened the door, and Chaz peeked in behind her, Finn next to her. She said, "We heard a scream."

"You did?" I looked at Gus, who I now realized had most definitely been looking at me with question *and* concern, not just question. "I'm sorry. I didn't know I screamed. I guess I was just dreaming . . . but I'm fine." I smiled. "I had a very full day yesterday. I think my head was just processing everything. Again, sorry."

"Okay." Viola stood there a long moment, Chaz behind her, both of them with concerned eyes. Gus whined once, Finn panted.

I tried to remember the dream, the scream, something. Maybe it was a good thing I didn't remember it. I felt great this morning.

"Hungry?" Chaz finally asked.

"So very hungry."

"Okay," Viola said. "Meet us in the dining room."

I got ready quickly and then took Gus and Finn outside. I stood next to the Benedict House's parking lot with my hands in my pocket and my face aimed at the sky. The sun was shining and warm on my face, even if the air was still chilly.

"Beth," a voice called.

I opened my eyes and then shaded them with my hand. Gril was walking toward me.

"Good morning," I said.

"Morning."

"Did you find anyone at Elijah's?" I asked, resuming the conversation from the previous day's call.

"No, but I'd like to talk a bit. You have time?"

"I do. What some breakfast? Viola's latest client is a great cook."

"Sounds good."

Viola and Chaz greeted us as we made our way back inside with the dogs. I watched as Gril looked at Chaz with the extra scrutiny he always had for one of the clients. He always let them know immediately that he was the law, even above Viola. So if they were afraid of her, they should be doubly afraid of him.

Chaz seemed a tiny bit uncomfortable under Gril's gaze but remained friendly as he gestured at the buffet-style spread he'd set up.
"Eat up."

"Thank you," I said.

Gril only nodded his thanks.

After a shared look between Viola and Gril, Viola instructed
Chaz to grab the dogs and told us they'd leave the food and the
dining room to Gril and me. A few moments later, it was just us as
Chaz took both of the dogs back outside, and Viola went back to
her office.

There weren't quite as many food choices this morning, but Gril
and I each had a waffle, which Chaz had left in a food warmer. I put
whipped cream and butter on mine; Gril put only syrup on his.

I spoke up before Gril could even taste his food. "Gril, what does
Orin really do? Where does he go?"

After he chewed a bite, his eyes brightening from the flavors,
and swallowed, he said, "I don't know specifically. There's a clearing
near his house where a helicopter has picked him up a time or two,
but I don't have any idea what he does when he's 'on assignment.' I
don't know if the helicopter was here recently."

"A helicopter. Wow. He so doesn't seem the type."

"He's the smartest human being I've ever met," Gril said. "He
and I moved here close to the same time, and he came to me about
clearing out the space for the helicopter. He gave me documents that
ordered me to approve all of it. Who am I to argue with the United
States government?"

"He must know what he's doing, but I hope he hasn't gotten in
the middle of my mess. Why would he have recently written that
number on the yellow pad?"

Gril shrugged. "Maybe it wasn't written recently. Who knows
when he last used it?"

It was a point I had considered. Orin didn't take notes. He could
remember anything and everything. Maybe the impression of the
number was from a long time ago, during a moment when his mind
was being used for something else. Maybe the original writing had

actually been my mother's when she'd stopped by the library and left it for him on her way to wherever she'd gone.

"That could be true. He memorizes everything."

"He does." Gril sighed. "Honestly, I'm not worried about him too much, particularly since you talked to him."

"Who do you think I saw at Elijah's? The man at the library? Could they have been the same person? Am I making a mystery out of something that isn't a mystery?" I asked.

"Could be any number of people. We have folks moving through all the time. Some want to get away; some are on the run. The weather is clearing, which makes it easier. There are too many possible scenarios to guess without something more solid, but I'm still checking manifests. I've got people on the alert, Beth. Walker will not make his way here without me knowing."

I had considered that the person I'd seen might be Walker, but that hadn't felt completely right. I'd been anxious the day before and had apparently had nightmares about something, but no, I'd been confident in the idea that I hadn't seen Travis Walker. A year earlier, I wouldn't have wondered if I was overreacting or overreaching on something, either. I would have been convinced it was Walker. It felt good not to carry the weight of paralyzing paranoia.

"Why did you want to talk to me? Something going on with the investigation into Kaye's murder?"

"Nothing new. Donner told me you were there when Cyrus came in."

"How's Cyrus?"

"He wasn't talking when I made it into the office. Now we can't find him."

"Oh no." I put my fork down.

Gril shook his head. "He's hiding . . . or something. Are you sure it wasn't him you saw at Elijah's?"

"I'm not sure, but . . . it's impossible to say. I thought maybe it could even have been Warren, but the trees are dark, it was raining." I paused and thought back. "I'm positive that the man I saw at the library wasn't either of them."

"And that man just said hello to you?"

I cringed a little. "I know. There's no real reason for me to turn those things into something bothersome, but I'm sure I didn't recognize him. And that stack of books . . ."

"Beth, you are known around here, but not as Elizabeth Fairchild but as the woman with the scar. Folks know that woman as Beth."

I nodded.

He smiled. "Lots of folks around here have a small limp. Shoot, sometimes I do." He paused. "Sometimes both sides."

I nodded again.

"And, even though they might not know you're Fairchild, lots of people like your books. I suspect that the stack was put there by a fan and that man was just saying hello. If they were one and the same, I can't tell you."

We heard the front door opening and the return of Chaz and the dogs. Those dogs were getting more walks than they'd had in a long time. Sniffing out where we were, they bounded in to enthusiastically remind us that we adored them. Chaz waved another hello as he passed by the dining room doorway.

"How did you end up with two dogs?" Gril asked as he scratched behind Finn's ear.

"Oh. I should probably let you know what I did."

"Uh-oh."

"I really do think it'll be okay."

I shared with Gril the truth about what I'd done at the Miller's place. Well, almost the truth. I didn't tell him that I went inside the house. I said I opened the door and Finn came out on his own but that my note said that he was out and about. Plausible deniability for him, I decided.

I tried to downplay the Oliphants' behavior because I didn't want Gril completely distracted, but he was immediately upset. His face reddened, and his eyes got sharper.

"They were just being idiots, Gril. I can handle them," I said with much more confidence than I felt, now or then.

"You shouldn't have to handle anything like that," he said. "No one should."

"It's okay, Gril. I'm okay. I got Finn out of there." I struggled for a change of subject. "Any leads on who shot out the bar window?"

"Yep."

I was surprised by his quick answer. "Who?" I sat up. Gus lifted his head to accommodate more attention.

"In fact, it was Kingston Oliphant," Gril said.

"Oh, that's troubling."

"He claims it was an accident—that he was loading his weapon into his truck and it fired accidentally. He took off because he was embarrassed but thought better of it when I was out there talking to all of them later. He thought I'd come back out to talk specifically about that."

"Is he in trouble?"

Gril shrugged. "Yes, but I'm not sure how much. No one got hurt. Yes, he broke quite a few laws. I might use that to question him further about Kaye, but unfortunately, guns get accidentally fired out here more than any of us would like."

"You think he killed Kaye?"

Gril bit his bottom lip and shook his head again. "I don't. I wish he was the one. He'd be easy to break, but I just don't think he did. I do, however, think that shooting the gun was him sending a message. He probably saw the Millers' trucks there earlier and shot the gun thinking no one would get hurt but just to let everyone know he was watching where they went."

"There was always a chance he could have hurt Benny."

"He could have hurt anyone. But he didn't."

"I never heard about the Millers and the Oliphants and their feud until these last few days."

"They've been behaving lately, but if Kaye and Cyrus were more than friends, things were bound to get out of control again. I need to find Kaye's killer and get that person out of here, which will not, by the way, defuse everything. It'll be tricky."

"Oh, Gril, I'm sorry. I wish I could help."

Gril shook his head. "Stay safe. Be careful. I have to get back at it, Beth."

I nodded. "I hear you."

"Right." His breakfast barely touched, Gril stood. The dogs and I saw him to the door.

Sixteen

I took time to get cleaned up, not just presentable by plopping on a hat, and then met Viola and Chaz back in the dining room. The dogs were spread out in the hallway, fast asleep.

Chaz's skills were going to cause me to size up in jeans if he stayed very long. Lunch, which seemed to occur right after breakfast, was Philly cheesesteaks. I'd never had one from Philadelphia before, but if they didn't taste like the ones Chaz created, the City of Brotherly Love needed to level up.

"Are you sticking around here the rest of the day?" Viola asked me.

"Do you need me to?"

"No, but I want you to be careful. I got a call from Ike Miller. He asked if the dog was here."

"What did you say?"

"I said that the dog was fine. He wants to come get him."

"He can't have him yet. Should I stay here to let him know that?"

"No, I told him that the dog had been meant for Kaye and that you were in charge of deciding where he goes now. He won't come get him, but that doesn't mean he'll just go away."

"I'm sorry I put you in that situation," I said.

"Don't worry about it. No skin off my back," Viola said.

I suspected she was just saying that to make me feel better. Taking the dog had been a selfish act, and I hadn't given one moment's thought to how it might affect Viola. I should have, but even with that guilt, I wasn't ready to give Finn back to the Millers.

"Gril will support you on this. Elijah's files were in writing, after all."

I shared with her my conversation with Gril regarding how I'd taken the dog, giving her an even further diluted account of the meeting with the Oliphants, attempting to make Blair and Kingston sound almost friendly. She didn't buy it.

"That will never happen again," she said. "I will make sure of it."

I shook my head. I'd told her because I wanted her to be aware. It was another moment I should have thought through better. Of course, she would be angry about their treatment of me, but I also thought she should know. "Viola, no, I'm fine. I just want you to be aware, just in case any of them say or try anything."

She huffed one angry laugh. "They wouldn't dare."

The phone rang in Viola's office. The distant jingle still carried the old aggravating ringtone of my childhood. I always smiled when I heard it, but not today. Along with Viola's new anger, I was worried about what news might come with them today.

She stood from the table and wiped her mouth with a napkin. "Eat your lunch. I'll be right back."

I watched as she left the room and then Chaz came out of the kitchen and joined me at the table.

"I've been eavesdropping a little," he said. "Your friend Orin is an adult, right?"

"Sure."

"Well, you just can't let yourself worry about what trouble other adults are getting themselves into or if it has something to do with you. People are going to do what people are going to do."

"I hear you."

"Anything you can do to help him?"

I laughed once, but of course Chaz had no reason to know the extent of Orin's security clearance. "He's much more skilled and much smarter than I'll ever be."

Chaz smiled. "There you go then. Now, about these people out in the woods. They are terrifying."

I thought for a second. "Yes, I think they are, but I also think it's just a matter of staying away from them."

"You need to watch your back, Beth. I might not be a violent criminal, but I've been around a few. I'm not saying you should kowtow to them, ever, but you should always be alert."

"I appreciate that." I looked at my plate. I'd only eaten half of the food. This was a new occurrence for me. I'd become very good at cleaning my plate. "The sandwich is great. I'm just full."

"I understand."

I sat back in my chair. He didn't seem to be in a hurry to get back to work on whatever he was prepping or cooking now.

I said, "How did you get caught, Chaz? You've said you became impatient too quickly. Do you mind elaborating?"

Chaz smiled sadly and then looked off into the distance a moment before back at me again. "I was there, sitting right there at the computer that would make me a rich man. All I had to do was click on TRANSFER. I heard people coming. I had a choice to make.

"I could press it and risk that those people would catch me—and they would; there really was no doubt. There was no escape from where I was. They would most likely see me and inquire as to what I was doing in there. One of them would at least check the computer screen and see what I was up to. I shouldn't have even been in that small room. Or I could just close the transfer page that I'd worked so hard to set up and lie and tell them I'd received a notice that something wasn't working correctly and I'd just come in to try to thwart any problems.

"I would probably have had to wait another six months to a year for such an opportunity to present itself again, but it would have eventually. I just had to play the role well, so they believed me. I just had to ignore that TRANSFER and act like I was one of the good guys."

"You clicked it?"

"I did." He hung his head in shame for a moment. "And then I hid under the desk."

"You did?" A smile pulled at the corner of my mouth.

"In case you're wondering, I was caught immediately—spotted the second they walked into the room. The desk had only a panel along its front. No one could have feasibly hidden under there."

"Chaz," I said, shaking my head.

"I know. It was dumb."

"Well, yeah. Do you know how hard it is to be a successful criminal?"

"Viola has already given me the statistics. But I was pretty dang close. I might have gotten in trouble for being in that room, but if I'd just backed out of the transaction, no one would have ever been the wiser. I could have lived to try another day."

I shrugged. "Speech time. I think you'd do better trying to make a living with your food. It's some of the best I've ever tasted."

"I love cooking, but there's much more money in embezzlement."

"Also more prison time."

"Only if you're caught."

"We could do this all day," I said as I took another bite. My stomach wasn't interested, but my taste buds wanted one more go at the sandwich.

"I know." Chaz smiled and looked around. "This place is wonderful. Maybe I'll just stay here forever."

"I've heard other clients say the same thing, but you don't get to make that choice. I suppose that once you've served your time, you could choose to come back. But I think that once you get back into the more active world, you'll want to stay there. Viola told me that no one has ever come back, even though many say they will."

"I might be the first."

"Honestly, I think we'd like that."

He smiled, seeming to appreciate my words. I heard my grandfather's voice in my head.

They are criminals, Beth. You've got to quit being so nice to them.

Sure, I'd been fooled a time or two, been kind to someone my grandfather had arrested only to realize they were working to get my sympathy and trying to find a way to use it.

But it was the moments that actually made a difference that I tried to remember the most, the times when I saw something in one of the prisoners that made me think that if they could just get one good break, they'd find a path of redemption. I couldn't help but think that one good break might begin with someone being kind.

If Chaz was fooling me, he was doing a great job of it.

"I'm going to clean up and then take the dogs for another walk," he said. "And, in case you're wondering, that is a life I could get used to."

I studied him. Yes, I liked him, and I loved his food, but I wasn't ready to trust him completely. If he knew about the money bag taped to the back of my toilet, he'd probably try to find a way to steal it. I thought of letting him know just to test him.

Beth, my grandfather's voice admonished in my head.

I hear you. I hear you.

Seventeen

I packed my backpack and made my way down the hall, stopping outside of Viola's office.

"May I ask who called?"

"Sure. Just the folks up in Anchorage, asking about Chaz."

"He seems to be doing okay?" I asked.

"He's doing great." Viola's eyebrows came together.

"This bothers you?"

"Something bothers me, but I'm not sure what it is yet. I'll figure it out."

I nodded. "I'm going to drive by Orin's place."

She frowned. "Why? No wait, I know the answer to that question. You just want to check on things, see if there's anything there that might indicate where he's gone."

"Kind of. I've never been to his house. I want to see it."

She nodded. "All right, I should warn you, do not go inside Orin's house. Not unless you use a specific key tucked under a potted plant on the west side of the house. You will set off alarms if you try it any other way."

"But if I use that specific key, I won't?"

"That is correct."

I hesitated. "Thanks?"

"You're welcome. Be careful out there, Beth. I have a hard time believing all this isn't something between the Millers and the Oliphants, and you've inserted yourself into it, whether you meant to or not."

"I'm aware."

"And I don't think Orin is involved in any way, or I wouldn't have told you how to get into his house."

"Actually, I'm trying to figure out why you did tell me."

She nodded. "I guess maybe I'd drive out there myself to see what's what if I had the time, but I don't."

"You want me to see what's what?"

"I want you to be careful, but if you happen to come upon something that helps us understand what Orin is up to, I'd like to hear about it."

"Won't he be mad you told me about the key?"

"No. He might actually be surprised that he didn't tell you himself yet."

"Got it." I was glad to have a task, particularly one Viola approved.

Chaz was in the kitchen, cleaning. I waved goodbye at him and then bid the dogs adieu. I vowed to walk them both more if Chaz had to suddenly leave.

I knew where Orin's house was even if I hadn't been to it or driven by it yet. There was not a lot of just driving around in Benedict. You got where you needed to get and then you got back as quickly and as easily as you could.

As I steered the truck down the road the direction of the community center, I saw something I hadn't noticed before.

Off to the side of the road, near the shoulder, an area of ground had been disturbed. It looked as if someone had tried to clear away the foliage back from an old stump. And then someone had purposefully placed a rock on top of the stump. I wondered if someone had had an accident at that spot; perhaps someone had died. Was it like I'd seen in Missouri, where traffic accident deaths were frequently marked with signs, crosses, or balloons? I filed it to the back of my mind to ask Gril about it.

I glanced toward the community center as I passed, my heart sinking again for Kaye and what had happened to her.

There were no vehicles in the parking lot, but today I had no desire to drive any closer to where Kaye had been killed. However, I remembered wondering what might have happened on the other side of the river. So once I passed the center, I changed course and turned onto an unpaved road that I was pretty sure would lead me to that other side.

The packed dirt road was well used. People drove along this stretch enough to make the ride somewhat smooth. I didn't understand exactly where it led other than hopefully to where I wanted to go.

I moved along slowly for ten to fifteen minutes before a curve veered to the right. I continued forward and less than five minutes later came right to the area I thought was directly across from where Kaye had been found. It had taken longer than I'd predicted to circle back.

I stopped the truck and hopped out, taking high steps to avoid getting my ankles tangled in the overgrowth.

I came to this side's berm and looked down. There was the water—fuller and moving faster than it had been the last time I'd seen it. I zeroed in on where Kaye's body had been found, though the area was even more restored to normal—the slides less obvious, the impressions in the creek bed now covered by the rising water. I leaned forward, looked to my right, and spotted the community center.

Could someone have . . . what?—thrown a rock from here and hit her in the head? It seemed too weird to continue to contemplate, nevertheless to consider all the angles, I did. And from what I could discern with what I knew, it could possibly make sense.

I examined the ground at my feet. I hadn't been careful to pay attention for any footprints. "Dammit." I knew better.

But I didn't see anything really. I'd disturbed nothing from what I could tell.

There were no footprints, nothing to indicate anyone, including me—my feet weren't sinking into the ground at all—had made an impression. I walked along the edge about twenty feet and then back again, still seeing nothing.

Whatever idea might have taken seed in my mind didn't have any roots to it. I shook it off and looked across the creek again.

"What happened, Kaye?"

There were no answers here from what I could tell. I got back into the truck. The road was wide enough that I could easily turn around, but I felt like exploring even more. I continued in the same direction. Maybe I could find another shortcut.

After another ten minutes through only woods, I decided I was probably just wasting my time.

"One more minute," I said aloud.

And that's all it took for me to come upon something at least a little interesting.

I'd become accustomed to things that weren't quite natural. A grouping of obviously crushed leaves and branches, for instance, might indicate that a wild animal had used that spot for a bed. So I should be alert for the animal and its potential offspring.

What I saw now wasn't crushed leaves and branches, but there was something unnatural about some of the bushes between two trees on the left side of the road. It was as if someone had cut away enough to serve as an opening to something beyond. The woods were too thick to see what might be beyond, but I was certainly curious enough to look.

I grabbed my bear spray and made sure my small, probably ineffective, knife was in my pocket and got out of the truck. The ground was still solid under my feet as I made my way toward and then ducked into the opening.

A tunnel *had* been formed. The walls were made of natural twine someone had taken the time to weave and mold into an archway. I had to duck to move, but it was a wide enough path. Once I'd traveled about thirty yards, I looked behind me. There was enough curve in the tunnel that I couldn't see the opening any longer. That made me nervous, but I trudged forward, still hunched over because of the low ceiling.

Another twenty yards later, I came upon the reason for the secrecy. I exited the tunnel and stepped into a clearing, a well-hidden pocket with enough elbow room for about four or five people if they were inclined to sit on some exposed tree stumps or the ground as they gathered around the object in the center of everything.

"A still?" I said aloud.

In fact, I'd seen plenty of them in Missouri. Milton had been a small town, and there had been plenty of folks living in the woods surrounding it. Stills weren't as uncommon as maybe they should be considering you could get beer and booze at almost all of the corner marts and gas stations.

A still was a sort of hillbilly rite of passage in my home state, even though the end products I'd tasted had all reminded me of paint thinner.

This still had probably been here in this clearing awhile, living through winters and thaws, but it was relatively solid. Nevertheless, it was ancient, homemade-looking. I touched one of the old coils—it was surprisingly well soldered into place on one of the cone pots. I didn't sense it had been used recently, maybe even ever, but with a little elbow grease and some extra solder, it probably could be. I was sure any antiques dealer would love it.

Was this a strange sight in Alaska? Last I knew in Missouri, all a person had to do to operate a still was be twenty-one years old. I didn't know Alaska laws. Was this someone's legal or illegal hobby? Could it be more than a hobby? Did people make money off these sorts of things out here?

It seemed pretty harmless, but it did give me pause to wonder if someone who owned it had somehow seen or been involved with Kaye's murder because she'd . . . what, discovered it? It was a weak lead, but I'd mention it to Gril as soon as I could.

I couldn't find evidence of anyone else having been there recently. Shortly, I left the clearing through the tunnel, now anxious to get out of there. It wasn't a long journey but being hunched over didn't make it easy. As I veered around the curve again, I heard noises coming from where I'd parked the truck.

"Oh no," I said, speeding up when I should have probably slowed down. I grabbed the bear spray from my jacket pocket.

Before the tunnel's opening, I stopped and leaned out to see what was going on. It was as I'd thought: wildlife. A mama bear and two cubs were curious about my truck.

I was relieved that they were black bears, not grizzlies, but a bear was a bear. And no matter how cute they were, I wasn't interested in getting to know any of them better.

I pulled back into the tunnel some and then wondered how good of an idea that was. Would they chase me farther into it? They—well, the mama—would win. I couldn't step out of there without them seeing me, though, so exiting wasn't an option at the moment anyway.

As I crouched, I wondered if I could go back to the still and then look for another way out.

I nixed that idea immediately. I hadn't seen anything but woods on the other side of the still. I'd get lost or run into other bears or other wildlife, I was sure.

I had to hope they would appease their curiosity and then move on and that they didn't smell me as much as I smelled them.

As I sat, I could lean to my left and observe. I watched the mama heave herself up and put her front paws on the hood of the truck. She was looking in through the windshield, seemingly disappointed not to see someone in there. Did I have any food that she smelled? I didn't think so. I'd been pretty careful not to keep any snacks around.

The two cubs were at her side, looking up at her, trying to figure out how to do the same trick. They weren't big enough, of course, but their attempts to lift their front paws so they could reach the hood were too humorous not to smile, even if my nerves were starting to fray.

They needed to move along.

One of the cubs peered over and noticed me, its eyes meeting mine.

Oh no.

It bleated a message to its family members but didn't seem to garner their attention. I reached for the bear spray and readied it.

For all intents and purposes, I was easy prey. I was trapped in a tunnel, my escape cut off by the very things that might chase me through the tunnel. I had some quick decisions to make. Did I want to stay here or risk a run to the truck door and hop in?

The answer was not easy, but it became much clearer when the mama bear noticed me, too.

Her nose was working a million miles an hour, but I didn't know if she found me because of my scent or if she actually saw me. Either way, when she lowered herself off the truck and took a step in my direction, I knew one hundred percent that I did not want to die in that tunnel. I needed to get out of there, no matter what happened.

As she took two big padded steps, her cubs by her side, I propelled myself out and into the open. For an instant, the plan worked. She was surprised by the maneuver and halted a moment, giving some thought to what she was seeing. But it was only for a moment.

She snarled, which was terrifying. I squealed and tripped over my own feet. I aimed the bear spray and tried to get to the truck.

She was quick, though, and she blocked me. For a long second, we stared at each other. And then she stood on her back legs and roared at me. I was frozen with fear, my finger immobile on the spray trigger. But then I yelled, too. We yelled at each other.

My yells were strangled with the tears that were springing out of my eyes, the mucus clogging my throat before I could process that I'd started crying.

She dropped back to the ground, her landing quaking the earth beneath our feet.

And then one of the cubs mewed and turned, hurrying toward the woods. The other cub followed. Mama gave me one last angry look before she turned and followed her babies.

I laughed as I shook, breathed noisily as I got into the truck. I fumbled the keys, dropping them twice before I managed to get them turned in the ignition.

I didn't remember getting out of there, but I did—more quickly than I'd driven in.

At the intersection onto the main road, I sat for a long time. I worked through the residual sensations left over from extreme fear and then an adrenaline drop. I laughed a little and sent some gratitude that I was okay out to the universe as well as that the animals were okay, having gone on their way without any of us incurring an injury. I didn't spend a lot of time out in the wild, particularly alone. I thought Tex would have been proud of the way I'd handled myself.

You gotta make yourself big, he'd once said as we watched some bears across the river behind his house. *They're all going to win a fight, but make yourself big and loud if you come across one.* He'd paused. *And you will.*

I suddenly missed him more deeply than I thought I would. It wasn't the bear encounter as much as that I wished he was there to talk to about everything. Intermittent email didn't make for an easy back-and-forth. As my frayed nerves wove themselves back together and he came to my mind as the person I most wanted to tell what had just happened, I came to a wavering conclusion that maybe there really was something to the two of us. I'd come to such a conclusion before but hadn't embraced it quite like it seemed I was doing at the moment. I imagined telling him as much. And then I smiled at what I was sure would be his response.

Uh-huh. Took you long enough.

My escape from the bears was now behind me. Another thing I'd learned here in Benedict: All's well that ends well. You have to keep going—the alternative isn't good. Keep moving.

I grabbed the steering wheel. I was exhausted, but I didn't want to go home. I'd come out to see Orin's place, and that's exactly what I was going to do. With Tex's voice in my head this time, I found some resolve.

Eighteen

found Orin's house more easily than I'd found any other place in Alaska. I knew the general area, and then a sign nailed to a tree announced, "Orin lives right down this way," with an arrow. Orin may have participated in covert operations, but he wasn't trying to hide.

His driveway was paved, which was a luxury not widespread throughout Benedict. Dr. Powder had a paved circular drive, but most I'd seen were gravel or dirt that had been tightly compacted from use over time.

I took the drive up to the house and laughed once when I could see the full structure. Surely this was a sight unequaled around here. Orin's house was done in the style of a log cabin but a very big one, three stories with edges too smooth to be made of real logs.

"Nice," I said as I parked and noticed the circular helipad next to the house. I laughed again. He wasn't hiding much of anything.

I parked the truck, got out, and looked up. There were various structures on the roof of the tall house, among them were a satellite dish and a telescope. I wondered about whatever else was up there and could not believe I hadn't been invited out to stargaze. Did Orin invite anyone out to his place? I hadn't heard about gatherings or parties.

I climbed the stairs up to a porch that took up the entire front of the bottom level of the home, which sat atop a rise in the land.

First, I knocked on the door and was not surprised when no one answered. I walked to a window to the right and tried to look in, then tried the one on the left. Both were covered by closed shutters.

I looked around for cameras, because if anyone had them, it would surely be Orin. But I didn't see any. I assumed they were there but well hidden.

I stood on the porch, my hands on my hips. Going into Orin's house was a ridiculous idea. Why in the world would I ever think that was even a semi-appropriate thing to do?

It was the wrong thing, even if Viola had told me where a key was located.

I wasn't even all that worried about Orin anymore. If this was the way he lived, I just hadn't fully understood him. He could take care of himself. He'd answered his phone. I'd heard his voice.

I took the stairs back down to my truck and turned again to look at the house. No, I wasn't going to go get that key and go inside.

But then I saw something on the roof, a flash of movement.

"What?" I muttered as I hurried backward so I could get a wider-angled view.

I saw movement again—a person, I was pretty sure—but they were quickly heading toward the back of the roof.

"Orin?" I called, but whoever I'd seen was no longer visible.

Had they gone to the back of the house?

I stood close to the middle of the wide front yard. I couldn't manage a quick decision on which way to go around the structure, but I finally chose the way that probably also had a key under a mat.

It wasn't an easy journey to the back; the ground was uneven. But at least there weren't any fences blocking my way. Once I made it to the backyard, I came to a stuttered stop. A pole connected the ground to the top of the house, giving a quick escape to anyone who might be up there or might have *been* up there. I looked out into the woods, clocking what I thought was a retreating figure, dressed all in black.

It wasn't Orin; of that much I was sure. They were slightly bigger than Orin. Was it the person I'd seen at Elijah's? They were a similar size, at least from what I could tell. I wasn't going to give chase, but I knew I should do something.

I would call the police, but there was no signal in these woods.

Except, there probably was. I'd seen the satellite dish. I ran back to the front of the house and to my truck. I rummaged around in my backpack for my phone, finding it at the bottom.

I opened it to a signal, all bars. I hadn't seen that once since coming to Alaska.

I dialed the police station, and the biggest miracle of the day might have been that someone was actually there to take the call.

"Benedict police," Gril said.

"It's Beth. You need to get out to Orin's place right away. I saw . . . someone."

Gril hesitated, but only for a brief second. "On my way."

It didn't take him long to arrive, even if to me it felt like it did. I shut myself in my truck as I waited, afraid to lock the doors because there was a good chance I wouldn't be able to get the ancient mechanisms to unlock again. From the driver's side of the bench seat, I kept my eyes moving around the property and surrounding woods. I didn't see any other movement. I was *sure* I'd seen someone on the roof and then someone running into the woods, but as minutes ticked by slowly waiting for Gril, I began to question everything.

I was sure I'd seen the figure in the woods behind Elijah's house, but what were the chances I'd see the same person near Orin's? What were the odds, even in a place with a small population?

"You okay?" Gril asked when he arrived and we both exited our trucks.

"I'm fine." I told him quickly what I'd seen and then shared with him the notion that had come to me. "Maybe someone just knows which houses are empty, even temporarily?"

We hurried around to the back of the house, both gazing out into the woods. Gril put out an arm to keep me back as he stepped a little closer to the thick trees, though not past a natural tree line. He turned around and rejoined me only a second later.

He shook his head. "I don't know, Beth. You're sure of what you saw?"

"Pretty sure, but I hear your doubt and I get it. But, really, what are the chances it was the same person I saw at Elijah's?"

"Anything is possible. Did this person limp?"

"I tried to see, but I couldn't tell. Sorry."

Gril bit his bottom lip and seemed to ponder his next move. He didn't venture into the woods, which I was grateful for. I would have either followed him or been worried about him as he searched on his own.

"It could have just been someone being curious," he concluded a few moments later.

"Does Orin have cameras around? Maybe something got recorded?"

"I'm sure he does, but I don't have access to his stuff."

We peered into the woods for another few moments. There was no movement anywhere, not so much as a whiff of a breeze. Even the leaves weren't rustling.

Gril looked at me. "Though I can't get into his electronics, I can get into the house. He's even given me a key. I'm going to look around inside, and you can come in when I'm done if you'd like."

I nodded. "I'd love to."

Not only was my mission Viola approved, but now Gril approved, too. We walked back around to the front of the house, both of us stealing glances into the woods, but neither of us seeing anything bothersome.

I waited on the front porch as Gril went inside and searched, appearing in the doorway only a few moments later.

"Come on in, Beth."

I stepped into the main living space, which was a giant room filled with furniture and lots of other things: computers, radios—did

I even spot an old CB radio? The oily scent of old mechanical parts filled the air, not unpleasantly.

"What is all this? Is it the world's technology all in one place?" I asked.

"Not really. Sure, Orin has modern stuff, but he's a tinkerer. He likes to take things apart and put them back together again, maybe in new ways."

I was too awestruck to speak for a beat.

"You can see why he's not married, huh?" Gril said.

I smiled at him, but he wasn't trying to be funny.

He continued, "Orin is brilliant, Beth, but he's also obsessive. His traits have helped him have a successful, secretive, and probably dangerous career, but he's the first to tell you how difficult he would be to live with."

"Has he ever been married?" I didn't know anything about that part of his life.

"I don't know. I don't think so."

The kitchen looked to only be used as more space for electronic equipment. Gril led the way through the house, most of the rest of it was plain and bland compared to the main rooms. The three bedrooms on the second floor were neat and tidy, the beds made. The third floor was one large space filled with comfortable furniture, a huge television, an old pinball machine, and video game consoles.

"I watched a Super Bowl with him in here one year," Gril said as I took in the comfortable retreat-like space. "He doesn't even like football, but we had a good time."

From the third floor, we climbed a narrow staircase and emerged onto the roof. Patio furniture sat alongside the satellite dish and a telescope that could surely see to the other side of space, but there was no sign of anyone having been there recently. Nothing seemed to have been disturbed.

"Orin added this," Gril said as we both looked down at the metal pole. "I asked him once if it was for a quick escape or if he just thought it would be fun. He didn't answer. This could all be strange timing. People are curious." He shrugged. "Orin knows that. He doesn't keep any secrets out here, but he does keep a lot of equipment. Maybe someone did just want to explore."

"He doesn't have to have hard copies of secrets because he keeps everything in his head?" I asked.

"Something like that." Gril rubbed his hand over his beard and sighed. "He doesn't do what he used to do years ago, whatever that was. He told me that any assignment he's given nowadays is much less dangerous than the old days. In fact, he usually gives me a heads-up when he's leaving. He didn't this time, but since he answered his phone when you called, I believe he's okay. I'm on a contact list if something happens to him." Gril paused. "He's lived quite a life. I think he enjoys the less dangerous assignments, but he misses the old days. I bet they were pretty fun."

"You're still not worried about him?"

"A little, but he's a grown-up. I've got more important things on my plate. Orin would want me to find Kaye's killer before I even thought of trying to track him down."

I couldn't argue with that.

We debated sliding down the pole but decided to take the stairs. On the way back down to the main level, I told Gril about the strange memorial-like setup I'd seen by the side of the road as well as my discovery of the still. I didn't want him to know about the bears. He listened closely but didn't offer a comment when I was done.

"Do you know who the still belongs to?" I asked as we stepped off the front porch and toward our trucks.

"I can narrow it down a bit."

"Millers or Oliphants?" I asked.

"Maybe." Gril shrugged. "It's not a bad lead, Beth. Maybe someone was over there. I will check it out. I'm not sure I can imagine someone throwing a rock across the river and hitting Kaye so precisely, but again, anything is possible. I don't know about the memorial. I'll look at that, too, but folks mess around with stuff all the time, just to have something to do. Weather gets nicer, people roam around outside more, get creative 'cause they don't want to go back inside yet."

"Makes sense. Do you have anything from the ME about Kaye? Measurements, like the depth the rock penetrated her skull?" I cleared my throat. I'd spoken the words so clinically.

"No, not yet. Cause of death is blunt force trauma to the head, but I don't have a full report. I see what you're getting at, though. Those details would help us understand from where the rock was potentially thrown or how it made impact with her head. I'll try to push it."

I nodded. "Thanks for coming out here, Gril. I feel like I keep pulling you away from your real job for phantom sightings. I promise you I saw a person . . . people, I don't know."

"I believe you." He paused.

"What?" I asked when I felt like he was holding something back.

He shook his head and said, "Checking out trespassers is my job. Somehow, all of these things might be connected. Though you should call me any time, particularly if you see someone else or the same person again—at least make sure you're safe and out of danger if you can't get to a phone right away."

I nodded. Viola had said some of the same, though her warnings were more specifically about the Millers and the Oliphants. "Thanks, Gril."

We both got into our trucks and Gril followed me out of the driveway. I still wasn't ready to go home or get to work like I probably should have done. I'd all but forgotten about my book and the ending that hadn't felt quite like an ending. I had another idea, and fortunately, it seemed vastly safer than potentially running into Millers, Oliphants, or bears in the woods.

I steered the truck farther west and then stopped by Dr. Powder's house for the sole purpose of checking on Old Al. Mrs. Powder, Lynny, seemed in her typical cheerful mood as I came into the front room that also served as the lobby to wait for the doctor. No one else was there when I arrived.

"Beth Rivers, it's always so good to see you," she said with her Southern drawl.

"Same, Mrs. Powder."

"Oh, for heaven's sake, when are you going to start calling me Lynny? It seems everyone does but you."

"I don't know. It feels somehow disrespectful."

"Pshaw." She waved my comment away. "Do you need to see the doctor?"

"Actually, I was hoping to see Al."

"Oh! Yes, he did mention that you were up at his house with him and made him soup." She stood from where she'd been sitting behind the desk. "He's upstairs. Follow me."

She set a small sign on the desk that said, BE RIGHT BACK. HAVE A SEAT. YELL IF YOU'RE BLEEDING OUT and led me up the stairs to the second floor. Though this wasn't an old cabin, the house wasn't anything modern like Orin's. It was fashioned like an old brick two-story, and I always thought it seemed so homey.

I followed her to the back bedroom, where Al, dressed in sweats, was standing at the end of a bed covered with a patchwork quilt, holding on to the brass footrail, and lifting his legs, one at a time.

"Goodness, you're doing so much better," Lynny said.

"I'm ready to get out of this place," Al said, as if he might have said the same thing a few times recently.

"A couple more days," Lynny said. "Beth came to see you. Can I bring you both up some tea?"

"I don't want any tea," Al said.

"I'm good. Thank you," I said.

Lynny left the room, pulling the door closed behind her and sending me lifted eyebrows when Al couldn't see.

"You look so good," I said and I plopped my hands on my hips. "How are you ninety-four?"

Al didn't want to smile, but he couldn't help himself. A small table and two chairs had been tucked next to a bay window. He signaled to the setup. "Have a seat, Beth."

When we were both sitting, he gave me a long look. "Thank you for taking care of me."

"Oh, you're welcome. I'm really glad you're so well."

"I was well before, too," he said. "I don't know. I got a cold or something and that put me down. I didn't eat right, and it just cycled into whatever it was when you found me. I won't let it happen again, but I'm not sure I'm going to get the chance. I suspect forces are working against me."

"They can't stop you from going home," I said, not knowing exactly who "they" were.

"They kind of can. I can't walk back up there. If no one helps me get back, I won't be able to make it on my own."

"Well, maybe that's a sign that you should move closer to town."

"That's what everybody keeps saying, and I don't like it one little bit."

"I'm sorry, Al."

"Getting old is a pain in the ass, Beth. Try not to do it."

I laughed. "I'm not sure I like the alternative."

"No, probably not, but it sure isn't fun having your freedom taken away."

I bit my lip. "You seem to be okay, Al, and Orin was pretty convincing when we were walking up to check on you. You've made your own choices. You should be able to live however you want."

"I agree. Now, if you'd share that with all the powers that be, it'd be helpful."

I shrugged. "I'll do my best, but I'm not sure anyone will listen to me."

"Thanks." Al looked toward the shut door and then back at me. "Did I imagine that crazy story you told me about how you got here?"

I shook my head. "Nope, it was all that and more. I tried not to leave anything out, but I still haven't remembered everything."

"Gracious. How are you doing? I don't think I asked that specifically."

"I'm doing better. I'm sad and angry at the moment but I don't think either have anything to do with me."

"I heard about the young woman who was killed. Kaye Miller?"

"Yes."

"You were friends?"

"We were acquaintances on the way to being friends."

"I'm so sorry."

"Me too."

"That feud between those families. I knew it would turn dangerous one day."

"One day?" I asked. "It was violent before now, wasn't it?"

How well Al and Viola had known each other back in the day clicked back into place in my mind. They'd been like family, or so she'd said. She'd also mentioned that she couldn't talk to Al back then about what had happened to her, but that didn't mean they'd been out of each other's lives.

"Oh, you mean Zevon?" Al said.

"I heard about his death."

"Right. Well, I don't think Ike Miller was Zevon's killer. I think that's just been another excuse for them all to behave badly."

"Isn't that what most people *do* think, though?" I wondered enough about Viola's secret to ask some questions, see if her version really wasn't considered.

"Gosh, I don't know anymore. It's been so long since I've talked to anyone about it."

"Who do you think killed Zevon?" I asked.

Al shook his head. "I don't know, and I never cared all that much. Ike was accounted for during that time. I'm not completely hardhearted, but I just figured they all brought it on themselves. They were both unruly groups back then. No law here; no one to keep them in line. Most of us just tried to ignore them and cut a wide path."

"Ike's key was found near Zevon's body?"

"Well, anyone in either of those families could have had that key, taken it. No, that wasn't strong enough evidence. I remember thinking it was planted."

"But the Oliphants think it was at least one of the Millers, right?"

"That's what they say," he said as if he didn't buy into it. "Everyone knows that a woman was somehow involved. If I were to speculate, and I did back then, I would guess Zevon was killed because of a battle for one woman's affections."

"Whose?" I asked cautiously.

"Camille, of course."

I was shocked. Viola hadn't mentioned Camille's name at all when she'd talked about the origins of the feud, but Al wasn't talking about the feud, he was just talking about Zevon's murder. Viola had mentioned that there were others in their group of about ten, but Camille's name had never come up. If everyone thought Camille was somehow involved in Zevon's death, it was no wonder that Viola got away with what she got away with.

"Was her choice between Ike and Zevon?" I asked.

"No, no, you apparently don't have the story. That's what I mean when I say anyone in either family could have killed Zevon."

"What's the whole story?"

Al sat back. "It's been a long time and I'm not sure I still have all the details in here"—he tapped the side of his head—"but both Blair and Zevon Oliphant were interested in Camille."

"Brothers?"

"Sure. It happens. We're a small community."

"Was it speculated that Blair killed Zevon?"

Al hesitated. "I think that saying that it was speculated would be giving it too much weight. Lots of things were discussed and wondered about, but no answers were ever discovered. No one really investigated it. It's the version that sticks out most in my mind, but that doesn't mean it's the same version that other folks held on to. The feud goes back further, I suppose."

Viola sure hadn't mentioned this version, although what Al was saying made me think it was all just too much of a mystery to have anything solid. The key was all they had, but even that wasn't considered solid evidence.

"Beth, it wasn't the first time someone had gotten away with murder out here; won't be the last, either. I'm sure there's more to come. Gril is here now, though, so real investigations will happen. It won't be as easy to kill as it used to be."

The wild, wild northwest, I thought. "Al, why would someone have killed Kaye?"

His eyebrows rose as if he was genuinely perplexed. "I have no idea."

"No, I'm not looking for anything specific. What would a reason be, any reason?"

"I see what you're saying." Al sat back in the chair again and rubbed his hand over his clean-shaven chin. "Okay. Well, if she was disloyal in some way, but that's a pretty big spectrum."

"Particularly if she was disloyal with an Oliphant?"

"Well, sure, of course."

"Okay, I thought about that one, and there's a rumor that she and Cyrus Oliphant might have had more than just a friendship."

"That would do it."

"Right. Okay, let's switch it up. Why would an Oliphant kill Kaye?"

"Just to get back at the Millers," Al answered quickly.

"Right, but let's try to go deeper," I said. "You know these families. Can you think of something that might not be obvious?"

He thought for a long moment. "That's kind of what I've been trying to get at. The feud goes back a long time. If she told a family secret to the other family, that would cause quite a ruckus."

"Like what? Do you know any secrets?" I asked, though I wasn't hopeful. Secrets were secret for good reasons.

Al's eyes unfocused as he fell into thought again. A few seconds later his eyes popped up to mine again. "Where was Kaye found?"

"Out near the river behind the community center."

"The Oliphants had a secret out that way a long time ago."

I nodded. I was sure I was onto something with the still now, but I wanted him to say it.

He huffed once. "Another tale as old as all time around here. There's a still out there. I bet it hasn't moved."

I nodded quickly. "Yes! I saw it."

Al chuckled. "Bet it hasn't been fired up to this day."

My enthusiasm stalled. "Why do you say that?"

"It's there to pull you off a scent. The secret's not about the still, Beth. The Oliphants found some gold up in that creek probably about fifty years ago and put the still there to make people think that's why they spent so much time in those woods near that creek. Nobody cares about moonshine." He looked at me. "I don't remember how we all learned about the still or the gold, but a long time ago, we all somehow knew what was going on. Since she was found where she was, there's a chance that Kaye's murder has something to do with gold—maybe they found more. The water is thawing. It's running fast, but maybe the Oliphants or maybe the Millers found more gold. Money is a tale as old as time."

I was completely shocked. Gold? It hadn't even crossed my mind. I hadn't seen any specks of anything in the creek, but I'd been looking for prints and evidence, not gold!

As far as I knew, it hadn't crossed anyone's mind.

"I see," I said, my mind processing the new information.

Al's face was serious. "You should call Gril. Get him out here. I have a few things I need to tell him. He wasn't here back then. I should let him know."

In a haze of confusion, I did exactly as he said.

Nineteen

In a twist that I could only call fate, I managed to again reach Gril in his office. He said he would head right over.

Al explained some of the panning process to me as we waited for Gril. Al had done his share of panning but had never found even one small nugget.

I knew there was gold in Alaska. When I thought about it, my imagination conjured up images of people dressed in layers of animal hides bent over the water. I'd seen pictures.

But panning for gold was a tedious activity, not made for the impatient or weak of back. And very few people actually found gold.

Al told me that over the years there had been rumors about the Oliphants finding gold. The creek was part of public land, and as he explained, to take possession of gold you find while panning on public land in Alaska, you must have a permit. He went on to tell me that back in the day, the Oliphants didn't want to acquire such permits because they didn't want everyone else to know that they'd found gold.

"But, how can you use the gold if you don't do the right things to acquire it?" I asked.

"You can get away with anything if you know the right illegal way to do it, and the Oliphants probably know some of those ways. They must've known how to sell their gold to someone who wouldn't turn them in to the authorities. There's always someone willing to help you break laws if they benefit, too."

I nodded. "A fence?"

"Something like that, but you have to remember where we are. No one pays us much attention out here. Even less so back in the day."

Gril pushed through the room door and, whether he meant it or not, threw me an impatient look. He'd told me to call him, but it had been less than an hour since we'd seen each other. It might have been a bit soon.

"I know," I began. "But this might be important. Really."

"What's up?" he asked Al as he sat down on the edge of the bed.

Gril was more than a friend to me; he was almost a father figure. He'd certainly shown me kindness in ways he didn't owe me. But he had a murder to investigate. If I hadn't thought Al truly had something that might help solve that, I wouldn't have bothered him again.

"What do you know about the Oliphants' past with gold in the creek behind the community center?" Al asked Gril.

"Not one thing."

Al shook his head and then went on to tell him about the secret that hadn't ever really been a secret, at least back in the day. The Oliphants had taken gold from that creek. They'd set up the still and then manned it with someone "drunk on the moonshine" to make the area less desirable for others to explore as well as give them a reason for being out there. It had worked, and it had all been a ruse.

According to Al, no one knew how much gold the Oliphants had mined from that creek, but their behavior kept people away even after rumors of gold spread through the community.

Al leaned closer to Gril. "Some folks even said that the Oliphants bribed looky-loos with moonshine from somewhere, but I would bet you a dollar to a donut that that still has never seen a drop of the 'shine.'"

"I'd heard about the still, and Beth mentioned it," Gril said.

"I just came upon it today," I said. "It's not grown over in the clearing, but the area looks ignored."

"It's all an old story maybe," Al pondered. "Though Gril's been here less than ten years, I suspect many of us sometimes think about Benedict as before Gril and after Gril. It was wilder before, but the weather always kept things in check some. Things are much better now with you here."

Gril smiled weakly at the compliment. "All right, so if Kaye came upon the gold, that might be enough to anger the Oliphants?"

I think we all knew that answer.

"Yes, sir," Al said. "And maybe the Millers, too."

"Right. Both families would claim it was theirs if one of the family members found it. They think the land all around there belongs to them. I can see that reigniting anger, jealousy, and possessiveness."

"Absolutely," Al said.

I said, "If Kaye found gold, maybe that's why Warren's in hiding—unless something more terrible has happened to him, I guess. Maybe he's in trouble with his own family, too."

Gril thought for a long moment and then said, "It's all more to question them about. I appreciate knowing it." He looked at me. "Thanks for calling." He turned his attention to Al. "Thank you."

Al put his hand on Gril's arm as he stood from the bed. "Gril, I'd like to get home. I can't get up there on my own, but I'm okay to take care of myself once I'm there."

Behind his old and smudged glasses, I saw Gril's eyes pinch with what I thought was understanding or maybe sympathy. "All right. Can you give us a few days? I need to focus all my attention on finding Kaye's killer, but I'll get you back home. You have my word."

That was enough to allow Al to relax. "Thank you, Gril. At your convenience."

After Gril left, I told Al I needed to go, too. He tried to hide his disappointment, and I refrained from pointing out to him that he sure seemed to enjoy company for someone who claimed they liked living alone on a ridge in the middle of the Alaskan woods.

As I pulled the door closed behind me, I gave him one last look. He'd closed his eyes and was leaning his head back in the chair, a smile pulling at his mouth. The promise that Gril had made had given him an enviable peace that I suddenly wished I could someday have.

I'd talk to Leia about it.

Twenty

I needed to talk to Viola again. I headed back to the Benedict House, my mouth already watering at the thought of what Chaz might be cooking for dinner.

As I came upon the spot I'd noticed with the rock on the stump, Chaz and the dogs appeared. The dogs were sniffing around the ground while Chaz studied the stump.

He saw me as I brought the truck to a stop. I parked and hopped out.

"Beth, hello!" he said, happily. He really did seem to be happy and to love it here, and the dogs only added to his joy.

"How's it going?" I asked.

"Great. The dogs and I were curious about this monument."

"Bizarrely, I was, too, earlier today. I wondered if it was a tribute to someone, but I have no idea."

Chaz nodded and then shrugged. "Interesting."

"You want a ride back to the Benedict House?" I asked as I greeted the dogs, who were equally happy to see me.

"That feels like cheating."

"I understand, but it's not too far."

"No, thank you. We all need the exercise," Chaz said as he patted his flat stomach.

"What's for dinner?" I asked.

"Lasagna, but it won't be like any lasagna you've ever had. And for dessert, there will be banana pudding, again unlike any you've ever experienced."

"Sounds great. Maybe I should walk, and you drive the truck back to the Benedict House."

He laughed but didn't respond. He turned his attention back to the stump.

"I don't know that this is a tribute to someone who was hurt," I said. "It might just be that someone decided to put a stone atop a tree stump."

"Yeah, I don't think so," Chaz said, his face changing to a tortured expression. "I think it's something more."

"You sense that?" I was surprised by his reaction.

"I don't know."

We looked at it a moment longer before I told him I'd see them all back at the house. I hadn't felt the same things he felt—I'd felt nothing, no sadness—but his reaction got my attention. Was he especially tuned in?

I liked him. I even sensed empathy. He wasn't a sociopath, but he was a criminal. I needed to remember that. Even after I drove away and I could see in my rearview mirror that he still hadn't moved away from the spot.

I found Viola in her office, squinting (through glasses) and frowning at her computer screen.

"Everything okay?" I asked as I took a seat, not waiting for an invitation.

"Spreadsheets are torture," she said. "Why can't I just do things the old-fashioned way with a ledger and a pencil with a good eraser?"

"Who's stopping you?"

"My accountant in Juneau. He has asked me to do it this way."

"I can help if you want."

Viola turned to face me. She took off the glasses and pinched the top of her nose. "Thank you. Let's see if I can get it figured out. If I can't, I'll take you up on it. What's going on out there?"

"So much."

"I'm listening."

I told her what I'd done, leaving out the run-in with the bears. I also held back telling her what Al had said about Camille—it didn't seem important at the moment, and I would never want to say anything that even slightly sounded like I was accusing her of a lie. It hadn't been a lie anyway, just her version. And since she'd done what she'd done to Zevon, her version was probably more accurate.

Viola sharing what I thought was the only real choice she'd had in a horrific situation hadn't done one thing to change how I thought of or felt about her. However, I had spent a moment wondering if maybe it should have, as if I should be more bothered by what she'd done than I was. I just wasn't.

"Gold. Yes, I remember those rumors, but it was a long time ago, Beth. You think maybe Kaye came upon more gold and the Oliphants didn't want her to have it."

"Or the Millers didn't want her to tell the Oliphants, tell Cyrus." I shrugged. "Lots of maybes."

She shook her head slowly. "Gold. Could it be?"

"It feels like a possible motive."

Viola sighed. "Well, I'm glad Al is doing better."

Ah, there was the lead-in I was looking for. "Viola, I have an idea."

She nodded me on.

"What if . . . I mean, you got the room next to me ready for my mother. . . . What if you rent it out to Al for a while?"

Viola's eyebrows furrowed. "What? You mean see if he wants to stay here?"

"Just for a little while. You were close at one time, right?"

"A long, long time ago."

"But you don't have a bad relationship now, do you?"

"I haven't talked to Al in months. Not only that, our last conversation was only us greeting each other as I came into the mercantile and he was walking out. No, our relationship isn't bad, but it doesn't really exist anymore, either."

I shrugged. "He's in a room at Dr. Powder's. He's doing fine, but I think he would enjoy the company and eating Chaz's food. Who wouldn't?"

Viola's eyes softened and she smiled to herself. "He was so good to me and Benny when we were kids." She looked at me again. "You know, it sounds like a great idea, I have to admit."

I smiled. "Glad to hear it. Want to call Dr. Powder and run it by him?"

She picked up the phone and dialed.

I'd been a part of a family all my life but not one that had meals together. My mother had often been gone, and my grandfather had been too busy to spend any time at the dinner table.

Since moving to Alaska, I had had a few meals with Viola and criminals passing through, but that night's might have been the strangest—and greatest—one yet.

Before I left her office, I mentioned to Viola that I'd seen Chaz intrigued by the stump at the side of the road. She hadn't noticed the stump, which made me think that it really had only been put together over the last few days. Viola was always driving the main roads; it would be difficult to miss. She wasn't bothered by Chaz's seemingly deep interest, but she did file away what I told her, thanking me for letting her know. She didn't bring it up at dinner, but there was plenty to observe.

Al didn't like Chaz, and Chaz tried too hard to change that. Viola didn't intervene, just watched the two men as they seemed to fall into an "old-fashioned pissing contest," as Mill would put it. I wouldn't have argued with her.

Al tried to question Chaz, and Chaz tried to remain friendly no matter the sense of interrogation that came with Al's tone.

The food was incredible and, as advertised, unlike any I'd had before. Everyone but Al ate plenty, but he ate some.

He was doing very well health-wise, though, and was grateful to stay in the Benedict House. When he'd arrived, he'd held on to Viola's arms with tears springing to his eyes. They'd hugged and then she'd shown him his room.

Finn had not moved from Al's side since the second he walked into the house, and Al enjoyed having him there. Gus had been torn between all the humans and gave us each some of his time.

I figured it would all work itself out.

After dinner, Viola and I made sure Al was comfortable in his room, and then we all went our separate ways to our rooms, Gus following me to mine. I was beat, so it didn't take me long to fall asleep again.

Gus woke me up with a paw on my arm and a whine.

"What is it, boy?" I said, noticing that it was about two in the morning. "Did I scream?"

He whined again. I didn't think I'd screamed. No one was knocking at the door to check on me.

"Need to go out? Okay," I said.

I rolled my legs over the edge of the bed. Gus didn't usually need to go in the middle of the night, but I was ready when he did. I grabbed a cap and jacket I kept nearby and slipped them on. I found some socks and put them on, too.

Gus was prancing in place by the time I was fully dressed.

"Let's go."

I unlocked my door and peered out into the dimmed-but-lit hallway. There wasn't a soul in sight. I thought about checking on Finn, too, but no sounds came from Al's room, and I didn't want to wake anyone else up if it wasn't necessary.

Once outside, Gus took care of business quickly. Too quickly. It was a beautiful night, with barely any chill to the air and not a cloud in the sky.

I walked out toward Ben, the bear statue that welcomed everyone to town, and looked up at the sky. The sight was breathtaking. A blanket of stars like I'd never seen.

"Wait," I said aloud as my eyes refocused. Not just stars. I was seeing colors waving through the atmosphere.

"Oh, Gus, it's the northern lights," I said as he took a seat next to me, wondering what in the world I was looking up at.

This was my first time seeing the phenomenon. Conditions had to be perfect, and tonight they were. The colors literally waved and undulated through the dark sky. The natural beauty of the moment seemed like something from a movie. It was breathtaking.

A tide of emotions washed over me.

I wasn't the same person I'd been when I first arrived, but I also wasn't turning back into the person I'd been before Travis Walker.

I was becoming someone new, even if I didn't quite understand who that person was or would ultimately be. I didn't know if she would be better or worse.

But she sure loved Alaska.

I sniffed. My eyes had adjusted even more to the dark, and I took in the other sights. The downtown store windows were all dark—somehow I'd missed when the bar's window had been fixed. I didn't sense anyone watching me, not even wild animals, which were surely out there and would notice me before I would spot them.

"We should go inside," I said to Gus.

Neither of us was excited about that idea, though. I patted my jacket pocket. My truck keys were right there.

"Let's go for a ride." I changed course.

Gus was agreeable, and we hurried to the truck. When I started the engine, I was worried I would wake either Viola or Chaz, but hopefully they'd go right back to sleep. I'd left in the middle of the night before, when sleep wasn't easy and story ideas wouldn't stop dancing around in my head.

I wasn't going to the shed, though, but to the community center. Once along the main road my headlights caught only the shadows of some bugs before they ran into my windshield.

"Wow," I said to Gus. "That's a lot of bugs. It's not even overly warm out yet."

I turned onto the road leading to the center. I had a million second thoughts. A murder had been committed out here, maybe because of gold. Did I really need to check this out?

I reached over Gus and locked his door and then gingerly locked my own, sending a prayer out to the universe that the pulls would raise again.

My headlights continued to lead the way. I was relieved when they landed on a familiar truck, even though it was tucked into the woods in a probable attempt to hide. Donner was there. I should have guessed that someone would be watching the place.

And my arrival was about to blow his cover.

I stopped my truck and thought about backing out, but my headlights shone through a side window of Donner's truck. From what I could tell, it appeared to be empty. Or maybe he was lying down, resting. Either way, I just needed to get out of there.

But then I wondered if he was okay. I stopped and told Gus to stay put. I managed the pull tab up on my lock—moving slowly and sending some gratitude out to the universe for hearing the earlier prayer. I hopped out and jogged over to Donner's vehicle and peered inside. He wasn't anywhere to be seen.

That probably meant that he was walking around somewhere nearby.

"Beth?" a voice whispered behind me.

I turned quickly. "Hey, Donner."

He was moving toward me, a small flashlight swinging at his side. "What are you doing?"

"I couldn't sleep. I thought I'd come out here, just in case there was something to see."

"You really can be your own worst influence. You know that, don't you?" Donner asked as he aimed the light down, away from my eyes.

I shrugged. "Well, I didn't anticipate interrupting you. Sorry."

Donner stood in front of me now, pausing long enough to sigh as if surrendering to the idea that I was there. "I'm going to take a look around the place. You're welcome to come but you have to keep up."

"I've got Gus in my truck."

Donner shook his head. "No, I don't know what wildlife is lurking. I could handle it for you and me, but I don't want to worry about Gus, too."

I wondered exactly what he meant by that, but I didn't push it. "Gus will be okay in the truck for a few minutes."

"Let's go." Donner turned, and I had to immediately take off quickly just to catch up. "There's a walking path around the center."

"Have you been here since Kaye's body was found?" I kept my voice as low as he kept his.

"At night for a few hours, yes, and I haven't seen anything, not even a wayward porcupine."

I'd seen a few of those in the last year. They were spectacular, but I didn't want to come across one at night.

"Any new leads?"

Donner stopped walking but kept his light on the path in front of us. "No, but your information about the gold might help get the job done."

"Al remembered it."

"Well, it really could help."

"How?"

"Not sure yet." Donner set out again.

And again I hurried to catch up.

"Shh." Suddenly, he put his arm out to stop me and flipped off the flashlight.

I stopped moving too, but my breathing and heart rate suddenly seemed loud in my own ears. I worked to quiet them both.

A twig snapped somewhere up in the dark middle distance.

"Get behind me," Donner whispered.

I did as he said.

We waited. I could tell Donner was listening. I tried to as well, but though I heard a million things, I couldn't make out any of them.

At a moment he must have known was right, Donner flipped on the flashlight.

A gurgled noise came from up ahead. I peered around Donner.

"Cyrus, it's Donner," Donner said.

"Hey. What's with the light? You're blinding me." Cyrus lifted his hands and squinted.

Donner lowered the light some. "What are you doing out here, Cyrus?"

"Trying to figure out who killed Kaye, which if I were to guess, is what you're doing, too." His eyes landed on me as I came around Donner. "Oh, there's a gal with you. Maybe that's not what you're doing."

"Put your hands down, Cyrus, and come inside and talk to me," Donner said. I heard weariness in his voice.

"You and I have already talked. Enough already."

"You didn't tell me anything, Cy. Now, if you're serious about finding Kaye's killer, sit your ass down with me and talk."

"What about the girl?" Cyrus asked.

"This is Beth. She was in the office the other day. She's out here on her own."

"She your girl?"

"She's a friend, who does happen to be around a lot." Donner paused. "Were you going to sleep in the community center tonight?"

"No."

"Just tell me the truth, Cyrus."

"I am, Donner. I came out tonight to see if I could catch whoever was here, and all I caught was you and the missus. People go back to where they've done things, and they always think the darkness is a good cover. I haven't caught anybody at all, except you two."

Donner sighed again. "Let's go inside. There's a coffee machine. Let's have some coffee and talk. Just us. Okay?"

"Only if she stays, too." Cyrus nodded in my direction. "She'll keep you civilized."

"Dammit," Donner muttered under his breath. "All right. Deal."

"I'll go get Gus and meet you inside," I said.

Donner nodded. "She's going to run to her truck to grab her dog. She'll be right in to join us."

"That works."

For a long beat, no one moved. Finally, I turned and hurried back. Donner aimed the light that way so I could better see, and then he and Cyrus followed the same path. They waited for me and Gus to join them before we all went into the community center.

I couldn't believe I was going to get to be in on this.

Twenty-One

Donner made the coffee as I gathered chairs and unfolded them. Cyrus wasn't sure what to do with himself, so he stood in the middle of the room with his hands in his pockets and looked uncomfortable.

I didn't know what to say that would be either Gril or Donner approved, so I remained silent. Cyrus didn't seem to want to say anything, either. He just watched as I set up the chairs and as I found a folding tray to add to the mix. Gus relaxed on the floor next to me.

Donner brought out three coffees a minute or two after both Cyrus and I had taken seats.

"Why are you looking around out here?" Donner asked Cyrus as he handed him a coffee.

"I told you. Because this is near where her body was found. I'm trying to catch her killer," Cyrus said.

"No, it's more than that. Why here, Cyrus? Give me something, a little more of the truth. If you really want to find Kaye's killer, you know we're on the same team here. Tell me something."

Donner sat down after he handed me a mug.

Cyrus set his cup on his leg and frowned at the ground near his feet.

"Cyrus, if you really want to find her killer, we need the truth. Why can't you see that?" Donner asked. "It's the only way. What are you so afraid of?"

"She and I weren't a couple, you need to know that."

"Okay, but I hear she was spending a lot of time with you."

Cyrus nodded. "She came to me first."

"First? When? Explain."

"She needed someone to talk to."

"About?"

Again, Cyrus hesitated. What *was* he so afraid of? Finally, he spoke. "A few months back I ran into Warren and Kaye at the mercantile. Kaye was always nice to all of us in public. She knew about the feud of course, but she tried to ignore it. I think she just wanted everyone to get along.

"I'd seen her with the dog and noticed that she sometimes came here to the community center. I think she liked the treadmill.

"Anyway, at the mercantile that day, I overheard her telling Warren that she'd been out with the dog near here and thought she saw something shiny in the creek. Something that might have been gold. I mean, I was right there, across a table filled with socks from them.

"Warren saw me and grabbed Kaye's arm, telling her to shush it up."

"Did he hurt her?" Donner asked.

Cyrus thought about that for a long moment. "I don't think he hurt her, but he surprised her. She yanked her arm away from him and told him to stop."

"How did he take that?"

"About as good as a Miller would."

"What happened next?"

"Well, to be fair, he did say he was sorry to her but then sent her a hand signal, like to tell her to stop talking now." Cyrus demonstrated the signal by putting his finger up to his lips and then slashing his hand through the air. It wasn't subtle.

"What did you do?"

"I smiled at them and told them to have a good day."

"Like a nice guy or a smart-ass?" Donner took another sip of coffee.

"I'm always a nice guy, Donner."

Donner sent him a level gaze.

"Okay, so maybe I was a bit of a smart-ass. Warren knew I overheard."

"You're sure?"

"Yep, because that's the first night that Kaye came over to the house."

"She what?" Donner asked. He might have choked on his coffee if he'd been drinking.

"She came over to my family's house."

"That had to surprise everyone."

"Yep," he said. "You should have seen the commotion she caused. My pops and brothers were up in arms. 'What's she doing here?' It was embarrassing the way they behaved. Anyway, Mom at least had some manners and asked Kaye to sit and talk awhile."

"And?" Donner prompted.

"Apparently, Kaye had come over to apologize to me for the way Warren had behaved, but then the conversation just . . . changed. She and Mom got along really well."

"Your mom?" Donner said.

"Yessir, and that's who Kaye was visiting all this time. After the first time, it wasn't me."

"Hang on, hang on. What about the dog walks? Folks have said they saw you together."

"Maybe, but only by coincidence. We were both out at the same time." Cyrus shrugged.

Donner inspected him as if he didn't believe him. I didn't, either, but I knew Donner was on a pretty good roll.

Donner said, "Still, though, she came over that night to talk to you. Did you talk to her?"

"I did. I accepted her apology and told her she didn't need to give me one. I didn't tell her about any gold, though. Mom did. She told Kaye that, yes, there used to be gold in that creek, but that the creek belonged to the Oliphants, and she shouldn't let the Millers tell her any differently."

"Jesus, Cyrus, your mother lied to her?" Donner asked.

"I don't know if she thought she was lying. I think in her mind the gold in that creek does belong to us. It's been that way for so long."

"Because your family just took what they happened upon. That's as good as what you all did—you stole from public land. Gril and I got the story, Cyrus. Sure, there wasn't any full-time law enforcement out here then, but there's a Juneau file on the whole lot of your family. That gold was no more yours than anyone else's. And all you had to do was get a permit to mine and keep what you found."

"Permit? We don't do permits out here. You know that."

"You do now. Gril will be expecting it."

"Then everyone will know about the gold, and other people will get permits and they'll take it."

Donner leaned forward, his arms on his knees. "Which is the legal way it should be."

"Goddammit," Cyrus said, but there was more resignation in his voice than anger. "Good luck explaining that to my family."

"I don't have to explain anything. Neither does Gril. If you don't follow the law, you get arrested. If your family can't understand that, that's on them." He paused and then shook his head. "Doesn't matter. Tell me about your mother's friendship with Kaye."

"I think I'm done talking now." Cyrus put the cup on the floor and stood.

"Sit down," Donner demanded.

The tension in the room ramped up. Donner wore a weapon, but he hadn't drawn it. I didn't see a weapon on Cyrus, but I would have bet he had one.

"Arrest me."

"I'm going to take you up on it at some point, Cyrus. Sit down and tell me about Kaye and your mother. Unless you killed Kaye, you have nothing to hide anymore. I now know about your family's shenanigans with the gold. Talk to me."

Proving that he wasn't as dumb as he'd made himself out to be so far, Cyrus sat.

"My mom reminded Kaye of her mom. It's that simple. Well, that and my mom liked having some female company for a change."

"What'd they talk about?"

"I don't know. Cooking, cleaning, stuff like that probably."

I couldn't help but roll my eyes.

"Did you ever overhear them talking about those things?" Donner asked.

"No."

"What did you hear them talk about?"

Cyrus pulled in some air through his nose and let it out the same way. "For one, Warren. And what it would take to leave him and that family."

"I believe we've just come upon what some people might call the nitty-gritty, Cyrus. Tell me more, and then we'll go talk to your mother. The more you talk, the more sleep she'll get tonight. Keep going."

"Kaye wanted away from them," Cyrus said, but his tone had changed. Sadness lined his words.

I looked at Donner, who, if I was correctly gauging the suddenly deeper furrow of his brow, heard the same thing. He waited, but I couldn't.

"Cyrus," I said. The two men looked at me like they'd forgotten I was there. "What the fuck happened to Kaye before she was killed?"

I had zero authority, except that I was Kaye's almost friend, and maybe that was a rare thing. I suddenly realized that while I'd had a desire to form a deeper relationship, we might have already had as much of a friendship as she'd been able to have while living in the Miller household. Sure, I might not have had legal authority, but dammit, I had a right and a responsibility to help a friend.

Cyrus almost rolled his eyes at me.

"Hey!" Donner said, getting everyone's attention. "Spill it, Cyrus."

Cyrus nodded. "Yeah, yeah. Okay, Kaye and my mom talked about babies. I think Kaye was pregnant, and for some reason, she didn't want to tell Warren. Hell, I don't know. Ma won't tell me shit. She probably won't tell you anything, either."

My heart sank and my stomach churned. Pregnant. I even heard Donner almost gasp.

I turned to Donner. "Where's her body?"

"In Juneau."

"Autopsy find a pregnancy?"

"Not that I'm aware of."

I nodded, grateful Kaye's body was still available. I looked at Cyrus, who was looking everywhere but at Donner or me.

I was suddenly so angry at these people, the Millers and the Oliphants. It was a fiery sensation that might only be salved if Kaye were still here. Since that wasn't happening, I wanted all the answers.

"Sit still, everyone. Don't move a muscle." Donner took out his phone and moved to stand in the back corner of the center's main room, where there must have been a cell signal. He called Gril and told him to meet him out at the Oliphants' place.

After Donner made the call, he told Cyrus he was driving him home and that he would be talking to Cyrus's mother right then and there.

"I'm going, too," I said as we stood outside the community center.

"Beth . . ."

"Don't even, Donner. I owe this to Kaye."

He looked at me, clearly not understanding what I was saying to him, but either knowing he couldn't stop me or not wanting to put up the fight.

Making sure Cyrus wasn't in earshot, he said, "I had to leave a message for Gril. He might not make it out there when we're there."

He'd faked the conversation, as I suspected he'd done before.

"I'm going, Donner."

"All right, I don't want Cyrus to give her any warning that we'll be talking to her, so we're doing this now. It'll be good to have a girl there anyway. You might be able to talk to her better than I can."

I didn't tell him he should refer to me as a woman. My anger was otherwise directed.

"I'll follow you."

Twenty-Two

The Oliphant place was not like the Miller place, but it was just as improvised. I parked my truck behind Donner's in front of what must have been the main house.

There were six cabins spread out on the property, none of them striking me as cute or appealing. They were put together with one clear goal in mind—making sure no one would be tempted to go into any of them. KEEP OUT signs were posted everywhere, some whose words or graphics were more threatening than others.

Late night had turned to morning, but that didn't seem to deter Blair Oliphant from greeting us with a large shotgun. As both Donner and I brought our trucks to a stop, Blair emerged in full gear from the front cabin.

"I won't be long," I told Gus. I hoped he wasn't keying in on the giant wave of nerves that had come over me.

The dog's attention was on Blair. He seemed curious about the man. I petted Gus's head.

"It's okay. It really is." Gosh, I hoped so.

Gus remained sitting up and alert as I got out of the truck. I didn't lock him in, but if anyone so much as touched my dog, I'd grab a nearby gun and shoot them.

"Cyrus, what's going on?" Blair asked.

"I'm here in a legal capacity." Donner stepped in front of Cyrus.

I thought it was interesting that Donner didn't tell Blair to put the gun down. I wished Blair would put it down.

"You have no legal authority on my property," Blair said.

"We're gonna play it that way?" Donner asked. "Are you sure you want to, Blair? How hard do you want to make this on yourselves, because even if you don't accept that we or the Feds, I might add, carry authority over you, we, in fact, do, and we will throw all your asses in prison before you can even reload."

They faced each other. I hoped Donner knew what he was doing.

"Blair," a voice said from the door of the cabin. "Stop it. Let them in."

We turned to see a woman in a robe at the door, her long gray hair only sort of pulled back into a ponytail. I'd never once seen her anywhere around Benedict.

"Morning, Esther," Donner said, his voice still stern but friendlier.

"Good morning, Donner. Blair, put the gun down. I knew they'd be out here at some point, though I am surprised it's so soon. Don't suppose you had something to do with that, Cyrus?" Esther said.

Cyrus shrugged. "Sorry, Mama. I tried to get away from them."

"Come in," Esther said.

I followed Blair, Cyrus, and then Donner into the house as Esther remained on the rickety porch, watching us pass.

"You are?" Esther asked me.

"Beth Rivers."

"Esther Oliphant." She offered me a small smile. "I'm very glad you're here."

That was a surprise, but as I considered her words, I wondered if Kaye had mentioned me to her.

"Nice to meet you, Esther," I said.

"Same."

She followed me inside and then walked around everyone, leading the way through a messy front room to a surprisingly big and messy—though not really dirty—kitchen.

"Sit down, everyone. I've already made a pot of coffee, and I have some banana bread I whipped up yesterday." Esther signaled at the faded wood table and chairs.

I wondered if she was always the boss. Blair leaned his gun against one wall and took the chair in the corner. Cyrus kept his eyes away from his parents and took a seat opposite Blair. Donner sat in between Esther and Cyrus, and I sat on the other side of Blair, which put me in between him and Donner.

We fit snugly around the round table.

"Cyrus, grab coffee for everyone," Esther said right after we'd all sat.

Cyrus stood again and started gathering the coffee things.

"You said you expected us out here," Donner said to Esther.

"I did."

"Why didn't you just come to us or tell us everything on one of our previous trips?"

"You had to figure some things out first." She looked at Cyrus as he wrangled coffee and mugs.

I looked, too. Cyrus's back was to us, but I saw it bristle slightly. I couldn't tell if Esther was angry that her son had shared things with Donner or if it had been part of some plan. I also wondered if Esther had been afraid to come forward because of Blair and whatever iron fist he might sometimes rule with. Maybe that's why she'd given Cyrus this task. I did sense she was very much in charge, but Blair was no shrinking violet.

"And"—Esther continued when it appeared that Donner wasn't quite buying what she was selling—"we're all here now, so let's move forward."

"All right," Donner said. "Start from the beginning of your relationship with Kaye."

Cyrus handed out coffees and then sat again as Esther nodded slowly. "It hasn't been a long one."

"She's been married to Warren for ten years or so," Donner said.

"Yes, and I first met Kaye about three months ago."

"That *is* pretty recent."

"It is. She was out walking her dog, one she got from you." Esther nodded at me. "My god, she loved that animal, and he loved her. Finn, that's his name?" I nodded and she continued, "Finn will mourn for her. I hope he's in good hands."

"I took him from the Miller house," I said.

Donner furrowed an eyebrow in aggravation, but Esther smiled.

"Good girl," she said.

"Anyway, I was out back in one of our greenhouses. They aren't much use to us during the winter, but I still love to be out there in them, even if I'm just cleaning up. I was there when I saw Kaye and Finn walking by. I stepped out of the house and said hello.

"At first, she jumped and apologized. Said she must have gotten off her route. She didn't mean to be trespassing. I felt her fear. It was real, and it shook me up." Esther leaned her arms on the table and crossed them. "Something came so clear to me at that moment."

"What was that?" Donner asked when it appeared Esther had fallen into thought.

She looked up at him. "How utterly ridiculous we were all being. This stupid feud, all of it. I asked her to join me for some cake here in the house." Esther laughed. "She said 'no thank you, ma'am,' and hurried off.

"I wanted to yell after her and tell her to come back, but I didn't want to scare her more. So I thought and thought about what to do."

Blair cleared his throat and shifted in his chair. Esther looked up at him.

"No, my menfolk were of no use to me on this one. I had to figure it all out on my own."

Again, Blair shifted, but I didn't think we'd get any details regarding how unhelpful he'd been.

"Well, let me rephrase. My menfolk, other than Cyrus, were of no use to me. Cyrus is my baby, the youngest, and maybe it's because it's like they say: that first pancake is your practice pancake.

Cyrus is the best man I've raised, though lord knows I've tried." Esther sighed.

Cyrus put his hand on his mother's arm, squeezed it once, and then pulled it away again. Again, I wondered if there would be any fallout from Blair regarding this obvious play of favorites or how much of Cyrus's behavior had been a ruse to get us out here. Though they were healing quickly, he still had the black eye and the cut lip. Who'd given those to him? That answer might never become clear, but my suspicions were changing from a Miller to an Oliphant.

"So I asked Cyrus to track her down, apologize to her, and tell her our intentions were only friendly." Esther looked at Cyrus.

"But it worked backward," he said. "I happened to see her in the mercantile with Warren and she came here to apologize."

"But that probably wouldn't have happened if I hadn't said hello to her earlier," Esther added.

"Then what?" Donner asked.

"We struck up a friendship. I was more like her mother than Camille ever was. We got along."

Donner shook his head slowly. "I don't know . . . That had to be pretty risky on her part."

"She *was* afraid of us and what her family would do or how they would react if they saw her interacting with us, at least in a friendly way."

"How did you convince her otherwise?" Donner asked.

"I told her we'd never tell her family that she was visiting us," Esther said.

"And did everyone keep that promise?" Donner asked.

Esther surveyed the people in the room. Her eyes landed on Blair.

"I never said a word, Es, you know that. None of the boys did," Blair said.

"Well, there you go," Esther said. "No one said a word."

"What did you all talk about?" Donner asked Esther.

"We talked about all sorts of things. Some about her growing up down in the forty-eight and how she got up here. Did you know she answered a personal ad that Warren had placed in the paper?"

"Yes."

"Alaska," Cyrus said as if that explained it all, and it kind of did.

There were more men than women out here. I'd heard a phrase: *Where the odds are good, but the goods are odd.*

My favorite people in the world were here, but they—no, we—were all a little odd.

"Right," Donner said. "So, let's go back to when she came over to apologize. What happened that day?"

"She and I had snacks, talked a little, and then she went home. We got into the other stuff later on."

"What did she say about Warren specifically?" Donner asked.

"Well, she told me that she really loved her husband. She loved Warren, but she was a little afraid of him because sometimes his family was just . . . not right."

"Did she say any of them hurt her?" Donner asked.

"No, but that didn't ease her mind much. She was always aware they could, and they might."

I wondered about the differences between the families. The things Esther was saying about the Millers would have been assumptions I'd made about the Oliphants. Was that fair? Probably not, but I couldn't deny my own prejudices, I supposed. Though I could choose not to vocalize them.

"Go on," Donner said.

"We talked about a lot of things about the family, but she never went too deep. I know she didn't want to bad-mouth any of them. I tried not to, but I've had enough run-ins with that group for a few lifetimes. Once we got through the initial getting to know each other, though, we . . . I guess we became friends." Esther smiled sadly. "I haven't had a female friend in a long time. It was very nice."

Donner nodded and then looked at Blair. "And how did you feel about this?"

Blair made a distinctly unpleasant sucking sound with his teeth. "At first I didn't like it. Not one bit. But when I realized it was pretty harmless and Esther here was enjoying her time with the girl, I stayed out of it."

Donner looked at Esther. "Did he?"

She nodded and then sent her husband a semi-glare. "He did. I'm not sure I gave him any choice, though. You know," Esther continued, "I'm not being held here against my will. This is my family. I wouldn't be here if I didn't want to be, so, Donner, if I were you, I'd quit looking for a reason to dislike us."

"I'm just trying to find a killer," Donner said evenly.

"There is nothing I would love more than for you to figure out who killed Kaye."

"Well, so far, nothing you've said seems to help much."

"I told you she was a little scared of her family."

"And I registered that." Donner sat forward, pushed his mug toward the center of the table, and put his arms atop it. "But you could be making it all up. Besides, I'm not sure you've told me anything that would get her killed by her own family. I can see them being angry at her—but killed? There has to be more."

"I'll get to the brass tacks, then."

"Please."

"At one point she started talking about a baby."

Donner put his hand up. "What? Like she was already pregnant or just thinking about it?"

Esther frowned. "That she was pregnant."

Donner nodded.

"At one point she said she wasn't feeling great and maybe she was pregnant, ha-ha, that sort of thing. I took her seriously, though, and asked if she really thought she was. She said, 'Oh, no, just kidding,' but then one day she said she was having trouble sleeping and she put her hand on her stomach. I asked if it was that baby again keeping her awake at night. She looked at me like I'd just shared state secrets or something. Afraid, almost angry. I changed the subject."

"Did she look pregnant?"

Esther shook her head slowly. "I looked, but there was no belly.

You knew I was pregnant about five seconds after I got that way. My stomach just appeared. It was winter, though, and she always wore big sweatshirts and things. And, Donner, we never brought it up again, so I don't know anything more about it."

"She never drank," Blair added.

We turned our attention his way.

Blair shrugged. "I offered her a beer sometimes, and she always declined."

"She might not have liked beer," Donner said.

Blair sniffed again and shrugged. "Maybe."

I saw something in Esther, something I thought Kaye might have seen too, something friendly and motherly at the same time. She was someone I could imagine Kaye being drawn to.

"What else, Esther? I need to know anything else you can tell me," Donner said.

"She was from Montana and grew up an only child to parents who weren't bad people but didn't have much time to care for their daughter. She loved the idea of adventure in Alaska, marrying Warren, and being a part of a big family. I don't think she and Warren had a perfect relationship, but who does? I don't think that means he didn't kill her, though. I don't know where his loyalties really lie, with her or his family, but I've seen those Millers defend one another no matter the destruction it caused them."

Separating the facts from the Oliphants' desire to somehow throw the Millers under the bus was something I was sure Donner was up to.

"That's all I've got, Donner," Esther said. "I was fond of the girl. I'd wish for a daughter-in-law just like her, but I don't think my boys will ever get married."

Cyrus remained stoic. He knew this wasn't the time for that sort of conversation.

Is that the way they planned to live their lives? Single men out in the woods? I suddenly understood why Warren had placed an ad for a wife. Why he might have been looking for something different than being single out here.

"What about the gold?" Donner asked, looking back and forth between Cyrus and Esther.

"I heard them, her and Warren, talking about it, but I don't think Mama and Kaye ever even talked about it at all." Cyrus looked at his mother.

"No, sir, not once," Esther said.

My gaze went to Blair. He'd told them all to keep their mouths shut. Sure, Esther might be in charge, but Blair had his own forms of intimidation. I looked again at Cyrus's black eye, his lip. If Blair was responsible for those injuries to his own son, then I was impressed by Cyrus and Esther's manipulations to get the law out here, now with the knowledge of the pregnancy. But Esther was lying about the gold. I had no doubt.

What were the real reasons for Blair not wanting them to tell the police? The gold? I hoped there were no repercussions for Cyrus and Esther.

"Thank you for your honesty," Donner said. He looked at Blair. "Let me tell you all right now: if I see or hear about any other injuries to anyone in your family, Blair, I will put you on a plane to Juneau and let them get the truth out of you."

Blair lifted a haughty eyebrow and sniffed again.

"I mean it," Donner said.

"I'll make sure that doesn't happen," Esther said.

"Thank you, all," Donner said. "Gril will be here soon. Don't shoot him."

"We won't," Esther said.

We stood and left the house, surprised to find the other brothers all sitting on the front porch with their guns across their chests. Donner didn't act the least bit intimidated, and I worked not to, but I was sure my eyes went a little wide at the guns. There were so many. I gave Kingston as stern a glare as I could. He ignored me, but Esther didn't.

"Beth, I heard about your time with my son and husband on the Miller property. It will never happen again," she said. "You have no need to worry."

I just looked at her and nodded my gratitude.

Donner walked me to my truck, which was behind his, but he kept himself between me and the weapons, which I appreciated and worried about. I knew this could have all been some sort of setup, and I also knew that even though Donner had left a message for Gril as to where he and I were going, we could be shot and hidden somewhere before Gril could even make it out to us.

"Thanks for letting me come along," I said as I sat in the driver's seat and scratched behind Gus's ears. He'd been resting and was no worse for the wear.

"Beth, I've got work to do, and I don't want to worry about you."

"You don't need to worry about me." I glanced toward the porch where they all stood, watching us. "They aren't aiming this way, at least."

"Not yet. Drive out. I'll follow. Meet you at the police station. I'd like for both of us to talk to Gril if he's there."

Only a few moments later, we were out of sight of the Oliphant compound. With an *oof,* I exhaled a relieved breath out of my lungs. I'd been on alert, but I'd had no idea how stressed I'd been.

Gus whined as I laughed with some more release. I looked at him.

"I'm fine." Even as I drove, I pulled him close to me. "I'm glad you're with me."

He licked my cheek, and everything was right with the world, at least momentarily.

Twenty-Three

It had started to pour by the time Donner, Gril, and I all parked our trucks in the gravel lot outside the police station.

"Come in with me," I said to Gus.

We all hurried inside. Gril hadn't gotten any of Donner's messages yet, and we managed to tell him everything before he even tried his voice mail.

"You think the Oliphants were telling the truth?" he asked Donner.

"I think some of it was the truth but not the whole truth. I think Kaye was pregnant, or she told Esther she was."

Gril picked up the landline on his desk and dialed some numbers. A moment later, he asked to speak to Christine Gardner, the medical examiner in Juneau. He was disappointed to be sent to voice mail.

"Christine, Gril here. I just received some information regarding the body we sent to you a few days ago. Kaye Miller. I know there's a backup there, but I have another favor. I don't need the full report quite yet, but I'd like to know if she was pregnant as soon as possible please. Okay, thanks. Talk to you soon."

He hung up the phone.

"I don't know if anyone else knew about the possible pregnancy,

Gril. I haven't talked to the Millers. And Warren is MIA. Who knows what he knows?" Donner said.

"We'll have a chat with the family as soon as I hear back. I'd like to go in with confirmation one way or another."

"Me too," Donner said.

Gril looked at me. "You okay?"

"I'm fine. I'm surprised about Kaye, but maybe I shouldn't be. Gril, I really didn't know her that well, but I think she was using me as an excuse for when she went to visit Esther. I thought it was Cyrus she was visiting, but I don't know now."

"She wouldn't want the Millers to know she was visiting any of the Oliphants."

"Motive enough for murder?" Donner asked.

"Maybe," Gril said as he sat back in his chair.

"What?" Donner asked him.

"I hadn't seen Kaye for a few months before she was killed. I keep trying to get my eyes on people all year around out here, but some folks really do want to be left alone."

"There's only so much you can do," Donner said.

"Isn't that why we have the Death Walk?" I asked, but I knew the answer.

"Yes," Gril said. "It took me five years to get everyone aboard. People fought me for a long time, but even Al would have been there if he could have. I wish I would have made more of an effort."

I shook my head. "No, Gril, they all keep to themselves. It's the way they live."

Gril kept stealing glances at the phone, but it didn't ring. I realized that though Gril and Donner wouldn't have minded if I waited for an answer, they'd now prefer if I left them to whatever other work they had to do.

"I'd better let Viola know we're okay," I said to them as I petted Gus's head.

No one stopped us from leaving. They told me again to be careful, and Gus and I drove away.

There was nothing about the Benedict House that day to indicate it was a place for parolees to reform.

Everyone was happy and in great moods.

Of course, Chaz was cooking again.

"Hi," I said as Gus and I walked into the dining room. It appeared that no one had even heard us come through the front door. They were all surprised to see us.

"Beth! Hello," Al said as he stood from the table. Gleefulness emanated from him. "Come sit and join us. Hello, Gus."

I wanted to ask who he was and what he'd done with the old curmudgeon we'd found a few days earlier.

Chaz and Viola also greeted me. Chaz filled my plate with more breakfast food than I'd ever eaten, but which I knew I would conquer easily.

"Thanks," I said.

"Where have you been?" Viola asked.

If Chaz wasn't there, I probably would have told Viola and Al everything, but I didn't think I was supposed to share police investigations with other criminals. I didn't know the rules, but it was only common sense.

"Working some," I said as I sliced my fork through some fluffy pancakes. "What'd I miss here?"

"I took Finn for another walk, but we both missed Gus," Chaz said as he made his way back to the attached kitchen.

"Sorry about that," I said. I stopped before I stuck the pancake bite with the fork. There was something about that, about Gus missing the walk with Chaz and Finn this morning.

I couldn't place what my mind was working through, what my gut was trying to tell me. *It couldn't possibly have anything to do with Kaye's murder, could it?*

I looked at Chaz. What was going on? Was I just trying so hard to find an answer that my mind glommed on to the nearest criminal as a somehow guilty party?

That was pretty unfair.

"You okay, Beth?" Chaz asked as I was still scrutinizing him.

"I'm fine." I scooped up the food and took the bite. "Oh my, Chaz, once again, how do you make everything so much better?"

Chaz shrugged and smiled. "Thank you."

"He should open a restaurant, right?" Al said, all signs of him not liking the younger man now gone.

"Yes," I agreed.

"But he should do it in Juneau or Anchorage or someplace bigger than here," Al said.

"You and Viola have told me that I won't be able to stay here forever anyway."

"You won't," Viola said. "That's just the way it works."

"Have you never worked as a chef, other than in prison?" I asked him.

"Never. Not officially. Even in prison, no one gave me the title," Chaz said.

"How did you get to be so good at it?" I asked.

"Just a hobby that I practice every day." Chaz smiled sadly. "Even when incarcerated."

No one laughed, but we all returned sympathetic smiles. No, that wasn't quite right. Al and I smiled sympathetically. Viola didn't. She gave him one of her suspicious side-eyes. It was a quick maneuver, but I knew it and I knew I'd seen it.

As I enjoyed the food, I wondered what I'd *actually* missed. Viola was a pro, and she didn't immediately believe anyone, let alone all of what her clients told her. I'd ask her about it later, but something was up.

"Hello?" a female voice called from the direction of the front door.

We'd all been talking so much, we hadn't heard anyone come inside.

"We're in the dining room," Viola said as she stood to greet our visitor.

But she didn't make it out of the dining room before Camille Miller appeared in the entryway.

She looked around the room quickly, her eyes landing on Finn.

"You took my dog." she said as she took a step toward Finn, who was sitting happily next to Al.

"Hang on there, sister." Viola stepped in her way.

"Get out of my way, Viola. That's my dog, and I'm taking him home."

I stood now, too. "No, you aren't, Camille. I'm in charge of where that dog goes, and you aren't taking him today. He was Kaye's."

"He was the family's."

I shook my head. "No, that's not how it worked. He was Kaye's. I will determine where he goes from here. That's my responsibility, and Gril will back me up."

"Gril," she huffed. "Like he has any say whatsoever."

Viola cleared her throat. "Gril has all the say, Camille. And for now, this dog is staying here. If you'd like to adopt him, put in your application with Beth and she'll consider it."

"I'll do no such thing," Camille huffed. "She came into my house and took him from me."

"The dog was outside," Viola said. "That's on you. He shouldn't have been left outside."

He hadn't been, but I was mightily impressed by how well Viola kept the lie going. Even I had to take a moment to remember how it had truly happened.

Fortunately, Finn being outside wasn't too far-fetched.

"He was on our property, then. She trespassed to get him," Camille said.

Al and Chaz had been quiet and observant through these contentious moments, but now Chaz came around from the kitchen and Al, all ninety-four years of him, stood from his chair.

"You won't be taking that dog," Al said. "Get on home, Camille. Beth will do right by that dog, but your behavior isn't doing your chances any good."

Camille fumed, but then she took a deep breath and looked at me.

"Beth, I will take good care of that animal, I promise. I loved him as much as Kaye did; I promise that, too. I'm not happy you took him from me, but I want him back and if being nice to you will help me accomplish that, I'll do it. But not forever."

I didn't point out the flaws in her argument. I nodded. "I hear you, Camille, and I appreciate your effort to let me know how much you care for him. I will one hundred percent take that into consideration, and I'll let you know what I decide."

She was about to blow again, but maybe her better angels whispered something in her ear because she finally gave one last pursed-lips huff and left. We could hear her this time because she made sure to slam the door.

Just as I was about to thank everyone for their support, Viola's office phone rang, clanging away the contention-filled air. She excused herself to answer it, but a moment later, she called for me.

I joined her in the office.

"Gril. For you," she said, handing me the phone. She didn't leave.

"Gril?"

"Yep, just wanted you to know that Kaye wasn't pregnant when she was killed."

"That's a relief."

"Only initially. She wasn't pregnant, but there were indications that she'd given birth recently."

"What?" I sat down on the corner of Viola's desk as I digested the news.

"Yes, probably within a couple weeks of being killed."

"There's a baby somewhere?"

"That's what we're working with. She didn't say anything about any of this to you?"

"Not one word, Gril. Not one."

He kept talking, but I wasn't listening as well as I should have been. I was trying to remember something that would help me know where a baby might be. I had nothing, I was sure of it.

"Beth?"

"Sorry, I'm . . . what can I do, Gril?"

"Nothing. If there's a baby somewhere, I'll find her. Or him. I will."

"I believe you."

We ended the call, but I was so distracted by what he'd said that

I didn't hang up the handset. Viola took it from me and placed it in the cradle.

"A baby?" she asked.

"That's what Gril said. Do you suppose there's a baby out there?"

"I don't know, Beth, but you need to know that more babies get born under the radar out here than you might ever want to know about. It happens, but that doesn't mean that something bad happened."

I thought about Tex and the way he became the father of two girls—it wasn't a happy story how they got to him, but it had worked out well for everyone in the end.

"I get that," I said.

"Okay?" Viola looked at me with furrowed brows.

"I just wish I could help. Why didn't I know about this, Viola? I think Kaye was trying to tell me something on that last walk, but she just couldn't bring herself to do it. And then Warren showed up. God, where's the baby?"

I'd been to the Miller house. I'd kept to that front room. If only I'd been more like my mother, if only I'd searched.

I could see Mill now in my head.

See? Sometimes you have to make things your business.

If she'd still been here and with me, we might have found that baby.

Okay, I was overthinking this.

"I need to go . . ." I said.

I walked around Viola.

"Beth!" she called from her office. "Where are you going?"

"Not sure," I called back before I went into my room, shutting the door behind me.

I didn't know what I was going to do, but I had some ideas.

I added a pair of socks over my feet and made sure I had an extra layer of a shirt on underneath my sweatshirt and coat. I loaded my backpack with things I might need—snacks, a water bottle, a knife, matches, some hand warmers, one of those silver emergency blankets, and other emergency essentials. I'd been preparing myself for this sort of thing. I'd been getting in good shape and learning how best to survive out in the elements if I found myself out there.

Screw that. I was *putting* myself out there. I was taking a hint from my own mother and doing what I thought I needed to do.

Even if it wasn't quite the right thing.

Twenty-Four

parked my truck at the community center. I was the only vehicle there. I didn't bother locking it, but I did slip the keys under the floor mat. I didn't want to risk losing them somewhere out in the woods, and that's where I was headed.

Then I took a closer look inside the community center.

I pushed through the doors and made my way to the back of the main room, where the bedding had been piled up. I'd seen it but hadn't given it a second glance. I knew Gril had left it there just in case someone really did need a place to sleep.

Pinching only a corner of the green felt blanket, I picked it up and shook it out. Nothing substantial fell from it. I put it close to my nose and sniffed.

Mint. I was pretty sure I smelled mint. Whatever that meant.

There were no visible stains on it, but from what I'd been through with Travis, I knew there might be some valuable DNA somewhere in the threads. Sending these things to Juneau might be one of Gril's next steps.

There were also two pillows, with mismatched pillowcases: one dingy white, the other dingy beige. No visible stains on either of the cases.

I shook one of the pillows and thought that something didn't feel quite right, so I took out the pillow inside and then shook the pillowcase again.

Something fell out.

I tossed the pillowcase aside and crouched to see the small item. It was a matchbook, similar to the two I'd just put in my backpack, though mine were inside a small waterproof container.

The words on the matchbook read ROCKY POINT. That was it; nothing else. It sounded familiar, but I couldn't place why. I didn't have any way to google it at the moment, either. I wanted to take the matches, but thought I should leave them for Gril. With a pen I grabbed from a nearby table, I wrote the words on my hand, then checked the other pillow but found nothing inside. When I sniffed it, though, I smelled a distinctly recognizable scent. Cigarette smoke.

I'd recognize that smell to the end of my days. Just catching a whiff now took me back to long car rides with my mother or my grandfather sitting at his desk in the police station. I'd never been a smoker, but I'd grown up with them.

Since smoking was prohibited in public places in Benedict, I didn't really know who smoked and who didn't, but if I came upon someone who smelled of cigarette smoke and mint, I was going to ask them about these items.

I made no other discoveries, even as I searched the rest of the center, turning on the bathroom lights and checking all the stalls, too.

I looked for indications that a baby had been present, checking the garbage cans for discarded diapers or maybe baby food containers, but found nothing.

Hoisting my pack over my shoulders, I set out from the center. I'd thought about bringing Gus, but I didn't want to have to worry about keeping him hidden. I had plans that included going into places I wouldn't necessarily be welcome.

I could see where I'd driven to on the other side of the creek, toward the still, but I wasn't going there.

Today I was going to take the path on this side of the creek, the side where Kaye was killed. My first destination was the Miller compound, and I wasn't even sure I could get to it this way, but I thought it was a distinct possibility, and I wanted to see if there were any clues out that direction.

Had Gril or Donner walked this path? I had no idea, but I really didn't think they had. Gril was a good officer of the law and Donner was at least a great interrogator, but with such limited resources, Gril might not have thought it necessary to take a walk this way.

I did.

Or I told myself that it was important.

Tex had taught me a lot about being out in these woods. I appreciated his lessons, but hadn't yet had the chance to apply them.

When I came to a fork of sorts in the path, I stopped and reached for a red ribbon in my pocket. I had a bunch of them.

I tied the ribbon around a nearby branch of a tree that would guide me back to where I'd come from. For good measure, and just in case someone wanted to remove the ribbon, I took out my knife and carved a small arrow into the bark.

I continued on, marking my path along the way, probably for about forty-five minutes when I finally came upon civilization, though it wasn't the civilization I'd been hoping for. At least not at first. I'd planned on casing out the Oliphant compound at some point but hoped to do so at the Millers' first. But this trail had taken me right to the Oliphants.

"Damn," I said to myself as I hid behind a tree, realizing the direction I'd gone.

At least I could now visualize the woods better.

So be it, I thought. I wove my way, tree by tree, closer to the compound. I'd come up the side of all the cabins, so I could see if anyone went in or out of any of the doors.

I crouched low, getting down on my knees. I grabbed some binoculars from the pack and surveyed the property.

Trucks were parked here and there, but there was no sign of other vehicles. If Gril had come out here, he was gone by now. Smoke curled up from chimneys on all the houses. It might be June, but it wasn't warm enough not to have heat.

I'd been so focused on just looking around that when I heard the noise of a door bursting open, I had to lower the binoculars to determine which house the noise had come from.

It was the main one, and Cyrus was the one making all the ruckus.

"Cyrus, get back in here," Esther said as she came out onto the front porch. She was fully dressed, her hair now pulled back tightly.

"Mama, this is all bullshit, and you know it. It's not right."

"Goddammit, Cyrus, get in here before Gril or Donner drive up here and wonder what in the Sam Hill is going on."

"I'm done talking about it, Mama. Done! I know what I need to do, and I'm going to do it. Right now."

"Cyrus," Esther pleaded. "You'll get yourself killed. Don't do it! We will figure it out."

As Cyrus reached for the handle on his truck door, Esther moved quickly to grab a shotgun leaning against the front of the house. She wasn't going to shoot him, was she?

She didn't, but she did step off the porch and shoot the gun up into the air, looking as close to any real-life Annie Oakley as I'd ever seen.

Cyrus jumped at the noise and then released the door handle. He slumped into a defeated posture before he turned toward his mother again.

The other cabins' doors were opening, and I saw Kingston jog out of a cabin behind the main house, spitting a wad of tobacco as he hurried to join his mother. Blair also came out of the main house, but he remained on the porch, leaning on a railing as he scowled out at Cyrus.

"Cyrus, you can't put us all in that kind of danger. You know you can't," Esther said.

"This has gone on too long." He swept his hand through the air. "It's all gone on way too long, and nothing good can come of what's happened. I don't mean to put the rest of you in any danger, and I'll make damn sure they know it's just me. But I've got to do something. For once in my pathetic life, I've got to find a way to do the right thing, my own safety be damned. Don't you understand? I can't live with myself if I don't try."

I was putting meaning to everything I heard, but still nothing was all that clear. I really didn't know what Cyrus was referring to. I hoped someone would say something that would help me better understand what was going on.

"Son," Blair called. "Don't think you can come back here if you leave."

Esther turned around and faced Blair so quickly, I could almost see the air move around her.

"Shut up, Blair. You don't get to speak about this. Do you hear me?"

She was angrier at her husband than she was at Cyrus. That was, of course, intriguing, but I was more intrigued by how Blair responded to her.

He didn't say a word. He just kept leaning as he stared at her.

Esther turned to face Cyrus again. "You are always welcome in my home, Cyrus. Always, but you will do us harm if you do this. There's no way around it."

"I don't have any choice, Mama. You're going to have to shoot to stop me."

Cyrus and his mother looked at each other for a long moment. Finally, Esther put the gun down on the ground.

"Think hard about it," she said. "I'm proud of you for being a man. Just . . . just try to come home safe and sound. Do you hear me?"

"Yes, Mama, I do."

Without a word to his father or brothers, Cyrus got into the truck and drove away.

Kingston, his hands on his hips, looked at his father, who just shook his head, then they went back into their respective cabins.

Esther picked up the gun and made her way to the front porch, where she sat in a rocking chair, holding the weapon across her body as she slowly rocked.

I lowered the binoculars, feeling like the show might have just ended, at least for now.

My mind had turned Cyrus's behavior into something that had to do with Kaye and probably the baby. But what I'd witnessed might not have anything to do with Kaye, and Cyrus might not be headed over to the Miller compound.

From my low position on the ground, I looked behind me, seeing nothing but the woods I'd just come through. I'd thought I was headed toward the Millers'. Evidently, I wasn't as ready for this outdoor adventure as I'd hoped.

I couldn't picture how to get to the Millers' other than walking back the way I came, getting in my truck, and driving over there. I knew I wasn't good enough at my outdoor explorations to just walk around and hope for the best.

I had witnessed an argument, though, and it might prove to be important at some point.

I sighed. At least I hadn't seen any bears yet.

I took my own advice and turned to head back to my truck just as the main cabin's door opened again.

"You coming with me?" Blair asked Esther.

She gave him a look that might have been worse than if she shot the gun at him, but then she softened. "I'm coming. I need some stuff."

For the next thirty seconds I thought I saw the depth of their marriage. They'd been fighting angry at each other just a few minutes earlier, but that dissolved, and with his hand at her back, Blair walked his wife to the passenger side of his truck before he got into the driver's side.

I would have loved to hear that conversation, but something told me they weren't going to further discuss whatever it was Cyrus was doing. They'd moved on.

And their cabin was now empty.

I didn't feel the same surge of Mill's righteousness as I'd felt earlier, but if she were here, she'd have made her way inside the cabin.

I stood and repacked the binoculars. I swung the pack back over my shoulders and boldly emerged from the woods, beelining it to the main cabin. It wasn't just the ghost of Mill's bad behavior guiding me. I wanted to know what had happened to Kaye. I wanted to know what had happened to a baby.

No one burst out of the other cabins, a gun at the ready, so I was pretty sure I hadn't been seen.

I climbed the porch steps and went inside.

"Hello?" I said, because even though I shouldn't be there, announcing myself was probably safer than surprising someone.

No one answered.

I'd spotted a desk on the far wall when we'd been there earlier. I hurried to it.

It might have been the nicest piece of furniture in the house. I lifted the roll top, exposing the insides.

Everything was neat and tidy—stacks of papers, magazines, a current calendar. I didn't much care about their financial situation, so I didn't look closely at papers with numbers, or inside envelopes that had come from a bank.

"Hang on," I said. "A bank?"

It was unexpected that the Oliphants trusted banks. I'd become so concerned about the baby that I'd forgotten about the other part. The part where they'd found gold and somehow managed to secretly monetize it, or so the theory went.

I grabbed a bank envelope. It was intact, having been opened at one time with a straight edge and the papers stuck back inside the envelope again later. I pulled out and unfolded the papers.

It was a savings account statement with some pretty big numbers. The Oliphants had over two hundred and fifty thousand dollars in this account. I had no idea how they'd gotten that kind of money, but it might not have been from gold.

It also might have been.

And I didn't much care about the gold or the money anyway, particularly when I noticed a brochure stuck in the back of the desk.

I put the statement back how I found it and reached for the brochure, which featured an angry man pointing from the page with a dialogue bubble coming from his head.

Did your sperm boldly go where it shouldn't have?

"Okay," I muttered as I opened the brochure.

It was a guide on how to get out of taking care of a child you'd "accidentally" fathered. Basically a list of reprehensible things to do and say so that you didn't have to "fork up any money for some brat you didn't want in the first place." Not surprisingly, there were diatribes about women not doing what they know they can do to not get pregnant, like jumping up and down after the act, etc.

It always surprised me that people like whoever made this brochure could still get away with this ridiculousness.

I put it back and had an urge to wash my hands. I closed the roll top and continued to search the house.

There was only one bedroom and one bathroom, both of them small.

Though my mother would have searched the nightstands, I wasn't prepared to. I did open the medicine cabinet in the bathroom.

I spotted pain relievers and a prescription for Blair from a Juneau pharmacy for a statin, but that was it.

Standing there in that bathroom, I had to check myself, though. I was doing something I'd told Donner I wouldn't do. I was projecting my experiences on people who had never lived anything near the life I had.

I'd scrunched my nose up at the idea of trapping animals. I still did, but that was the way some people put food on their table. Donner had simply shrugged and told me that if I was going to live here, it would behoove me to be open-minded about all kinds of things I hadn't considered before.

He was right, but I did have a limit. That brochure would never be something I could accept. To be fair, I didn't think Donner would be able to, either.

From the front of the house, I heard the door open. I caught my reflection in the medicine cabinet mirror. My eyes got big, and my face went very pale.

I heard someone walking around out front. I had nowhere to go. I had to hope they wouldn't come into the bathroom.

With no other choice, and as quietly as I could, I jumped into the tub and pulled the curtain shut. This was not the way I wanted to die, but not hiding didn't seem smart, either.

Someone started whistling and heavy footsteps brought them into the bedroom.

"There you are," I heard a man say.

I was pretty sure it was Kingston. I heard creaking, and then I thought I heard the dial of a safe. A few seconds later, a clunk.

"And they'll never even notice I took you," Kingston said before breaking into another whistling tune.

The closing of a heavy metal door and another clunk reached me in the bathroom, followed by more footsteps making their way out of the bedroom and then the house.

I didn't notice I'd been holding my breath until I let it out. Thank goodness he hadn't needed to use the bathroom.

I propelled myself out of the tub and into the bedroom. A serene picture of a waterfall hung on the far wall. I hurried to it and then pulled on one side. The hinged side swung it wide and exposed a safe.

"Now, that's what I'd expect," I said, thinking that Mill would be extraordinarily proud of all that had just happened, though she wouldn't have been half as freaked out as I'd been.

At that moment, I realized I was balancing on a thin wire. I wasn't sure if I needed to be more like her or be glad I wasn't. The answer was always fuzzy.

I closed the picture back over the safe. Okay, Kingston was probably stealing from his family. Did I care? Not really, but I would certainly remember the moment. Maybe I could use it against him if he threatened me again.

I needed to get out of there and probably get back to my truck and park closer to where I knew I could get to the Millers' place. I liked what I was learning, and I wasn't ready to give up expanding my knowledge.

I hoped again that no one was watching me leave, but I kept up a confident stride on my way back to the woods. Well, maybe stride wasn't the right description. I full-out ran.

Twenty-Five

The ribbons got me back to my truck, though the trek took longer than I wanted it to. As I climbed into the passenger seat, my progress was further thwarted. Someone had stuck a piece of paper under one of the windshield wipers.

I hopped out and grabbed it, my heartbeat speeding up in anticipation.

In a scribble I didn't recognize, it said, *There are wild animals in these woods. Stop exploring.*

"What?" I said into the quiet.

There still wasn't another vehicle in sight. I didn't see anyone. No one. I looked at the note again. I didn't recognize the writing at all.

I took a few steps away from the truck and investigated the woods again.

"Show yourself," I called into what truly felt like a void.

No one came out from behind the trees or from the community center. I felt distinctly alone and spied on at the same time.

Who was watching me? Why?

Another unnerving sensation washed through me. I knew this

feeling, this sense of losing control, and I didn't like it, but what used to scare me about it now only made me angry.

I gritted my teeth and got back into the truck. Again, I risked breaking the lock by pushing down on the tab, and then I reached for the keys under the mat.

They weren't there.

"No," I said as my unnerved feeling ramped up to full-on panic. "No."

I put my hands on the steering wheel and squeezed my fingers tight. I breathed in and out, working to relax my jaw as I noticed how tight my teeth were clenched. This was not going to get the best of me. Nothing was.

I suddenly knew that my keys were still under the mat. I'd missed them only because I'd come to expect the fear, the anger. No. I didn't want to do that anymore.

Slowly, methodically even, I reached under the mat and found the keys. That part of me that had been buried by the fear and anger had pushed itself through.

I put the keys in the ignition and turned hard. The gravel from the parking lot sprayed as I drove out of there.

I had to put the note to the back of my mind as I made my way toward the Millers'. It kept wanting to nudge its way forward, but I kept fighting it. I'd deal with it later.

I pulled onto the dirt road I'd taken to the Miller place before, but this time I stopped when I thought I was half a mile from the entrance to their compound. I pulled off to the side of the road. This time I put my keys in my pocket, adrenaline from those earlier moments still propelling me back into the woods. I was pleased that I'd been correct in my assessment—I was about half a mile away.

The scene at the Miller place was much busier than at the Oliphant compound. I spotted some of the Millers' trucks, as well as Gril's, Donner's, and Cyrus's.

Were they getting to the bottom of it, getting the answers? My heart squeezed at the idea that a baby was out there somewhere, maybe being ignored. Or worse.

There was a design flaw in their compound that the Millers should have recognized: I could walk toward the house without being out in the open for too long, lowering my chances of being caught. It only took a few leaps between the trees and the house before I was crouched below a front window. I was confident that I hadn't been noticed.

The window wasn't open, but I could hear the rumble of conversation inside. I tried to quiet my breathing and listen hard. It took a second, but soon I could distinguish different voices.

Gril said, "Have you seen the child?"

He was not happy.

I couldn't hear the noise of answers, so I assumed people were either nodding or shaking their heads.

I wasn't going to be able to get the information I needed unless I could see.

"In for a penny," I muttered to myself.

Leaning against the house, I slowly lifted myself up and tried to peer in. I knew immediately that no one was looking in my direction because everyone was looking at Cyrus, who had yet another black eye. Without a doubt, this one hadn't come from his family. I'd seen him leave them, and this was a very new injury.

I'd missed a lot, but I was sure it wasn't Gril or Donner who'd done that to him, either. More likely, it was good that they had come along when they had. They might have saved his life.

I saw that Ike had his arms backward around a chair, probably handcuffed. That was probably good.

"I haven't," Cyrus finally said.

"That child is not yours!" Camille screamed as she paced the front of the room.

"You don't know that, Camille," Cyrus said, his head bowed but his voice still strong.

I couldn't digest those words quickly because he kept talking, and as I listened it did occur to me that this was new—Cyrus had said he and Kaye weren't romantically involved. Was he changing his story or was he just trying to get under Camille's skin?

"That child was Warren and Kaye's." I saw spit fly from her mouth as she yelled again.

"Enough, Camille," Gril turned to her and put up his hand. "Honestly, it doesn't matter who that child 'belongs' to. We need to find it."

"Her! It's a her!" Camille yelled again.

"All right." Gril looked at Camille. "So you have seen *her*?"

Camille looked as if she realized she'd been caught in a lie. "No, I haven't seen her, but I know it's a girl."

"I don't believe you, Camille," Gril said. "Tell me where she is." He looked around. "What is wrong with all of you? This is about a baby, a child. We have to do the best for her."

"The Oliphants can't have her," Ike said from his position in the chair. "She's ours. She's Warren's."

"I understand, and that's the way it will be," Gril said.

I knew he was just trying to work them, attempting to find the child. Unfortunately, so did they. They didn't buy into his easy concession.

"Isn't that something you'd like to know for sure?" Cyrus said. "We'll get the tests done. We'll find out."

"Don't trust any of that bullshit. No one should," Camille said.

"I want to know if she's my daughter," Cyrus said. "If she isn't, I'll step away. I promise."

"I don't trust anyone but us. She's ours," Camille said.

As I continued to listen, flashes of the time Donner and I had spent with the Oliphants played through my mind, and I realized, if only with a brief moment of clarity, that not only was the moonshine setup a diversion but the gold was, too. This was all about a child, one who might belong to Cyrus. Why hadn't the Oliphants just told Gril as much?

One look at Cyrus's face probably answered that question.

I wondered what Gril was going to do. Arrest them all? I thought it was a distinct possibility.

I watched as he turned and made his way to a chair around the table. He spun it around and sat, leaned his elbows on his knees.

"We need to get an answer here, folks," he said, settling in as if he wasn't leaving until he had one.

"We don't know where she is," Camille said adamantly.

Gril nodded. "All right, here's the deal. There's a baby out there somewhere. If she disappears, I'll have you all arrested for murder and shipped to Juneau. I've lost my patience. No one will have patience for a dead baby. But the other answer we need is who killed Kaye. Someone in this room knows what happened to both of them. If that child is alive, I want her in safe custody immediately. I want that truth, and I want it right now."

He very well might have them all shipped to Juneau, but I didn't think much would come of that. Without solid evidence, they'd be shipped back pretty quickly.

"I don't know what happened to Kaye," Cyrus said. "I've asked my family and they all say they had nothing to do with her murder. I'd tell you, I really would. I . . ."

"What, Cyrus?" Gril asked.

"I loved her."

"God! He loved her, another man's wife. He loved her!" Camille was still pacing and still raging. "I'm sure your family was just as thrilled as we are about your . . . involvement with Kaye. It sickens me, and I'm sure it sickened them."

"It didn't." Cyrus looked at her. "My mom really liked her. Told her to get away from you all, in fact."

Camille lifted her fist and rushed toward Cyrus. Donner stepped in front of her and held her back.

"Stop it, Camille!" Gril bellowed. "No more."

I cringed as I watched. None of this was going well. Answers weren't being uncovered. Donner pushed back on Camille, forcing her farther away from Cyrus.

A long moment later, Gril looked at Cyrus. "Why did you come here?"

"If that baby is mine, it's my responsibility to take care of her. I came to get her."

"She's not here! She's somewhere with Warren, we think," Ike said. "We don't know where they went."

"I don't believe you," Cyrus said.

"Cyrus, we've searched the whole property. There's no sign of either Warren or the baby," Donner said. "I could believe that they are together somewhere."

Cyrus scrutinized Donner.

"He's telling the truth," Gril said. "We've searched the whole place, and you should have just left it up to us."

"What kind of a man would do that?" Cyrus asked.

A smart one, I thought. Nevertheless, I understood what he was saying.

"You're getting out of here, going home," Gril said. "We'll handle this, and we'll make sure we figure out who the baby's father is. I swear, Cyrus."

"You won't put a hand on my granddaughter. If Warren comes back, I'll tell him to run so far away that you'll never find them," Camille said.

"And I'll have you locked away for that," Gril said.

"I don't care," she retorted.

I looked closely at her and thought that maybe she really didn't. She was motivated by her hatred of the Oliphants. She didn't even want them to have a child her daughter-in-law had given birth to, even if it was more their bloodline than hers. She'd taken ownership of Kaye, too.

There was never going to be a way to broker a peace between these two families. If Cyrus was telling the truth now, Kaye had been unfaithful to Warren, which, in itself, was ammunition for destruction. Not to mention the timing—they'd been seeing each other for at least nine months, probably right about when winter set in hard. A baby might just ruin them all.

Where would Warren go? The possibilities were both limited by the geography and also limitless because of the vast wide openness. Gril would have made sure to tell the people running the ferry and the Harvingtons to let him know if Warren tried to get away using those modes of transportation.

I had an urge to talk to Viola, to ask her if she had any idea of secret Miller hiding places. I was sure Gril didn't know Viola's history with this family.

I'd come out here to snoop. I'd planned on trying to get inside, just like I'd done at the Oliphants, but there was no way to do that. I'd spied, and if Gril caught me, it might mean an end to our friendship.

I crawled away from my spot under the window. Once I was close enough to a tree, I stood and brushed myself off.

In the distance, I saw movement. My first thought was to wonder whether this was a wild animal, not the person I thought I kept seeing everywhere. But the shape was distinctly human, and they were dressed in black. They were far enough away that I could wait them out from behind the tree. I tucked myself behind one and peered around the trunk as the figure approached.

They were recognizable in that they moved the same way the person outside Elijah's and maybe the one on Orin's roof had moved.

"Mill?" I said quietly to myself, even if that didn't quite jibe.

It came to me then—mint and cigarettes. Those were classic Mill scents. Had she been hiding in the community center? Why wouldn't she just let me know where she was? She was up to something, and she wasn't going to show herself to me, even as she was spying. I was going to have to catch her.

I took off in a run. It wasn't easy in these cramped woods, and the person ahead of me noticed me, turned, and ran away. They were faster, more agile, even as they limped a little.

I closed the space somewhat and managed to catch another full-on look at them. It wasn't my mom. *Was it?* I did the best I could to catch up, but when I got to my truck, I lost sight of the direction they'd gone. Breathing heavily, my thighs burning from the journey, I looked around but couldn't see anyone. They were either hiding or gone.

Had they left me the note?

If it wasn't Mill, was it Orin? I didn't think so. I knew it wasn't

Warren because he was so much bigger than the wiry, agile person I'd seen.

I'd have to figure out a way to set a trap.

I had other things to do first, though. I got into my truck, dug my keys out of my pocket, and quickly made my way back to the Benedict House.

Twenty-Six

found Viola quickly, but before she would talk to me, she made me sit down in her office and "pull myself together." I did the best I could. Then I tried to keep a level tone as I told her everything that had happened.

"Well, first of all, I'm glad you got out of there. You are correct, Gril would be upset at you for eavesdropping and putting yourself in that situation. He had enough to worry about. Secondly, holy Moses, what a mess. A baby? The father could be Warren or Cyrus? This just isn't good."

"I know. Can you think of any Miller family hiding places?"

"I have no idea," Viola said. "It's been a long time since I might have known about a Miller hiding place. I wish I could help." She frowned. "Honestly, no sign of the baby anywhere?"

I shook my head. "No. I don't know for sure that anyone actually knows."

"My goodness, that's . . . well, shocking and awful at the same time."

I nodded and reached into my pocket. I handed Viola the note that had been put on my windshield at the community center.

"What's this?"

I gave her the details.

"You're being followed?" she asked.

"That was my first thought, but if it's who I've been seeing, *I* came upon *them* at Orin's and Elijah's. They might think I'm following them."

"I don't like it." Viola handed me the note. "You need to tell Gril."

"He knows about the people I've seen, but I'll tell him about the note at some point. He's got a lot on his plate. I thought it might be my mom, but the person isn't really built like her, not even like a woman at all. They seem male and agile, which also kind of rules out Orin. I don't think he's all that agile."

"No, I don't think he ever was."

We both fell into thought for a moment, but then I held up the note again. "I'll tell Gril tomorrow."

"Good."

I took a deep breath, wanting a distraction. Similar to my writing, thinking about something else sometimes helped other answers surface. "What's going on around here?"

Viola smiled wearily. She tried to lighten the mood. "Viola's halfway house for criminals and old farts? Everyone is behaving themselves."

"Did Chaz take the dogs out again?" I petted Gus with my toe. He was lying on the floor at my feet.

"He did, and he promised to cook more tomorrow."

"We're all going to be very fat," I said with a happy smile.

Viola glanced at her door and then leaned over her desk to talk to me quietly. "He'll be leaving in a couple of days. I don't want him to know yet."

"Oh. I think we'll all be disappointed."

"Our first male prisoner was a success, or they've found a more appropriate place for him, I don't know which it is."

"It hasn't been inappropriate. I think it's been fine."

"They do like to keep the boys and girls separated, and it's for good reasons. This has probably been a one-off."

I nodded. "I still miss Ellen, and I'll miss Chaz. I think I'm looking forward to whoever comes next."

"It's an adventure, that's true."

"How about Al? Do you think he can go home soon?" I asked.

"He can go anytime someone can get him up there," Viola said. "But I wish he wouldn't. I wish he'd just stay here."

"That's just one more person for you to take care of."

"I don't mind taking care of him. He took great care of me and Benny, and it's been good to remember that and maybe pay it back a little. Though it's more than a debt owed, he's a good person, and I like having him around. I think I forgot that, but it's been good to remember it, too."

"He and Finn get along. I'll hint around that Finn and he can hang out here together," I said.

"I don't think Camille will like that," Viola said.

"No, she forms attachments in unhealthy ways, though. Her sense of 'ownership' of Kaye is bothersome enough. I'm not going to let that family have that dog. Ever."

"What if Al does go home? Will you let him take Finn?"

"That's a good question," I said. "I don't know if Al can handle it, but I could run up there every week or so and check on them. The exercise would do me good."

"Think about it. I'm not going to require that he leave, either Al or Finn."

"Two dogs? That's a lot for someone who hasn't had them before now."

"I don't care. We've got the room. You do more than your part. I'm totally on board with the idea."

Surprising me, tears sprang to my eyes. Her words were sincere. How had I been so fortunate to find this place, find these people?

"Beth? Are you crying?"

"No." I wiped away a tear before it fell down my cheek. "Of course not."

"I forget sometimes," Viola said.

"You forget what?"

"I forget that we haven't been doing this forever. I'm not one for thinking about the past or the future, I'm very much someone who lives in the moment, and this moment is right. You are here, and that's what's supposed to be. I know other people have a longer perspective, so sometimes I forget you managed to find this place by sneaking on to a doctor's computer in St. Louis. I haven't forgotten about what you've been through, but it's not happening now, so it's not at the top of my mind. I hope I don't behave unsympathetically."

I got up from the chair and made my way around the desk. As she sat in the chair, I leaned over and hugged her. "You are anything but unsympathetic. Thank you for everything."

She patted my back uncomfortably. She wasn't a hugger. "Okay, yes, you are welcome. It's all good. Thank you."

I released her, and we told each other good night. I patted my leg and Gus joined me at the doorway.

"I'll see you in the morning," I said.

"I'll be here." Viola smiled, and this time it reached her eyes.

My dreams were out-of-control, vivid scenes that didn't make a lot of sense when put together.

I could have awakened myself sooner, but I didn't want to. Even while asleep, I was sure these images in my brain were trying to tell me something. I just needed to pay attention to what the message was. No, my subconscious knew something, and if that fact or those facts could become uncovered, a mystery might be solved.

Flash of the creek, flash of gold, guns, trucks, the safe, gold again. Gravestones. *Gravestones?* My dream self said aloud. *Why gravestones?*

My eyes popped open, and I sat up in bed.

"No, that can't be it."

I swung my legs over the bed and switched on the light. Gus was up immediately, looking at me with a concerned question. *What's up, human?*

"Oh, Gus, that can't be it, can it?" I pleaded.

He whined at my tone. It was four in the morning. The sun would rise soon, but I didn't want to wait for the sun. I needed to know.

I got dressed, and Gus and I hurried down to Viola's room. I knocked loudly.

She answered a moment later, wearing a long nightgown, her hair a mess.

"Beth? What?"

"I need you to come with me." I swallowed hard. "And we're going to need a shovel."

To her credit, she only gave me a moment of uncertainty, then she nodded and said, "I need a minute."

Viola gathered a shovel and a full toolbox without asking what we were going to be up to. Silently, we loaded everything into the back of my truck and then got inside.

"No Gus?" she asked when the doors were closed.

"No, not this time."

"Okay, what's up?"

"First of all, I hope I'm wrong about something." I steered the truck out to the main road and took a right.

"That does not sound good."

"Remember that tree stump I told you about, the one Chaz was intrigued by? It caught my attention but only because I didn't think I'd seen it before."

"Okay. What about it?"

"I'm about to show you."

"Why?"

"I can't . . . You'll see."

It didn't take us long to get there.

Viola looked out the windshield and then back at me. It took her a second, but I could tell she had come to the same conclusion I had.

"Oh no, Beth, you don't think . . . ?"

"That's what we're here to find out."

We grabbed the shovel and hurried out of the truck.

Twenty-Seven

Together, Viola and I stared down at the tree stump with the rock atop it. It didn't have to mean anything at all, but my thoughts—my dreams—were telling me I needed to take a closer look. It was still dark, but I'd grabbed a flashlight from the toolbox and aimed it in that direction.

What if it was some sort of tribute? What if it was a tribute to someone who'd been buried there? A gravestone. For a baby.

Viola and I looked at each other and then back at the improvised sculpture.

With her toe, she pushed away some leaves that appeared to have been piled there purposefully.

"The ground has recently been disturbed," she said. "Shit."

Digging at that spot had taken place probably within the last week. I grabbed the shovel from her hands, but she held on to it, too.

"I really do think we need Gril," she said.

"I don't disagree, but I can't not dig. I'm sorry about that, Viola, and I appreciate you coming out here with me, but I have to know. And I have to know now."

The face-off didn't last long. She let go of the shovel a beat later, and then aimed the flashlight for me.

"Be careful, Beth."

"I will be."

I lifted the shovel.

"Stop!" a voice called from the gloom.

I knew that voice.

"Orin?" I said, the shovel coming to a halt.

He emerged from the woods. "What in the hell are you two doing?"

"Where have you been?" I asked, though relief that he was there now seeped in and loosened my limbs some. No matter the odd circumstance, it was good to see him alive and well. I also determined that he was not the person I'd been seeing—Orin was taller and thinner and didn't walk with a limp.

"Beth, I work sometimes. It's what I do. My assignment has been around here this time."

"You left me up at Al's," I said. "It was okay, and it worked out, but why are you hiding?"

"I'm only hiding from one person," Orin said. "And you're about to mess up my mission."

"Orin," Viola said. "Would you mind telling us what's going on? We really do think we have a good reason to dig here."

Orin's long braid moved down his back.

He sighed, but didn't immediately offer up an answer.

"I wanted to dig here because I'm worried someone might have buried a baby here, Orin. Why should I not do that?" I said.

"What? A baby? Whose?" he said.

For someone usually in the loop, he'd been out of Benedict's for a few days. As quickly as I could, I told him what had been going on, though the speedy story didn't allow the reverence it needed.

"Good lord," Orin said. "I had no idea. The Oliphants and Millers all keep to themselves so much. I haven't seen Warren or a baby anywhere, but I'll keep an eye out. Why did you think the baby might be buried here?"

I shrugged and looked at the odd sculpture. "It's a new thing, this setup. I noticed it even though it's not all that noticeable. My dreams told me to come look at it."

"Your subconscious is working overtime," Orin said.

"Well, maybe."

"You should have just told Gril, but I understand your need to know. It's not a burial site, not for a human, that is. Something is buried there, yes, and my job is to catch the person who buried it. That's what I've been doing."

"Who?" I said at the same time Viola said, "Oh no!"

I looked at her.

"Chaz?" She was still looking at Orin.

"Yes, but that's all I can tell you. Now, please leave and let me keep watching this spot. He brings the dogs by here all the time. He'll dig it up soon enough."

"What is it?" I asked.

Orin shook his head. "Can't tell you that."

"But he buried it here?" Viola asked.

"No, he was working with someone back in Anchorage. They buried it here for him. I was called to find and follow them right when I came down from Al's. I'm sorry I abandoned you both, but I was in a . . . I felt I had no choice."

"Oh, Chaz is good, slick," I said.

"He's not that good, but I have to catch him in the act if we want any charges to stick."

I leaned and looked behind Orin. "Are you staying out there?"

"I am. I have a nice, cozy setup. I'll show it to you another time. Come on, ladies, I need you to leave. Your housemate will be out here with the dogs any minute."

"I'll tell him he'll be leaving Benedict soon. Maybe that will force him to dig," Viola said.

Orin thought about it for a minute. "Make it casual if you can, Vi, but that sounds like a good idea."

"Wait!" I interrupted. "We like Chaz."

Viola and Orin looked at me. Orin spoke first. "That doesn't matter."

"Of course it matters!"

"Beth," Viola put her hand on my arm, "we aren't out to get Chaz, but both Orin and I have to follow laws. Our jobs mean we have to do things that we might not want to do because we like someone. This isn't news to you."

It wasn't.

I looked at Orin. "You can't tell us what's buried under there?"

"Later, I will tell you. But not now." He paused. "Beth, you can't let him know about this. I promise you, it's important. I will explain it all later, but please don't blow this for us."

Another thought occurred to me. "Is the person who buried it still out here? I saw someone at Elijah's, someone on your roof—I even had Gril come out to take a look—and then someone in the woods yesterday. And someone left a note on my truck."

Orin's eyebrows came together as he shook his head. "No. I watched them board the ferry. You saw someone at my house? There was a note?"

I nodded. "It's okay. We'll deal with it later. We'll leave you to it."

"Thank you. Just . . . be safe."

"We will," Viola said.

"All righty then." Viola nodded at Orin. "I'm damn glad there's no baby buried under here. That would have made some very bad news, and we don't need more of that."

"Go, please, and maybe push him along, Viola." Orin turned and disappeared back into the woods.

It wasn't as dark as it had been when we first arrived, but even with the long braid, Orin melted back into the natural backdrop.

Viola said, "Let's go, Beth." She took the shovel from my hand and marched it back to the truck.

I followed behind after a long beat later.

"I'm so relieved there's no baby buried there, but I'm sad about this," I said when we were on our way back home.

"I know you won't believe me when I tell you this, but it will be good for Chaz to get caught again. He's not a bad guy, but he's got to stop being a criminal. He'll learn there are no shortcuts, or he won't."

"He needs to hit bottom?"

"Something like that. It's a little different, but I guess the impression needs to be made deeply. He can't keep breaking the law and hoping to get away with it. I've told you this before. There are very few successful criminals."

"Yes, you have, but I think I want him to be successful."

"That's why I have the job I have. I don't get attached that way."

I held back a laugh. Yes, she did. Even if she didn't want to admit it. I wasn't going to be the one to point it out to her, though.

We made it back to the Benedict House just as Chaz was wrangling the dogs outside.

"Don't screw this up, Beth," Viola said right before we got out of the truck.

"I won't." I meant it, even if I didn't want to.

"Where did you two go?" Chaz asked as we approached him and the dogs.

"Early morning workout at the community center." Viola crouched and gave attention to both Gus and Finn, managing tandem neck scratches. The dogs both leaned into her hands.

"Wow, that's impressive." Chaz smiled.

I smiled and squeezed his upper arm, a little too flirtatiously. "You've inspired us."

He looked at my hand on his arm and then at me. "Yay me."

"Hey, Beth, I need to talk to Chaz. Go on in if you don't mind." Viola stood up straight.

I didn't think I'd ruined the chance to catch Chaz, but no one could have missed my awkward moment. "Sure. Have a good walk."

I hurried inside and shook my head at myself as I closed the door. If I could be fired, Viola might do that today.

"Good morning," Al said as he came down the hall.

He wasn't walking like a ninety-four-year-old. He moved well, with confidence. In fact, if I wasn't pretty sure it hadn't been him dressed in black out in the woods, I might have had some suspicions. He was built like the man I'd seen.

"You are doing so well!" I said.

"I'm getting back to my old self."

"Your old self is pretty spry."

"Yes, ma'am. Is Chaz cooking again?" He put his hand on his belly.

"He's walking the dogs, but maybe when he gets back." If he wasn't arrested.

Viola came through the door. "Good morning, Al."

"Vi."

She looked at me and did a tiny eye roll, so tiny that I didn't think Al even noticed. Then she looked at Al. "I need to talk to you."

"Okay." His eyebrows came together. "What's up?"

"Come to my office. Beth, thank you for the morning. I'll chat with you later."

I was left standing there in the entryway all by myself. I won't lie. I did have the urge to run after Chaz and tell him not to dig up whatever it was. I also wanted him to tell me what it was.

Instead, I made my way into my room and repacked up my backpack.

If I couldn't find the baby or Kaye's killer, maybe I should try to get some work done.

Twenty-Eight

stared at the piece of paper I'd threaded through the typewriter. I had nothing. It happened sometimes, and I'd been writing for so long that I knew what to do to combat it. Just start. Put something on the page and then later cull for the one or two words you might want to keep.

But this nothing wasn't a normal nothing, which for me was something like a long tunnel with a lot of blank space but something there at the end that I'd get to eventually.

This one felt like a well—though it wasn't empty, just deep and dark, hiding things that didn't want to be seen. Sadness filled the spaces inside with part of me that mourned Kaye's death and another part that was worried about a baby. I couldn't dwell on Warren's potential fate or Cyrus's growing list of injuries or the man in black. It was too much.

I wondered if Leia was available, but then I decided I should first try to figure out some of this stuff on my own and use some of the tools she'd given me.

My writing block was probably because of everything else anyway.

The good news was that even though Viola told Chaz he would be leaving today—which wasn't necessarily true—he reappeared back at the house with the dogs in tow just as I was heading to my truck. If he'd dug up the item, Orin hadn't taken him in, or down, or whatever the plan might have been. It had been difficult to hide my relief, so I'd just hurried away and took off.

From deep in my backpack, my phone rang. I'd take any distraction, so I grabbed the pack and dug for it.

"Hello?" I answered without looking at the caller ID. Very few people had this number, and there wasn't one I didn't want to talk to.

"Beth, hello," Detective Majors responded.

"Detective, what's up?"

"I have news."

"Okay."

"It's good news."

I laughed. "The suspense is killing me."

"We got him, Beth. We got Travis Walker."

I dropped the phone onto my desk. My throat tightened.

"Beth?" Detective Majors's tinny voice from the cheap speaker reached me. I had quite literally been stunned by her news.

For another few beats, I couldn't move.

"Beth?" she called again.

I managed to pick up the phone. "I'll call you back."

I sat the phone on my desk, and my brain, which had been so tired just a moment before, whirred back to life.

Memories flooded me. I'd remembered some things from the three days with Travis, but it had been a slow process. Now it was as if someone turned the camera back on and everything came back to me at once. Or maybe only almost everything.

I'd been in my office at my house in St. Louis. It was a great house (still is, even if I had thought about never going back to it), and I was sitting at my desk, working away. I was wearing a Beatles T-shirt and some old sweats I'd cut off for shorts.

My office was one of the top floor bedrooms that looked out to some Missouri woods. The room itself was plush with seating or standing work options and comfortable furniture for writing, reading, or napping. The shed wasn't even as big as my home office, and yet I suddenly realized how much more I loved working from this place.

That day, the doorbell rang. I ignored it. I always ignored it. I even had a NO SOLICITING sign posted in the long window next to the door.

It rang again. And again.

"Jesus," I said as I propelled myself from my chair and wound my way downstairs, wishing I'd installed one of those front-door cameras.

Through that same window that held the sign, I saw a man holding a small bouquet of daisies. He seemed slightly nervous, and my heart went out to him.

A fan.

How sweet.

But also kind of weird that he was at my house. How did he know where I lived? Did he look familiar? Maybe a little.

I peered out the window. I didn't open the door immediately. *I didn't open the door immediately!* I hadn't remembered that part. At least for an instant or two I'd been careful.

Good job, me.

"Elizabeth?" he said as I waved at him. I heard him through the glass. "Hello!"

"Hello," I called back.

"Here. For you." He extended the flowers to the glass.

"Thank you." I nodded and then pointed down toward a large decorative vase. "Could you just set them there?"

"Of course," he said immediately.

That was it. That was the moment everything changed. His quick move to do as I asked made him seem harmless. This guy was here to deliver flowers. I asked them to be set in a vase. They were just flowers, and he was just . . . a guy.

I opened the door. "I'll take them."

I saw it then, a glimmer of satisfaction that brightened his eyes. But the door was now open, and he was quicker than I was.

In a flash, he grabbed my arm and pulled me from the doorway. I'd screamed, but I lived on a secluded, well-treed property. It had cost a fortune for that kind of privacy, the same kind I had much more cheaply here.

As he hoisted me over his shoulder and carried me to the back of the van, the flowers fell from his grip, making a bread-crumb trail from door to door.

I'd struggled. I'd fought. But it had done no good. He threw me into the back of the van, locked it, and then drove us out of there in less than a minute.

I continued screaming, yelling, trying to get at him, but he'd put up a sheet of Plexiglas between the back cargo area and the front seats. Given enough time, I could work the Plexiglas away and then somehow do harm to him, but a screwdriver would sure help.

It hadn't mattered anyway. Once outside of the city, he'd pulled over and come around to the back again. He opened the doors, and I tried so hard just to run away and get out of there, but he was stronger and faster than me. I'd never bothered getting in good shape, building muscles.

That's when he'd tied my wrists and ankles together, telling me over and over again how I was his now to do with whatever he wanted. I was his and he was never going to let me go.

He gagged me with an old sock and a bandana. He knew how to park in the back of parking lots when he went into restaurants to get the greasy food he loved to eat but didn't share with me. He kept me in the back most of the time, but after he tried and failed to rape me, he moved me up to the front seat.

He had slapped me a few times and thrown me around some. He'd tried to feed me, but when I wouldn't eat, he stopped trying and just used the food to torture me.

By the time I'd realized I could throw myself out of the van, I'd been ready to die, ready to kill us both if that was necessary.

But that's not what had ultimately happened. I'd gotten away. Maybe not quite unscathed, but here I was living a life. A life I loved. Maybe even more than the life I'd had before.

Back in the here and now, I realized tears were streaming down my face. If it was true, if the police had truly caught Travis Walker, I was free to go home. I was free to . . . do anything at all, go anywhere.

I'd never felt anything like it. It was like flying, soaring, maybe even dancing. I'd ended the call so quickly that I didn't have the details, but hearing those words, that they *got him*, was like flipping another switch and turning my life back on to living mode. Oh my god. I could go home. I could go anywhere I wanted to go—and Travis Walker wouldn't be there, because he'd be locked away in prison. Hopefully forever. This was what real freedom felt like, and though I wouldn't wish what I'd gone through on my worst enemy, what I felt now was so, so sweet I wished everyone could feel it.

I wiped away some tears and blew my nose, then I picked up the phone.

"Beth, are you okay?" Detective Majors answered before the first ring was finished.

"I'm fine. I just needed a minute. Tell me what happened. You really caught him?"

"We did. He's behind bars in a place you won't believe."

I had to squeeze my eyes shut and swallow hard. "I'm listening."

"Milton."

"What?" I smiled as I sniffed. My hometown. It did seem fitting. "Tell me the details."

"He couldn't stay away. We'd been zeroing in on an idea that he traveled a certain route over and over again, including Milton, but we couldn't quite get the pattern. He's been in Missouri this whole time, hiding but still with the same van. He's so arrogant.

"Anyway, he was gassing up in a corner gas station. Stellan was there, too. Inside, not working, so he was dressed in civilian clothes. He was paying for a coffee when he looked outside and saw the van. He couldn't believe there would be more than one of those old things on the road, but he also couldn't believe it was Walker, either. Nevertheless, he made his way to the station's front window and just watched for a moment. When Walker came around the van,

Stellan choked on his coffee. Then he apparently threw it down, ran outside, and tackled Walker. Took him down right there in the gas station parking lot."

Stellan was Milton's police chief, a position my grandfather had held for years.

"That's incredible." I laughed.

"Right? So Stellan grabbed some rope from inside the station and tied his hands and feet until one of his other officers could get there. It was quite a thing."

"Had he been shot in the leg?" I asked, wondering if Mill had actually managed to do what she'd been on the run for doing.

"Yes. Shot through and through, and healed as well as it's going to heal. Here's the thing. He claims not to know who did it to him. Just some crazy woman in the grocery store parking lot. We have no witnesses. We have no idea who shot him."

More tears flowed down my cheeks. My mother, wherever she was, was free now, too.

"No suspects?" I said, asking only to hopefully hear what I wanted to hear.

"None at all, I'm afraid."

"Well."

"Well, is right. We'll be transporting him to the Missouri State Penitentiary as soon as we can, but I wanted you to know."

"When did this happen?"

"Just this morning. I got off the phone with Stellan and then through a couple update meetings only thirty minutes ago. He's behind bars, Beth. Locked away forever, I'm sure."

"I hope so." I laughed. "I can imagine Stellan tackling him."

"I'm sure it was a scene and a half. Stellan is so excited that I'm not sure we'll be able to stop him from floating away."

"I'll call him."

"Sounds good. I've . . . Well, I've got nothing on your father yet. I'm working on it, but nothing at all."

"I understand. I'm so . . . god, Detective Majors, I don't know what I am. Happy, relieved, all of it."

"It's a good day, Beth, a damn good day."

"It is."

We were both silent a moment, the things that had brought us together still palpable over the distance, but now there was an even heavier dose of gratitude on my part.

"You can come home, Beth, if you want," she said a minute later.

"Right. I . . . don't know what I'll do, but I'll figure it out."

"That makes sense. Let me know if you need anything."

"I need updates, any sort you want to call or email me with. I'd love to know what the news is saying down there, too."

"I'll keep you in the loop. It's going to be all over every media outlet very soon, I'm sure. I don't even know yet if anyone managed to catch any footage on their cell phones, but we'll probably see that before we even see anything else. I'll forward you everything."

"Thanks."

Another silent pause stretched.

"You okay?" Detective Majors asked.

"This might be one of the rare times in life that something has exceeded expectation, Detective. I knew I'd feel free and safe once he was caught, but I actually feel freer and safer than I could have imagined. It's quite wonderful."

"Yeah, it is. It's the best."

We disconnected the call, and I thought about what to do next, with this new freedom.

Maybe just enjoy its sweetness for a little bit.

Twenty-Nine

called everyone. First my mother, who didn't pick up, so I texted her, hoping she'd somehow get the message. Then my neurosurgeon, Dr. Genero, who actually squealed over the phone. I called Orin, leaving a message on the regular library landline, not his fancy satellite phone, and then I called Stellan.

"Beth?" he said when his receptionist patched through the call. "We got him."

"Sounds like it was a one-man operation. *You* got him, Stellan."

He laughed. "Well, I did make a mess with my coffee."

I let him tell me the story again, and I savored it just as much as I had when Detective Majors had told me.

"Did you get hurt at all, tackling him, I mean?"

"No. I played linebacker in college. I know how to do it right."

I smiled. "Is he talking?"

"No, he's asked for a lawyer. I'm not pushing it, though. I want all of this done as right as right can be. I don't want any excuses for any sort of mistrial or such nonsense."

"I'm going to have to come back there for a trial, aren't I?"

"Probably. That going to be okay?"

"Yes." Honestly, I couldn't wait to do whatever I had to do to put him away forever.

"Can you tell me where you are now?"

I opened my mouth to tell him, but something stopped me. "I will. Soon. It's been a secret for so long that I need to pry it loose, not just yank off the Band-Aid, you know?"

"I do."

"Do you mind emailing me with any updates, though?"

"Not at all. You can count on it."

"Stellan. Thank you. I'm so grateful."

"Well, me too. I can't believe how it happened, but I'm just glad it did. I hope this is just a nasty chapter you can put behind you now."

"Me too."

When we ended the call, I thought about who else needed to know. The obvious choices were Viola and Gril, but my captor's capture seemed much less important than finding Kaye's killer or tracking down a baby, or whatever Viola was doing with Chaz. I couldn't wait to tell Tex, but I didn't know if I should email him or tell him in person when he and the girls returned next week. I'd think about it.

I'd been absently twirling a pen in my hand and suddenly dropped it. I crouched to reach under the desk. As I bent over and leaned down, I put enough pressure on the office chair to send it backward, crashing against the wall. I landed on the floor, my right hand and both my knees hitting the hard surface none too softly.

"Jeez, that was graceful," I said aloud.

I was cramped in the small space, but as I looked down at my hand, something occurred to me. I lifted my hand and stretched my arm as far to the right as I could and then spotted where on the floor it would land if it did so while being stretched.

"Oh no," I said aloud, knowing my grandfather would have much sooner caught what had just become clear to me, what I should have seen.

"Shit, shit, shit," I said as I stood.

I gathered my backpack, hurried out to my truck, and made my way back to the community center, my mind replaying things over and over again but not able to visualize the scene like I needed to.

Once parked, I jetted out of the truck and ran along the berm until I came to the spot where Kaye's body had been. It had rained, and the creek had indeed risen. The indentations that were there before weren't visible at all any longer.

But from up on the berm, I crouched and estimated the angles.

"Oh, Gramps, I'm so sorry," I said aloud. He would never have missed this.

And then I spotted something else, something shiny along the creek. It was just a small speck, but I was pretty sure it was gold.

We'd all considered that Kaye had been next to the water because of the gold, but the gold might not have had anything to do with her murder. What suddenly came to me clearly, though, was that she hadn't been here alone. I could "see" now how there had been two people crouching right next to the creek—not standing, but crouching side by side.

If I'd been trained as a crime scene investigator, I would have better understood the distance from her body the handprint had made. I'd assumed it was Kaye's because it *could* have been hers from when she fell. But it was more likely that it belonged to someone who'd been next to her—the location was just a little too far from where Kaye's hand could have reached. Or so it seemed. I'd still need the measurements.

I realized that of anyone, Tex would have figured it out immediately. Though he wasn't formally trained, he knew everything about tracking, about understanding the interruptions that humans and animals put into the environment, and about what they meant.

The other part that had tripped us up was that the handprint belonged to someone with a small hand, probably a woman—which might be why we'd all thought it was Kaye's.

If a woman had killed Kaye, which one? I'd narrowed it down to two—Camille or Esther. They were equal suspects in my mind.

I glanced along the water now seeing specks of gold here and there, or maybe that was my imagination. It was a beautiful creek in a breathtaking setting, but sadness overwhelmed me.

"Oh, Kaye, I'm so, so sorry," I said.

The wind whispered through the trees, which I interpreted as a nudge from her to keep on doing what I was doing.

I sniffed away some more tears that hadn't quite fallen yet. "Got it." I turned and hurried back to the truck. I sat there for a long moment, snippets of scenes from the past few days coming to me. I had to weed out the unimportant things and focus on the most important problem. Where was the baby? Probably with Warren. Okay, where in the world was he?

I whittled away even more. Where could he go? Not far, particularly with a baby in tow. He'd need shelter. He couldn't just hide in the trees—not with a baby.

I had an idea, but it would be unwise to execute my plan without help. Well, it would be unwise for me to do anyway, but I wasn't going to let that stop me. It wasn't a solid idea, but if I took away everything else, it kind of made sense to me, and it all began with the Death Walk.

I made my way back to my truck and went to find Gril. I hoped it might make sense to him, too.

I didn't find Gril, but at least Donner was at the station. I didn't tell him about Travis Walker—we'd all discuss it at some point, but it wasn't important right now. I didn't share with him what I'd overheard as I'd spied under the Millers' window, but I did give him my thoughts on the handprint.

"I think you're right," he said as we peered at the pictures from the crime scene on his computer. "We all thought it was Kaye's print, but I think you're absolutely correct. Someone else with a small hand was next to her. Nice work, Beth."

Donner wasn't one to compliment unless he really, really, really meant it.

"Thanks," I said. "Okay, so do you think the killer was Camille or Esther?"

"I think you're also right about the killer being female, but it's a mistake to automatically and immediately assume it was one of them."

Case in point. "Of course. Never assume, but I think they're good possibilities." In fact, I thought they were the only possibilities, but I got what he was saying.

I still hadn't shared my plan. Donner wouldn't approve anyway, even if he thought it was a good idea. He'd wait for Gril's approval.

But time was ticking, and it could rain at any moment.

"You think Gril will be back soon?"

"I don't know," Donner said as if he'd had to tell me that a few times even though he hadn't.

"Right. Where is he?"

"Millers and Oliphants again. He took off out of here an hour ago."

That was about the same time Chaz had taken the dogs out for a walk.

"Do you know if he's talked to Orin today?"

"No idea."

I wasn't good at waiting, but I wasn't sure exactly what to do next. I sat back in the chair on the other side of Donner's desk.

"Okay," I said as if I were starting a meeting. "We think Warren might have been sleeping in the community center, right?"

"Some nights, yes." Donner looked at me as if he didn't want to discuss this further.

Nevertheless, I persisted. "Do you suppose he's really at the Miller house with the baby? They're able to hide when people come looking?"

Donner sat forward on his chair, swiped away a notebook, and then leaned on his desk. "No, I don't. Gril and I have searched that place up and down. He's just trying to get someone to break and tell him where they are. I was just about to head out to do the same with the Oliphants. I've watched the community center, too. We also had a trap set up there that no one knows about, but it hasn't been tripped."

"Tell me more."

"Nothing sophisticated but something that would at least inform us that someone had been there when we couldn't watch it. I need to go, Beth."

I nodded. "Donner, whatever happened to the people who didn't show up at the Death Walk? I mean, the couple you mentioned. I can't remember their names."

"The Abacos?"

"Yes."

"They were fine. They just forgot."

"How does anyone forget that? We posted about it everywhere." I waved away my own question. "Doesn't matter." I paused for a long moment, and then I looked up again. "What would you say if I told you I think I know where Warren and the baby are."

Donner squinted. "Where?"

I stood and shook my head. "Come with me or don't. I'm not telling you so you can tell me we'll wait for Gril. I know where that baby is, and I'm going to get her. With or without you."

Of course, I knew he'd come with me. I really hoped I was onto something, but I wasn't sure at all.

Thirty

Donner drove.

"We should have brought an ATV," he said as he looked up at the rocky ridge.

"I don't want to announce our arrival. I think it will be better this way." I got out of his truck and led the way to the path up the slope.

Not only had he come with me, he'd agreed that I might be onto something. Warren was on the run, but where in the world could he possibly run? Right now only to homes he knew were empty. He had a baby to take care of. Oh, I hoped the baby was okay.

I couldn't pinpoint the sequence of events or the exact reasons, except that empty houses were places to hide, and I would bet that Warren somehow figured out Al's place was empty. Word had surely gotten around that Al had been brought down and was spending some time at Dr. Powder's. I bet everyone knew he was now staying at the Benedict House.

There were lots of abandoned places in these woods, but not all of them were furnished and equipped with the things needed to stay safe from the environment. If Warren was on his own, he could use those ill-equipped places, but if he had a baby with him, he'd want more shelter.

Al's place was not only available, it was off all the beaten paths. The more I thought about it, the more it made sense.

Once we were by the airport, Donner used the cell signal to leave a message for Gril before we set off up the slope.

I wasn't in any better shape than I'd been a few days earlier, but I was in more of a hurry. Sure, I'd been concerned about the old guy up there then, but now I was even more worried.

I was easily able to keep up with Donner's sure and quick steps, though I breathed much heavier than he did. Neither of us cared; we just wanted to get to the top.

Once there, we stopped and kept hidden behind some trees. Al's cabin was far enough away that we couldn't look in the windows from where we were. There was no obvious activity. No one coming in or out of the door, no shadows moving over the glass of the windows.

"Stay here, Beth." Donner stepped around the tree and headed around the perimeter, probably planning to come up to the side of the house.

"No, Donner. No way."

"You might be putting a baby in danger."

"Or I might be able to help."

Donner sighed. "Be careful."

"You too."

We made our way around the perimeter, scurrying and then stopping for moments to stay hidden. Still no activity came from the house. I wondered if I'd been completely wrong about all of it. But I still felt something in my gut, something that told me I wasn't.

As we made it to the side of the house, Donner leaned in and listened next to a window.

"There's someone in there," he whispered to me. "I hear movement."

I nodded and strained to hear what he was hearing. All I got was the light breeze rustling the leaves.

Donner thought for a moment, and then he signaled me back behind a tree.

"Look, I'm just going to have to go in there. Surprise is the only way here." He spoke quietly. "But you can't come in. I'd be in trouble if you got hurt." He paused. "I'd feel bad about it too, but I can't let you."

He thought he was appealing to my sympathetic side. I could see through him, but he was correct, and I didn't want to be the reason for him getting into any trouble.

"I'll stay out here until you say it's clear," I said.

"Thank you."

I stepped back out from behind the tree so I could watch him open and then run through the door, his gun not drawn.

"Police. Show yourself!" he called.

I heard a noise like a man's surprise. Voices said something, then a gun fired. That was the end of me keeping any sort of promise to stay outside. I suddenly didn't care what might happen to me if I ran into a place where guns were being shot. Adrenaline sucks away all intelligence, apparently.

"Donner!" I yelled as I ran, coming to a stop right inside the front door.

Donner turned and looked at me. Cyrus held a gun pointed up at the ceiling.

"Cyrus?" I asked when I realized no one had been shot, except for the ceiling.

"Beth, get back outside," Donner said.

"No." I stepped next to him.

"Put the gun down, Cyrus." Donner turned his attention toward the man, who hadn't received any more injuries to add to his already black eyes and cut lip.

"Get out and leave us alone." Cyrus still kept the gun where it was.

Light streamed in through the hole he'd shot in the roof, highlighting a tornado of dust mites.

"Cyrus, we need to know what's going on. We need to know if the baby is okay. I know you didn't kill Kaye." Donner moved one arm in front of me and put the other hand up to Cyrus in a combined pleading and halting motion.

"I didn't kill Kaye! I loved her. I've loved her for a long time."

"I know. Okay, let's just get to the bottom of everything. I need to see that baby."

"You'll take her from me." Tears welled up in his eyes.

"Not if she's yours, we won't."

"She's mine even if she isn't mine! Goddammit, don't you see that? Kaye hated Warren. She loved me. I loved her. The baby is mine."

"You've got both me and Beth on your side." Donner lifted his hand a little higher. He still hadn't drawn his gun, and I kind of wished he would.

The screaming sound of a baby's cries came from the back bedroom.

I wanted to wilt from relief. She was okay.

"You're not on my side, Donner. The law has never been on my side. Never."

"I'm not really the law, you know that. I'm a ranger. I know what you're saying, and I promise you, I'm here for you, man. All the way."

"No one is taking that baby from me. No one." Cyrus made a move with the gun as if he was going to point it in our direction.

Out of the corner of my eye, I saw Donner reach for his.

"Come on, buddy, you don't want to do this," Donner said.

I didn't want anyone to do anything more with the guns. I didn't think about anything, most particularly my own safety. I just reacted. Maybe it was the way someone who'd vowed to never be afraid to fight again would react. Maybe it was stupid. Maybe it was anger. I did what I did.

I ran at Cyrus and tackled him just like a linebacker in a peewee football game, maybe like Stellan had Travis Walker. It didn't matter that Cyrus was bigger than me. It didn't matter that he was stronger or had a gun. I was quick, and I wrapped him up so well that he went down, losing his grip on the gun.

A few seconds later, Donner had him handcuffed and all guns were far from his reach.

"Goddammit, Beth, what is wrong with you?" Donner asked as he made sure both guns were out of the way.

"Sorry."

"And you?" Donner said to Cyrus. "If you weren't an idiot, we could have gotten this all figured out."

I wanted to add another punch to Cyrus's face. "Gril would have done anything to help you all. If you don't know that, then you *are* an idiot."

"Okay, Beth," Donner said pleadingly. "Enough."

The baby cried again.

Leaving Cyrus, who was handcuffed and seemed properly ashamed, Donner and I made our way back to the bedroom, where, thank all the things in the universe, we found a perfect baby girl.

She was swaddled in a blue crocheted baby blanket—I might have seen something like it on the side table in the Miller house the time I'd gone in for Finn. Also with her was a bag packed with the items needed to care for her, including formula and bottles.

There might be a question as to who the baby's father was, but there was no doubt that she was well taken care of. She had a head full of brown hair and big blue eyes, but she didn't look much like Kaye. She didn't really look like anyone yet.

When Donner picked her up, she stopped crying and gazed at him as if she was trying to figure out exactly who he was and why he would want so much beard. She couldn't have been even a full month old.

"Do you think Cyrus did something to Warren?" I asked.

"I think it's a good bet." Donner sighed, though I could tell he was immediately smitten with the baby. He handed her to me. "I've got to get Cyrus out of here and back down to the station. I'd like to keep the baby out of reach of everyone until I can get Gril up to speed. Can you take care of her here until I get back?"

"I don't know what to do."

"No one does until they're forced to learn. She's in good shape. I have to see if Cyrus will tell me what he's done to Warren. I can't be worried about you and a baby, too. You got this?"

"I don't got anything." I looked at her. She still wasn't crying again, but her eyes were now curious about me. Wait until I showed her my scar.

"You'll be fine."

"I'll be fine. We'll be fine." I ran a finger over one of her cheeks. She smiled. "Hurry back."

Donner nodded and stepped out of the room. As I sat on the bed, I heard him gather Cyrus none too gently, and the two of them left out the front door.

"Oh, little girl, it's so unfair. Your mom was lovely. I'm so sorry."

I didn't know how to tell the perfect human that I held that her being okay gave me more hope than I might have felt in all my days.

Time and life do go on. It's the craziest thing.

Thirty-One

need to call you something."

She blinked up at me, still curious.

I continued. "I can't keep calling you 'baby,' but I need to call you something today. What should it be?"

She might have shrugged.

I smiled at her tiny movements, her impossibly small fingers. Oh, and the toes. I had to peek at her toes. She was so little.

"When were you born?"

I didn't know a thing about babies, but I thought this one couldn't even be a month old.

"You are so . . . beautiful." I knew a few words of French. "Belle. That works."

Belle became restless and squirmed in my arms. I had no idea what to do, but I took it down to the basics. How was the diaper? Seemed just fine. Okay, she must be hungry.

I could figure this out.

Cradling Belle in one arm, I carried her and the baby bag to the front room. Making a bottle wasn't going to be as easy as turning on a burner.

A laundry basket piled with folded towels rested in the corner. It made a perfect spot for Belle to rest and watch me figure out how to make a bottle. Oh, and cry loudly while I was doing it.

"I know, I know. I will get this figured out."

I got the fire going in the belly of one of the stoves, and then found a pot and filled it with water from a barrel in another corner. Who filled the barrel for Al, and wouldn't he much rather live where he could do everything so much more simply?

Thankfully the instructions on the container of formula were easy to understand. When a baby is crying, nothing happens quickly enough, but somehow I did manage to get a bottle mixed up and then warmed. I even tried a drop on the inside of my wrist to test the temperature.

I gathered her from the laundry basket, and we sat on the end of the couch. Once I got the bottle into her mouth, I felt like I'd solved all the mysteries of the universe. She sure seemed hungry.

Once the bottle was empty, I worried that she'd want more, and I was mentally calculating the steps I'd need to take again.

But she fell into a deep sleep before I could even try to burp her.

For a long time I just looked at her. I'd never craved having a baby, but even I could feel my ovaries stand at attention.

We ever gonna do this?

"Probably not," I said quietly. "But I would love to be this little girl's aunt or something."

I happened to look up and out the front window. In the distance, at the edge of the woods and the rocky drop-off, I saw a person approaching. At first, I thought Donner had come back, but it took only another moment to realize it wasn't him, and he probably hadn't sent this person. Oh no, was it the mystery person in black I kept happening upon? No, in fact it wasn't.

Camille Miller was walking this way with what seemed like a clear goal in mind.

"Oh shit," I muttered. I looked at Belle. "Sorry." She was still asleep.

I got up and grabbed all the baby things and the laundry basket. I took everything and Belle back to Al's bedroom. I opened the closet and stuck the basket inside, then put Belle atop the towels again. She remained fast asleep. She wouldn't fall out. If she woke up, I was sure she'd wail loud enough for anyone in the near vicinity to hear, but I could hope that her full stomach would keep that from happening.

Just as I closed the door to the closet, I heard the front door open.

"Warren? It's me, honey," Camille said.

Silently and quickly, I debated whether or not I should just hide in the closet with Belle. Maybe Camille would just go away if she didn't see Warren or the baby. But maybe not. I decided it was better to play offense than defense on this one.

I stepped out of the bedroom and walked toward the front.

"Camille? What are you doing here?" I asked.

My appearance surprised her so much that she couldn't hide her reaction. Her eyes went wide, her mouth agape.

"What are *you* doing here?" she asked.

"Al asked me to come up and check on things." I paused. "Was Warren staying here?"

"No." She shook her head quickly, but she must have remembered that she'd just said his name. "I mean, I wondered. I was just checking."

"Interesting, because your tone sounded like you were expecting to find him here."

"I wasn't. Sorry to bother you." She turned and reached for the door handle.

"Why, Camille?" I said, stopping her. I couldn't let her go. I'd pegged her as one of Kaye's possible killers, but my money was firmly on Camille, even if I didn't quite understand all the reasons why.

She paused but didn't look back at me. "Why what?"

"Why did you kill Kaye?"

She turned and faced me. "I didn't kill Kaye. I don't know what happened to her."

"Oh, come on," I said. "I get it. She slept with another man—an Oliphant! I'd've probably killed her too if I'd been in your situation."

"I didn't kill her."

"Sure you did. You lured her down to the river, showed her where she could find gold." I was making this up as I took a confident step toward her because it really did seem like a plausible story. "Gold would have been her way out, wouldn't it? She didn't have any money. She couldn't get away. You told her you were going to show her a way, huh? I can see it now. You pretended to be on her side."

Camille's mouth pinched tight. "No."

"Yes." I took another step toward her. I smiled. "I know what it feels like to be angry, so angry that nothing but murder will solve the problem." I did know this, I realized. I'd wanted Travis Walker killed, but incarceration wouldn't be a bad solution, either. Nevertheless, I suddenly understood this horrible woman in front of me, which both terrified me and I hoped made her feel like she had a friend.

"You understand that anger?" Camille's expression softened.

"So much." I held her gaze. I was telling her the truth, and I would bet she could see it in my eyes.

"Then you know that sometimes you just have to do what needs to be done?"

"Yes! Totally." I did. Oh, how I did.

Camille smiled wryly. "I don't know how you figured it out, but yes, I lured her there. I had to get rid of her."

"Why?"

"She was going to take the baby and go away with Cyrus."

"I see. Do you think Warren is the baby's father?"

"He's the father in all the ways that count. He was Kaye's husband, and she should have been faithful to him. She's my granddaughter." Camille hit herself in her chest. "Mine."

"I get it," I said.

All that woman's anger, anyone's anger, needed for fuel was the belief that they were right. Just because someone else might not feel things the same way didn't make feelings any less real.

God, I'd seen that with my mother time and time again.

"I need to find them." Camille turned and reached for the door again.

I thought about how I could further stop her. I didn't have a weapon, and I wouldn't want to harm her anyway. She'd go into hiding too now if I let her go. I was testing Belle's napping ability, but I said, "Want some coffee before you go? I'd love to tell you my story."

"You have a story?"

"Do I ever."

She let go of the door again, but it was all for naught. From so far away in that bedroom closet, Belle awakened and screamed.

Camille and I looked at each other. I saw her face scrunch and light with fire. She came at me then.

Kaye had been my friend, not a potential friend but a real friend, no matter how little we knew each other. I knew that if she were there, she'd fight like she'd never fought before to keep her baby out of this woman's hands.

I channeled Kaye and I fought hard.

It was good old-fashioned fisticuffs. We punched and hit each other. When she tried to crawl away from my grip, I grabbed her and dragged her back.

I wasn't supposed to get in a fight. Well, Dr. Genero had told me, with a smile, that I wasn't to ever play football or hockey again. She said I could ride a bike, but only if I wore a helmet. She said if I ever bumped my head or got hit in the head, I needed to get to a hospital as quickly as possible.

I didn't try to protect my head with Camille. I just fought.

She landed a hard punch to my jaw and for a moment I blacked out and saw stars. I was a combination of woozy and insistent—telling myself to get it back together again so I could continue the fight.

Something like a whoosh sensation pulled air away from my body. From flat on my back my hands reached in the air, trying to find my assaulter but not touching anything. Finally, my vision cleared some, and I noticed my ears were ringing so loudly that I couldn't hear the words the person standing above me were saying.

Someone had Camille in a grip around her neck, holding her arms behind her back. I didn't quite understand how they were managing the hold. I realized they were dressed all in black, even a black hat and ski mask.

I sat up as my ears started to clear and I could hear the words between the two people.

"Let me go!" Camille screamed. "There's a baby here. I have to get the baby!"

"No way, sweetheart," the other voice said. It was male and somehow recognizable. Or maybe it was just the Missouri drawl that made me think I knew it.

I wanted to help the man keep Camille secured, but I couldn't quite get all the pieces back together that quickly.

I watched as he used a rope to tie her wrists and ankles and then tie her to one of Al's chairs. I didn't like watching that, but I had to tell myself it was better than letting her go.

When Camille was secure, I finally noticed again that Belle was still crying from the bedroom. I got myself up off the floor and took a wobbly step toward the hallway.

The man put a hand on my arm and said, "Sit. I'll get her."

Again, that voice. "Who are you?"

The man nodded but then hurried down the hall to gather the baby. I thought I caught the scents of mint and nicotine, and I decided this must be who has been staying at the community center.

By the time he returned, the full laundry basket in tow, Belle had somewhat calmed and my senses had come back to me. I was now worried he might try to take Belle. I hoisted myself off the couch, glad my head wasn't spinning quite so much anymore. No one was going to take that baby, unless they killed me first. Camille might have come close. I'd fight again if I had to.

He brought her over to me and had me sit again. He went to his knees, took the baby gently from the basket, and put her on my lap.

"She's fine. Right as rain," he said.

"Tell me who you are," I said after I made sure Belle was, indeed, fine.

He nodded and then reached for the ski mask. He pulled it off slowly.

A shock of thick gray hair covered his head. Lines framed his eyes and his mouth. His jawline wasn't as tight as it used to be. But I was surprised I hadn't recognized his eyes already.

The word choked my throat for a minute, but I finally managed to get out, "Dad?"

"Hey, Bethie, I can't tell you how good it is to see you."

God, I loved this man. He'd left when I was a kid, but I hadn't forgotten that love. I'd held on to it, making it bigger, making him better than he ever was. I'd been angry at him, too, though.

A surge of love spread through me, and tears welled up in my eyes. Because love was greater than anger, right? Maybe. At least it should be. And then, as carefully as possible over the baby in my lap, I pulled my bruised fist back and hit him hard in the chin.

Thirty-Two

"All right, here we go," Orin said before he plunged the shovel into the earth.

Viola and I were excited to see what he'd uncover. Chaz, and his amazing food, were gone. He'd never come for the item that had been buried here. Because he hadn't dug it up, he would probably be a free man soon.

Of course, maybe he'd planned it all just that way in case he was being watched. Maybe he thought that playing the long game this time was better than losing patience again and digging something up while he was possibly being observed. Was he going to come back sometime later?

Orin had been called in because Chaz had actually been successful in embezzling money from the tech company he'd been working for. Well, allegedly. In fact, it appeared that Chaz being caught was all part of the ploy, that he'd had a partner in crime, though that person was still a mystery.

Someone had taken money. Other law enforcement couldn't track the money to Chaz. He'd been sent to Benedict specifically because Orin was here, and Federal investigators on the case knew Orin's reputation. If anyone could catch Chaz or figure out who his partner had been, it would be someone with Orin's skills.

Orin hadn't managed to get the partner, and the only real way to prove Chaz's involvement was to catch him in the act of digging up whatever had been buried here—allegedly money. But he hadn't been caught. Whatever was buried hadn't been unearthed by Chaz.

It was an incredible day in Benedict, Alaska. The sun was shining and not a cloud was in the sky. It smelled like a Midwestern spring. It seemed so strange to recognize that milky, weedy scent and picture Missouri but think of Alaska as home. Could two different places be home?

As Orin dug, I closed my eyes and leaned my head back, letting the sun warm my cheeks. Things hadn't felt this good in a long time.

I'd finished my book. The day Belle had been found, which was the same day I'd punched my dad in the face, I'd spent all night at the shed rewriting that ending even while I'd battled a doozy of a headache. Inspiration. I'd take it, no matter where it came from.

It'd only been two days, but a lot had happened while I'd been writing and then recovering from my all-nighter and everything else.

Al was back at his home, and Finn was with him. They'd be fine, and I'd check on them both at least once a week. Al seemed pleased about the idea of my company. Regarding Finn's company, well, he was downright ecstatic. Donner was going to fix the hole in Al's roof.

My dad turned himself into Gril and was currently staying in a room in Gril's house. He'd been one of the people who'd stayed in the community center and Elijah's house until they started watching those places. He'd moved around for the last week or so, even spending a night in one of Orin's back rooms. He'd never crossed paths with either Warren or Cyrus, but he'd been careful. The matches I'd found had come from him, from Rocky Point, Mexico. I should have remembered that that was a place Orin had tracked him to, though it had been from a long time ago. I was simmering with anger at him but also excited about the chance to spend time with him—when I was ready and when I didn't feel like punching him in the face again.

Mill had called him months ago and told him where I was. Weirdly, from what I could put together, that call had also ended her obsession with finding him. She'd never gone down to Mexico for a showdown with him. Though I was glad about that, it was unlike her, and I hoped she was okay.

Gril couldn't find any old charges from his drug dealing days in Missouri that hadn't expired. Dad was in the country as a free man.

"So I just got confirmation this morning," Viola said, pulling me from my reverie. "The baby *is* Cyrus's. Despite his earlier lies, he and Kaye had been seeing each other for about a year in secret, even before Finn came into her life. The dog brought Kaye and Esther together, but good old-fashioned attraction brought Kaye and Cyrus together. He'll get to raise her, but oh boy, those families." She shook her head.

I thought about Kaye. I thought about Esther. Nothing about the situation was perfect, but Esther and Cyrus would take care of her.

Viola shrugged. "I suppose it's better than some options. They're quite a group, but Cyrus isn't the worst guy, and Esther won't put up with any crap."

"Still no Warren?"

"No, neither dead nor alive yet. Cyrus says he thought Warren might have gone up to Al's too, so he went up there to check. When Cyrus got there ready for another fight, Warren just gave up, claiming to not want to be responsible for another human life, that it was too much work. Cyrus told him to just go, that he'd take care of the baby."

"Does Gril believe that?"

Viola bit her bottom lip. "I don't know. I think he's glad to have found the baby. That was his big concern."

"Camille?"

Camille had killed Kaye. She'd also been the one to mark off Kaye's name at the Death Walk, even though the murder hadn't taken place until that night. Kaye had seemingly run away, taking the baby with her that morning. Camille decided that if everyone thought Kaye had been at the Walk, no one else would search for her. Camille would be left with hours to find Kaye herself. Somehow, I'd gotten the story right. Once she found her daughter-in-law, she had, in fact, lured Kaye to the creek to "show her the gold" but not so Kaye might have the means to escape, but so she would stay with the rich Millers, not leave them for the poor, backwards Oliphants. When Kaye insisted that she should be with Cyrus, Camille killed her, took the baby and gave her to Warren, who'd managed to hide the same way my dad and even Cyrus had been sometimes hiding—here and there, in otherwise unoccupied places.

"Oh, she's sure to rot in prison. She'll never see the light of day."

"Good."

"Agreed." Viola paused. "You going back home now? I mean, I know you'll have to go back for a trial, but will you stay there?"

I looked at her. "Honestly, this feels more like home now. I'm not sure. I guess I need to . . ."

She put her hand on my arm and smiled. "It's okay. I like that answer, and I hope you stay, but I know you have a lot to sort through."

"Thanks, Viola."

My dad had come over on the ferry three weeks ago. Though Gril had been checking manifests, Dad had created a few fake IDs over the years. "Lenny Mackinaw" didn't resemble anyone Gril was on the lookout for, and the name didn't raise any red flags. Gril made it clear to my dad that his real identity was going to be his only choice from here on out. I'd heard Dad was okay with that. I was sure we'd go over it all in detail. Someday.

Orin looked up from his shoveling duty. "I hope you stay, too."

"Thanks." I smiled at him.

Orin reached into the hole he'd dug and pulled out a metal cashbox. It was hinged but didn't appear to be locked. He glanced up at us. "Well, this is it."

We nodded and moved closer.

"Ready?"

We nodded again, even more eagerly.

And ever so slowly, he opened the case.

Inside was one single folded piece of paper. Orin reached in with gloved hands and grabbed it by its corners. He unfolded it and read silently for a moment. He looked up at us.

"It's a recipe for, and I'm quoting here, 'The On-the-Lam Lemon Cake.'"

"What?" Viola asked.

"That's what it says. However, it's not a traditional recipe, I don't think." Orin held the paper out for us to look at, but he didn't want us touching it.

The cake recipe ingredients read, "Two of the loveliest ladies; two great dogs; a strange house in the middle of nowhere, Alaska; and an old guy. Mix them all together, and you realize bad decisions might not always pay well, but they can lead to exciting adventures."

I looked at Viola and then at Orin. "You never caught him digging?"

"Nope, and I watched closely."

"Somehow . . ." Viola said.

"After he was taken away, maybe his partner came back. Damn," Orin said, but without any vehemence. Had he taken into account how much we liked Chaz after all? Had he actually looked the other way? I doubted it, but we'd never know.

I'll remember that moment forever, because regardless of the mystery of how the recipe actually got into the box, I realized something so deeply that I almost shouted it aloud.

We weren't anywhere near the end of this story, and that was a very good thing.

Acknowledgments

I am so fortunate to work with the best in the business. Thank you to my agent, Jessica Faust, my editor Hannah O'Grady, and everyone at Minotaur.

As always, I couldn't write books without the support of my family. Thanks to Charlie, Tyler, and Lauren. I love you all so very much.